SUNSET ON

THE PEARL
OF AFRICA

SUNSET ON

THE PEARL
OF AFRICA

PETER HUNT

Riverside Publishing Solutions

Peter Hunt asserts his moral right to be
identified as the author of this book.

Published by Riverside Publishing Solutions, Salisbury, UK

Printed and bound in the UK

Paperback edition
ISBN: 978-1-913012-06-9

CONTENTS

PREFACE

The Protectorate Printer annually produced a guide to the Country. The information on Mamba District ran:

In 1906, Capt. James Martinsen of the Protectorate Rifles, captured the native settlement of Romba while hunting elephant on leave. After some negotiation with the self-styled sultan of Bulikiki within whose nominal control the present counties of Bulikiki and GodiGodi lay, the Treaty of Romba was signed and subsequently confirmed by the Mamba Agreement of 1909.

The country of the Wamamba people to the south of Romba was later still incorporated into what is now Mamba District as a result of the report of the Gamage Commission of 1914. A photostat copy of the Treaty of Romba may be viewed in the Protectorate Museum, the original having been destroyed by white ants in 1949.

SEPTEMBER 1961

CHAPTER ONE

Garston Moorside's Home

Garston Moorside looked up at the sky from his garden. In a film, he thought, he might be discovered – *discovered* was the right word – by an aerial camera sweep of Romba that finally focussed attention on his tiny white-suited figure hundreds of feet below. All this would happen while the credits of the minor characters in this film were being displayed but when the Director and Producer were being acknowledged, the camera would move inexorably down, down, and he, Garston Moorside, like some old prophet, would almost rise to meet it in the air, until the whole screen was taken up by his kindly, intelligent face with its gentle, sensitive eyes looking concernedly out to the Bulikiki Hills.

If there was really no film, no camera and no public, it sometimes soothed to invent them. It was, after all, not difficult to become alternately one's own cameraman and one's own public; it was even easier to project Garston Moorside into the leading role. And it was becoming increasingly clear that if he didn't cast himself in the part, nobody else would.

His dog, Fox, started barking crazily into the snake hole by the culvert in the drive.

Garston walked slowly over to the spot followed by his absurd long shadow floating languidly across the impeccable lawn.

African sunsets, he thought, while the sun went down, might not be the drawn-out affairs you have in England but they were the only times for composing the soul. The night was at once too active and too complete, while the day was a hurried succession of decisions taken, letters dictated, people reasoned with until they had to be thrown out. Sunsets were the only times. He had once known some Keats on sunsets. Now, how had it gone?

However, it was futile and depressing to try and recall anything that he had tried to memorise years before. He had persuaded himself that his memory had lost its old activity. Maybe he too would soon be deprived of that bittersweet pain that always accompanied his meandering reviews of the past. It was a pain utterly vital to him: without it, a final complacency would set in like an ineradicable rot. Already in the last year, there had been a major abdication from his ambition to become a Provincial Commissioner after service as a District Commissioner. And, who knows? He might have ended up as a Colonial Governor. Alas, that seemed not to be.

CHAPTER TWO

Cedric in Court

If political events had made excuses easy in Garston's long and silent communions with himself, the raw fact remained that another had been appointed in his place. He dragged Fox away from the hole, picked up a stick and threw it for the dog to recover. Soon, he would persuade himself that all he now wanted was a quiet retirement growing watercress in Abinger in Surrey.

It occurred to him that lives were surely like rivers. They just rolled on down to the silver sea. And consciousness was like a twig being carried along with the current. To dredge a new channel for yourself, you had to have a flood. Maybe only a few people could make floods like that. But the similes were becoming confused and it was necessary to look for others.

Sisto, his manservant, came out, brilliant in his white kanzu and red cummerbund, his fez perched rakishly on the back of his head with its black tassel swinging almost sensuously in the air. Garston took his sherry and asked Sisto to thank the Memsaab for it.

Right from the start, he had wanted to make his mark. Looking through *The Times* obituaries, he had wondered through the years what his own would read like. Initially, he had supposed that it would be written by one of the paper's own journalists with the use of long-prepared material. Then, he conceded that it might, in the absence of an actual article, have to begin: "R.S.T. writes," while "U.V.W." would write in a few days later to add some intimate aspect of Moorside the Man not covered by his predecessor in his preoccupation with Moorside the Administrator. Now, for the most part, he did not read obituaries any more. It was like going through the honours list of an examination that one had failed years back.

Compose the soul or not, it really was getting dark now. The bougainvillea over the great water butts outside the house was losing itself in shadow. The match flame breathing over his pipe had a momentary glory among the towering enclave of cypresses that took up one corner of the garden. They seemed to have been placed contrapuntally to the thin white flagpole that now shot up dark against the unprivileged side of the sky where night was almost a reality.

"Damn!" said Garston, as he burnt a finger. But from the bowl of his pipe came an intermittent warm glow that cast moments of radiance round its rim.

He called Fox and slowly walked up the steps to the verandah of the rambling old bungalow that had housed successive generations of District Commissioners ever since Mamba had been roped into the Uganda Protectorate. Outside, a hyena howled in the hills.

There were some letters to write before dinner and Garston sat down at his desk. The Moorsides owned several pieces of furniture including this magnificent and grotesque Napoleon desk that Angela had insisted on buying at an auction one leave and then crating out to Romba. It more than neutralised the mundane effect of the government-issue suite. Then, the Asian community at Garston's last station had given him a silver inkstand when he left. It had become one of the very few objects allowed on the desk. Another was the knob-controlled calendar. He glanced at it and noted with pleasure that it was up to date. Sisto had learned that at last.

A whiskey and soda was at the ready. He really ought to start writing. But the prospect of addressing the Provincial Commissioner on the District Council estimates which were in their annual confusion filled him with irritation. He took his whiskey, left the desk and stood in the middle of the room, sipping away his sense of guilt. Some other time would do, maybe after Angela had gone to bed and was not fussing about the house to no apparent purpose in that annoying way of hers.

And, in any case, to think of the countless evenings he had spent on official correspondence! Everything ganged up on him during the day. He would start off well in the morning when dictation would flow easily. Then someone would call and the whole thread of his thought would be broken. That was the pattern for the whole day. It had become routine for him to bundle half a dozen files into the car when he left the office.

Not that he minded work. But it would be exciting to feel now and again that it led somewhere different from the mere satisfaction that ensued its completion. Famous men like Lord Lugard, Cecil Rhodes, Sir Harry Johnston and the rest – they at least must have known that different goal. They had not only first decided upon it – and this hurt – they were also in a better position so to decide.

Still, Gamage, the first District Commissioner of Mamba, had done a great deal at a lower but equally effective level. He had got the main roads built, the bridges put up, the missionaries made reasonable and, in the end, with a royal gesture, had pleaded against promotion so as to be able personally to supervise the introduction of cotton to the District. Gamage had had the vision to see that cotton could alter the whole economy of the people. And he was a legend among the three tribes of Mamba. Invalided home in 1937 and dead two years later, he was still the D.C.

remembered with most respect and affection in the District. Old Paulo, Livingstone Okot's grandfather, had been one of Gamage's lieutenants and he still talked of the man in a tone and with a deference never accorded to other officials, however senior. Garston remembered acutely how embarrassed he had been when Paulo was introduced to the Governor on his most recent tour. The bent old man had fixed His Excellency with his sunken, yellowed eyes and, through the interpreter, had said that although he was very pleased to see Sir James, he would like to make it clear that Gamage would be at Government House today, had God spared him.

But Gamage and his days were gone. In a year, perhaps, Garston's job would go to an African, he would be compensated out and the wind would still blow dust devils down the main street of Romba as though he had never existed. Eight years of his life had disappeared into the District, another ten elsewhere in the Country. He could flatter himself that the people had said that they wanted him to stay, that the District Council had passed a resolution appreciating his services – that, from an all-African body, was something.

But time was not on his side. Within a year, to put it conservatively, he would be on his way out.

Sisto came up to him and said that dinner was ready. Garston pumped more air into the pressure lamps and walked into the candlelit dining room.

Angela was already sitting silently at the polished mahogany table. Sisto and the second houseboy, Frederico, stood at their appointed stations, ready to hand round the vegetables after Garston had carved. It was always like this except when there were guests – a succession of stereotyped move-ments, and Angela sitting there, saying nothing, morose perhaps, disappointed clearly. Poor Angela. After all, she had good reason to be disappointed. He had always possessed the relaxed, confident air of the successful careerist. That was presumably one of the reasons she'd had for marrying him. It had taken several years for her doubts to crystallise. He was, in the event, second rate.

The mutton, if you could call it that, was particu-larly tough. Market meat had to be kept frozen for at least a week before it was tender enough to eat. Angela knew that but this joint had been bought only three days before. And, in any case, the knife needed sharpening. He looked angrily first at Sisto, then at Angela but he said nothing.

He had noticed how that, in recent years, all the minor irritations of daily life in Romba had become immediately associated as he met them with the major burden of his burning frustration. The little pinpricks all seemed to be directed at a running sore. And, even as he carved, he became aware of a very high-pitched whining noise in the room. Angela was running her wet finger round the rim of her wine-glass. He contemplated seriously smashing her glass against the table.

At least there were no guests tonight. Feeling as he did, that was a relief. At least twice a week there would be guests, and at least once, they would dine out somewhere. They were such an inbred lot in Romba. Everybody tried to keep up the pretence that it was ages since they had seen any of the others. Only when someone had a nervous breakdown, or something equally exhibitionist and unseemly happened, would a cry go up and the great fraud laid immodestly bare. For the rest, he quite enjoyed having guests. Angela was superb in her hospitality. And there was something rather special about the glint given off by their best Czech wineglasses and the crystal fruit bowl. Their furniture, their wine at dinner, the game he shot and had served up – all this attracted silent admiration. It was outside the ordinary run of Romba's standards. One had to admit that, at times, guests were a very tolerable facet of Romba life.

"I'm going to bed," yawned Angela, putting her coffee cup down on a Kashmir hand-painted tray.

"Goodnight, my dear," replied Garston, whose eyes, staring straight ahead of him, had become abstracted from his mental processes, "got some work to do".

This was the manner of the Moorsides' nightly parting on those evenings free from guests and invitations but presided over by the six green files in the Mercedes outside. He walked to the verandah and opened the door. The sky was alive with a billion stars. He could nearly always find Orion's Belt and the Pleiades but, this search over, he took little interest in the names of others, allowing the blackness, the distant noises within it and the effervescent little dots that penetrated it to enshroud him and merge with his deepest consciousness. But it was too dark, and he was too inarticulate to enjoy these mysteries. They always underlined his inadequacy.

It had not always been like that. At Winchester, as a boy, he had taken a hidden pride in being able to play games with all the unimaginative toughs, while cherishing secret thoughts only expressed in the company of the night. The greatness of a boy's vision had, it now seemed to him, challenged the greatness of the night and had not been overawed. It was only after leaving Oxford with a third that the male taste of failure had first suggested itself to him.

They called him a Senior District Officer nowadays. That was the equivalent of giving you a long service and good conduct medal, though it carried more pay. And then he had his M.B.E. He had done good solid work on building up the District Council in his previous District, and they put him down for one. And yet, whenever he threw his honour into the credit balance, he would remember a visit that he had once paid to the Jewel House in the Tower of London in the springtime of his career. He had been taking an important African chief around London, fulfilling one of those chores that the Colonial Office sometimes springs on officials taking long leave. In the showcases he had seen and explained to the chief all the various State insignia, from the dazzling and bejewelled stars to the humdrum polished medals. He had told his companion that the M.B.E. was frequently awarded to civil servants who had to be informed tactfully that they would not advance further in the service.

He put his third draft letter to one side, hoping that Diana Manley, his typist, would be able to decipher his writing which, tonight, seemed particularly disorganised.

Something kept gnawing at his stomach, urging him to abandon his letters and to walk about and think. He poured himself a brandy. He heard Fox stirring in his wickerwork basket in the kitchen and the sharp click of a bolt swinging home in the back door as Sisto locked up for the night and went off to eat his own supper. Yes – Sisto; there was a man who had achieved something! In Romba at least he had reached the top of his own line of business. District Commissioners were not necessarily the best payers of staff but jobs with them carried the highest status. It happened that Garston combined the two advantages and Sisto was able to parade through Romba on his off days, looking for all the world as though he had just emerged from a successful Lancaster House conference, never shedding his stifling blue waistcoat beneath a heavy jacket that had been run up by Noormohamed Jiwa, one of the least unskilful tailors practising in the township.

Then an idea came to Garston, not with any Damascus Road dramatics, yet simply, completely, and compellingly.

The whole evening had been preparing him to receive it, and when it came, it demanded no wild effusion. It had almost been expected. There was one road in Mamba that needed to be built just as much as the original arterial routes laid down by Gamage. But because the cotton had been carried along the old roads for so many years, nobody had given a thought to bridging the Koi River and pushing a road through the flat bushland in East GodiGodi county to the ginnery at Port Steamer. In any case, there had never been the money. But there were ways of raising money and that road could cut off at least fifty miles of the present run made by the cotton lorries that carried the northern crop. Cut your transport costs on that sort of scale and the co-operative ginnery would pay for itself in no time. Then again, you would ensure much more regular collection from the cotton stores, obviating the interminable delays suffered by the co-operative society's members at the present time, a factor slowing down enrolment. And, finally, you would secure the immense political advantage of making East GodiGodi more accessible to West GodiGodi at a time when the locals were clamouring for District Council attention and complaining that all the money went to Bulikiki people. It was mainly a matter of funerals: people could not canoe over the Koi for five months of the year – several were annually drowned in the attempt – and so their relatives had to walk the full distance to Port Steamer before ferrying across the Koi estuary where it joined the Great Mamba River.

Garston Moorside would build that road. Somehow, he would build that road. The idea was worth another pipe before bed.

CHAPTER THREE

Romba Town

The terrible sphere of the sun rose in indecent haste from the Great Mamba River far in the horizon, like a brilliantly incandescent balloon. For nearly an hour before, a velvet red glow, ever widening and mounting, had threatened the dark. Imperceptibly, the sky above it had paled to a light blue, killing the stars. And then the sun had arrived and set the seal on anybody's hopes that it would perhaps be a cool, overcast, comfortable day. That was not an unreasonable hope in the wet season but, during the dry season, nobody really believed in such days. One could find some cool in the hills but down in Romba, at the extreme south of Bulikiki and on the border of the Wamamba flats, the heat, with its nasty admixture of humidity, could be very trying.

The towering eucalyptus trees that flanked the golf course put out deep shadows. Doors on houseboys' quarters opened like lilies with the day, and black

figures dressed in singlets and underpants yawned up
at the sky and seemed to grab for it with straining
arms. Soon there was activity in the kitchens and
a hundred morning cups of tea were being poured
out by the side of semi-conscious heaps huddled
beneath thin coverings of bedclothes. Except that
John Fawcett, the O.C. Police, was already exercising
his bull terrier between number eight and nine holes.

A mile away, a few shutters were coming off in
the Bazaar. Poky shops on the verge of bankruptcy
nuzzled unashamed against the handful of big oper-
ators who financed the bulk of the District's trading
activity.

The first of the giants to show signs of activity
were Messrs. Patel, Patel and Patel: their shop on
the corner of Romba First Street monopolised the
European grocery business, while wholesaling to
African and Indian shops in the bush at near retail
prices. Next door, from Romba Express Motors Ltd.,
emerged part of a fleet of broken-down buses, each
with its highly theoretical timetable. The firm also
ran a garage where the right solution to a repair
crystallised, if it came at all, purely fortuitously
under the aegis of a mechanic called Hamisi, whose
knowledge of the uses to which a hammer could
be put was prodigious. Shariff Mohammed, the top
Arab, had for some hours that morning been baking
Romba's bread at his Superior Flour Millery. He too

possessed a sideline as the proprietor of the Happy Events Bar, a sort of legal speakeasy frequented by doubtful politicians, government clerks, prostitutes and plain-clothes policemen. Down on Romba Second Street, Gordhandas Jivandas competed with his Mamba River Club, while under the cover of a fizzy drinks works run in a backyard with the Health Inspector's disapproval, Muljibhai, the town millionaire, operated a complex network of trading interests ranging from tobacco to glass beads, from transport to coffins and cement. He was reputed to be immensely rich but, as his surplus wealth found its way to Swiss, Indian and Argentine banks, nobody really knew. Occasionally, he would make a takeover bid for one of the sordid little shops on the verge of collapse and heavily indebted to him. Rumour had it that he now owned about twenty of these shops throughout the District. An old man now, he delighted in lavish entertaining, while himself leading a life of utmost austerity. He was much given to philosophising on the fatuity of money.

Gordhandas Jivandas emerged from a door cut into his shutters and stood barefoot, unshaven, toothless and pyjama-ed in front of his Bar. He looked for a moment down the half-tunnel formed by the stone canopies that extended from each shop and were supported by pillars on the raised pavement. Then he went back to bed for a little while.

One by one, the African sewing-machine oper-
ators set up on the pavement outside their Indian
employers' shops and, sheltered from the morning
sun, began treadling away at the happy and outra-
geously coloured cloth.

Yusuf Fademulla, the Market Master, an enormous African with a terrible look and a completely
shaven head, shouted wild insults at his ragged assistants who had not cleared up the previous day's mess
to his satisfaction. Within the confines of the market
place, a tiny mediaeval town surrounded by a white
wall, he stumped about pointing furiously at uncol-
lected bits of spat-out sugar cane. There was one
arched entrance to the market, and when he had done
swearing, the redoubtable Yusuf sat in its shadow
at the seat of custom. There was already a queue of
women with baskets full of fruit and grain waiting on
his pleasure outside.

A small army of office boys was assembling at the
Government and District Council Offices on Street
Road. They mostly came on bicycles, wearing faded
fezzes and patched drill shorts and shirts. On the
breast pockets of some were inscribed the initials of
the office that claimed them. Johnson Ezekiel was the
doyen of them all, and he occupied a place of honour
in the D.C.'s office. He had been Gamage's first
bicycle runner and for a full eighteen years had been
in undisputed command of the three subordinate

boys who emptied the waste-paper baskets, carried files and took a commission on the vegetables that were sold to officers by hawkers at the door. Snowy haired, he bore himself with a quiet dignity admired by all his white superiors, accepting the burden that fate had laid on his shoulders with a proud reserve. But if his legs were brown and smooth, his knees were crinkled and grey-looking and the day of his retirement could not be far off.

Up on the small prominence known locally by some as the Bishop's Pimple, the Catholic Mission Church rang out for Mass. From the forecourt of the great redbrick church, Father Cincillati looked down upon Romba, nestling, as he felt, like an egg beneath Mother Church, an impression fortified by the shadow of the building which, with its Cross lengthening up the golf course, appeared to yearn for the souls of those who were at present irreverently cycling across the fairways to work. Not insignificantly, mused the Father, the Cross pointed straight at the scruffy white Mosque a mile away on the town boundary. And he went in to officiate.

The Protestant Mission to Mamba had its headquarters well outside Romba, and the tower of its old stone church could just be seen from the European estate emerging from a thick belt of eucalyptus that almost encircled the town. Denis and Moira Billman, just out from England, were reading their morning

Bible passage, while outside, the ancient Archdeacon Grantham was up on a piece of scaffolding on the mission's new water-tower. He was examining closely the cement work done by Class Six the day before and making a note that it would have to be gone over again. Gordon Rice, who taught technical subjects to the senior classes, looked at himself closely in the shaving mirror and thought that he was getting old.

Meanwhile, back on the Government Estate, Leslie Farrar, Garston's immediate subordinate, rolled over in his single bed away from the sight of his wife, who was sitting up straight as a ramrod sipping her morning tea. Thelma offered a slightly unpleasant image with whom to breakfast and his dawning consciousness, burying him in the pillow, he decided that he wanted no part of the spectacle. In consequence, he had to bolt his cornflakes and was late for the office.

Reg Blagdon, the Inspector of Works, was stomping about his ill-run bachelor household looking for a clean pair of socks and threatening to sack his houseboy for allowing nine and a half pairs to accumulate in the wash.

Blagdon lived on the new ring of economy-class bungalows. It was considered a jumping-off point for the Old Circle, which was made up of large single-storey houses standing in very spacious gardens that had received the loving care of generations of officials.

Venerable shady trees dominated rolling lawns. The rich perfume of frangipani blossom was suffused in the privileged atmosphere, and citrus trees bowed with the weight of their fruit. Orgies of violet, yellow and red broke out spectacularly against the profusion of green. In Dr Manley's garden, the lawn was set off by dozens of vivid red poinsettia streaked delicately with yellow veins. Farrar's garden alone had reverted to something like the bush from which it had been carved.

For the station's dogs, there was no Old Circle and no New Circle. Blagdon's gross dachsund, "Bert", was conferring with Garston's "Fox" and the Harriman's "Roddy" in his master's rubble-strewn garden. Harold Harriman, the Veterinary Officer, and Mavis, his wife, lived next to Garston on the Old Circle. Nobody really knew how they had managed to do that.

Stanislaus, the Romba Rest House Keeper, knocked gently at Judge Butterworth's door, heard the usual grunt and went back to the kitchen to help with the breakfast. The Judge, he knew, would be another half an hour before getting up. His Memsaab was not with him this time and Stanislaus was grateful. On her last visit, she had accused him of pilfering a pair of sunglasses, a pyjama cord, an earring and a twenty shilling note.

He had discovered all but the money in various parts of their room before they had left but the loss of the cash had hardened Mrs Butterworth and she had been unimpressed and ungrateful. The money would in any case never be found because he *had* stolen it.

In the adjoining block of the Rest House, Cedric Hamilton-Gandon, the new District Officer cadet, scarcely off his plane, was already dressed and nervous. He straightened his tie in the mirror and hitched up his knee-length shorts. Garston had told him briefly what he should wear for his first day in the office. Having decided that he looked alright, he gingerly touched a piece of cotton wool glued to a razor cut on his chin and went in to his place at breakfast.

About one hundred yards from the last shop on Romba First Street, where the town's half mile of bitumen road faded into an earth track, Reuben Onyango, the Nominated Member of Legislative Council for Mamba District, had built his new house. It had taken him eight years to complete and three of its windows were still without shutters: glass was in any case not in the tradition of this type of house. Bricks lay untidily about the forecourt. A few blood-red canna lilies shot up in the space around the building like indeterminate symbols of nationalism. A blue Consul stood in front of the door, while a boy, dressed only in a pair of torn red underpants, tried to remove the orange earth that had accumulated round the wheel hubs and on the windscreen. Normally, Onyango lived at his tribal home in East GodiGodi but when he was occupied with what he called his "mission", he often spent the nights in his Romba house, entertaining guests and useful informants. Very often, too, he would be in the Capital, warming his seat in the Legislative Council during sittings. Onyango's mission was at best ill-defined and forever the subject of his own fresh connotations and the interpretation of detractors. The only constant in his position was his avowed enmity for Garston Moorside and, even here, he had to be careful, for Garston had many friends among the people up and down the District, not least among them the powerful County Chiefs who required the D.C.'s continuing approval.

Onyango was preparing to tour Bulikiki, starting at Ogi and working south. Sitting on his native stool, in the attitude of Rodin's *The Thinker*, he wondered what he should tell the people. If nothing else, there would be an allusion to the District Commissioner's corruption in allowing Muljibhai a monopoly of the market for the coffee of non-cooperative society growers. He decided that he would put the amount of Rajbhai's bribe at £2000, roughly the cost of Garston's new Mercedes. He would have to be very discreet about all this, only opening his mouth in safe company. Maybe it would be best to circulate the tit-bit through the bars but indirectly, cunningly and obliquely. He did not want the Special Branch to catch him red-handed at this stage of the people's progress.

Onyango rose briefly from his stool and looked down at it affectionately. His grandfather had given it to his father who had given it to him and Onyango would give it to his own eldest son. It was part of the African culture that imperialism had never broken down. He wondered again about Garston and thought that it was not in the least beyond the bounds of credibility that he was in corrupt league with Muljibhai. And, as he started his car with a jerk, the boy in the red pants scarcely had time to take himself out of the exuberant path of the crusading war-horse.

CHAPTER FOUR

New Boy

"I think you'll like the place," Garston was saying to Cedric Hamilton-Gandon, who sat in front of the D.C.'s enormous mahogany desk.

"To start with, there's your work. I'll show you the map in a minute. Your course at Oxford pointed to some of the theory but my view of these courses is that they just don't measure up to the conditions on the ground. I'm giving you a portfolio of jobs that will increase in size and responsibility as you become more experienced. Originally, cadets were supposed to do nothing much in their first year except watch, and amend their "Laws". But I'm going to throw you in at the deep end, both because I think it will be more profitable for you, and because we can't afford not to, staff and time being as short as it is."

At this point, Garston took up his pipe and began an elaborate filling process without saying a word. Cedric fixed his gaze on two flies cavorting on the wall. At a table behind him, Diana Manley typed out Garston's drafts of the night previous, sighing deeply over the tedious deciphering process. Only when the smoke was spiralling sensuously towards the ceiling did Garston resume, little puffs escaping from the corner of his mouth between sentences.

"I remember when I first came out here, my first D.C. had no time for the feather-bedding of cadets either. He sent me out to make a map of a swamp. When I got lost, he waited five days after I was due in and came and looked for me. He never found me, and when I crawled back finally into town, I discovered that the bloody old fool had been picked up in the swamp with a bad attack of malaria and packed off downcountry to hospital. But don't worry, I won't come out and look for you."

Diana edged round the desk and queried a word on a draft.

"Obsequious," said Garston.

"But Okot doesn't know the meaning of that word and you said the letter was to go in English," Diana protested. "In any case, it's unnecessary to the meaning of the sentence."

"Obsequious," repeated Garston. Then he remembered he had not yet introduced his new cadet.

"Diana, this is Cedric. Cedric, this is Mrs Manley, our physician's lady and my esteemed co-adjutor."

Diana nodded and smiled.

"I hope you'll be very happy here, Cedric," she said. "I hope that you'll like Romba and Romba will like you."

Cedric supposed that Diana hadn't meant to be sinister but her last remark did little to make him feel at ease in Romba at that particular moment. Yet he admitted to himself that, for a middle-aged woman, she had kept her looks remarkably well. She had done her shining black hair into a chignon; her eyes were sharp, exciting, and she was wearing one of those floppy elasticated blouses that he associated with French laundry women from a Renoir that hung in a hired reproduction in his College Junior Common Room.

"You'll go out on safari a good deal," Garston resumed, "with Leslie Farrar to begin with, and by yourself when you've got the hand of the thing. In fact, I'm going to send you out with Farrar next week. By the way, what on earth is the matter with your chin? It worries me."

Cedric blushed and tore off the offending and forgotten patch of cotton wool. He started to bleed again.

"Better put it back on," suggested Garston. He lit his pipe in a humane gesture, for it had not gone out. "The main thing to remember is that you must learn the people," Garston continued. "In this job, you learn people just as you learn their language, which is a must, of course. In that connection, I suggest that you have a crack at Mamba first – the people down south talk it and a lot of the northerners have picked it up. Old Cincillati at the R.C. Mission will give you a hand."

The D.C.'s head disappeared in a cloud of smoke as he relit in earnest. "No, as I was saying," he emerged, "you must get the hang of the people. You'll spend a great deal of your time sitting in the office sorting out jokers who come to you with tales of bloody woe, tell you that a leopard has raped their old mum and ask if there is any compensation due. Some of their worries are idiotic and some are genuine and serious. The point is that they are all causing these people anxiety, and you've got to go in to them all to root out the trouble."

He signed a few letters and noticed that Diana had omitted the word "obsequious" from the memorandum to Okot.

"You know, time was probably when we whites first took control when you could get up and address a crowd of people who had spent all day sitting under a tree waiting for you to turn up, and tell them when you arrived that they were a bunch of illiterate, cattle-thieving bastards who should go back to their homes and wash at once. It wasn't true but it went down well. But you don't do that now. It doesn't go down well. You, for your sins, have come to the Protectorate during the golden dawn of freedom and every man his own politician or politician's stooge." He reached down under the desk, pulled down one of his long socks and scratched vigorously at a mosquito bite on his leg.

"Never mind, it should come easy to you. Others of us have had to adapt and it hasn't always been plain sailing. Particularly as one tends to have a great deal more time for the loyal, courteous old African of the old order who came to the D.C. when his gods failed, than for the smarmy detribalised political boys who hang around the bars planning riots. You'll notice the difference. You'll see it next time we have a march-past of ex-askaris on Remembrance Day."

"The Colonial Office people," ventured Cedric, seeing that Garston had leant back in his chair and appeared to have dried up, "said that the country was advancing very rapidly to independence. How rapidly, sir?"

Still staring at the ceiling, Garston opined, "In my view, very. There are always asses in the Secretariat who will tell you that we've another ten years to run out here and that people like yourself can expect a full career. It's my guess that we'll all be out within three years, me with a big cheque and you with sixpence. Can't imagine why they recruited you at all. Still, enjoy it while you can. It's changing but it's a good life and they're wonderful people up here."

He tapped his pipe-bowl on his shoe heel and showed Cedric the District on the wall map.

"So much for the work side of things. I'm putting you in an office with Morris Mbuya, nice chap, part of the stepping up of Africanisation in the service. He's a glorified clerk really but I'm hoping he'll turn out well. You'll have a house on the New Circle and you can leave the Rest House any time you like. The social life in Romba can be great fun. Join the club, play golf, tennis, even squash. There are a few non-government types about and they pep the place up no end. There's the deb's delight, Lacey, and old Uncle Burns; you'll meet them eventually. We're a small, tight-knit community and that sometimes leads to explosive situations. Some of the wives in particular have never settled down to Africa. But, for the most part, we rub along remarkably well."

As he was leaving his chair to show Cedric round the office, a clerk brought in a pile of about twenty files and deposited them in a precarious tower on the contents of an already overflowing in-tray.

"Look at it! Loaded down with the verbosity of the under-employed, and they tell you to do more safaris!"

Garston introduced his new cadet to the clerks and interpreters.

"Better watch that man Marciano," Garston warned, after Cedric had nodded to the Military

Affairs Clerk, an ageing and toothless figure in the background of the main typing office. "He never charges a soldier coming up on leave less than a shilling to see a white officer, sixpence for doing him a travel warrant. Only we can never pin him down. His accounts are perfect and the soldiers reckon he gives good service."

The Goan Chief Clerk, Mr Xavier Rodrigues, was deputed to show Cedric through the office filing system. He was a small, wisened man with greying hair. He wore an off-white cotton jacket with numerous letters bulging from the pockets. These letters were nearly all of a legal character, for Rodrigues spent his pay and spare time on suing and being sued. On several occasions, chronic indebtedness had nearly cost him his job but, being of a generous disposition, he himself was owed a great deal of money by defaulting acquaintances, and so the proceeds of one lawsuit offset the costs of another. Garston, for his part, was content to note that Rodrigues neither sold the office stationery nor hired out the township tractor as his predecessor had done but confined himself to the occasional interview.

"What's all this, Rodrigues?" he would shout, with the simulated fury of a judge's admonishment prior to the grant of a conditional discharge. And he would wave the latest summons high in the air, his pipe glowing with unnatural brightness.

"Sir, allow me to explain…" Rodrigues invariably would begin.

"Look, Rodrigues, all I know is that Mr da Pinto has been in to see me again this morning and asked me to sign the third civil summons on you this year."

Then would ensue an impassioned outburst from Rodrigues detailing the perfidy of the unseen creditor.

"…I am going to him as absolute friend, sir, and he is telling me that I can take the money for as long as I wish. And I am thinking that he is very kind man and is remembering the very great services rendered to his father by my father when they were doing business in same town. And now this very evil person is trying to play me very bad trick, isn't it?…"

"Look, Rodrigues, you're a bloody liar and always will be! Go away and bring me the file on the deportation of undesirables."

But Rodrigues never did as Garston asked.

While Cedric was looking through the filing system, Morris Mbuya arrived back from an inspection of drains in the township and Farrar drew up late in his monstrous Bugatti, the only one in the Protectorate. He strode past Mbuya's window, did not hear the African's "Good morning" and sat down heavily on his swivel chair in an office adjoining Garston's. Something inside Morris smarted for a moment; then he looked back at the woman petitioner kneeling on the floor in front of his desk.

"And what does she say that the husband did to her next?" he asked his interpreter.

"She says that he called her a very bad thing and started to beat her with a stick."

"And what did she do then?"

"She sounded the alarm and her friends came to rescue her."

"And the man?"

"The chief put him in prison and she is going to take a criminal case against her husband."

"Well, what does she want from me?"

"She wants a letter."

"What sort of letter?"

"She wants a letter that will tell the County Court Judge to transfer the case to another court, as the Chief in her area belongs to the husband's clan."

"But surely she doesn't believe that the Chief will be unfair, since he has already locked her husband up?"

The interpreter taxed the woman on this subject.

"She says that the Chief locked her husband up in order to enforce a debt owed to him from a previous civil case which he took personally against the man. As soon as the Chief confiscates her husband's two head of cattle, he will protect his fellow clan-member."

Morris began to write a letter but the woman began speaking excitedly and noisily to the interpreter who, in turn, replied to her harshly.

Morris sighed. "What does she want now?"

"She is being troublesome."

"I can see that. But what does she want?"

"She says that she wants the letter to be written by Mr Farrar because the Chief will pay more attention to him and because she saw Mr Farrar about the matter when he was on safari three months ago and because…"

"Shut up!" Morris interrupted. "She can have my letter or none at all." And he started writing furiously, trying to repress a mounting indignation welling up from unrecognised depths within him. He knew that she had a good point, this stupid woman. Beads of perspiration rested on the cicatrisation on his forehead as he handed his draft to the waiting interpreter. The woman slowly unwound to her feet and walked soundlessly from the office.

She was shown to a bench on the office verandah where she waited all day for her letter and was told to come back next morning.

"Take this to the Memsahib D.C. at once," ordered Farrar, handing Johnson Ezekiel an envelope marked O.H.M.S. and sealed with red wax. He was always playing practical jokes like that on Angela, particularly when he was bored.

CHAPTER FIVE

The Club

The Romba Club sat like an island in the centre of the golf course, immediately surrounded by sibilant eucalyptus trees under which sat an eternal gang of ragged small boys who were encouraged to call themselves caddies. They were supervised by a retired houseboy called Burton who had been given the job through the good offices of his brother Chalisi, the club barman. Burton had become an unmistakable piece of club scenery. Across the front of his greasy bush jacket were sewn the letters C.M. (for "Caddy Master"); his earlobes had been pierced in youth and then stretched to such a degree that the loops of skin hung practically to his shoulders, and he carried an officer-type stick under his arm in combination with a green fez on his head.

It was the evening of the annual general meeting, and the first cars were already drawn up in front of the cottage-style thatched clubhouse. A group of golfers was dawdling off the ninth hole in the last of the evening light. The hammering of the club generator started up and sent its staccato message chuntering down the fairways.

Chalisi was laying out the chairs ready for the meeting. He wore white overalls and brass buttons.

Blagdon, the Bar Member, called to him from the bar: "Charlsey! Come 'ere? 'ow come there's only three small beers in the Coca-Cola fridge?"

Without replying, Chalisi put ten more bottles into the cooler.

"Always the same, isn't it?" said Blagdon, turning for sympathy to Willie Ives, the Game Ranger. "Things are never quite right, are they?" Ives rotated his sleepy eyes away from a game of darts which he had been watching from his barstool and nodded agreement. He was already on his fourth whiskey of the evening and Blagdon handed him the fifth.

"Thanks Reg. I had a case in point today. Told my chief scout to clean up the shotguns in the store. Do you know what he went and did? Pulled the barrels through with sandpaper, said it made them shine more. I'm getting rid of him for that."

John Peebles, the geologist, edged up to Ives. His eyes protruded fish-like from an inflamed face; a red chest like underdone beef showed hairy through the long triangle allowed by his open, red-checked shirt.

"You don't want to go about dismissing too many people, Willie old boy," Peebles advised. "I had a letter written to my Director about me by my clerk last week. He sent me a copy of it."

"What was in it then?"

"Oh, he merely complained that I was in the habit of calling him old chap. He said that he had consulted his dictionary and discovered that chap meant the cheek of a pig. Very sensitive fellow, my clerk."

Garston arrived with Angela. She was wearing a tight-fitting and elegant green dress with a high collar around which curled a golden choker. Diana Manley nudged Christine Fawcett and they glanced over at her from the bookshelves.

"We're in our snake outfit again," whispered Diana.

"Well, everyone here except Borny and me is dressed up," said Peebles. "Can I use your house to change in, Reg?"

Peebles and Berg Björnsson, the Swedish diamond-driller who was working the Mamba borehole programme, were nomads in the District. Both men camped out in rest-camps or caravans and came into Romba when they could. Only, while Peebles was liked and popular, Björnsson was grudgingly tolerated.

"Come on, Borny," said Peebles, dragging off the good-looking, ill-shaven young man with a shock of fair hair obscuring his right eye. Unknown to himself, he was the centre of more than one Romba wife's fanciful and slightly adulterous daydreamings. As it was, he made no secret of his own arrangements. "Man," he was in the habit of saying, as he looked uncertainly through a whiskey glass at two or three in the morning, "you haven't seen a thing until you've gone native."

Peter Freeman, the young Agricultural Officer from Lancashire, was trying to make conversation with Mavis Harriman. But he was nervous and could think of little else to say except, 'have another drink', while she was unable constitutionally to do more in reply than smile wanly. He stood at the bar thinking how best he could put his points. A week before, he had steeled himself to propose an explosive amendment to Rule Two of the Club Regulations which laid down that Club membership was open to any person of unmixed European extraction regardless of nationality or creed. Freeman had been unable to obtain a seconder for his amendment, although Manley, the District Medical Officer, had been sympathetic and had promised to come along to see how things went. He hoped that the doctor would not be too inebriated to provide a coherent argument in his defence. He was, after all, much respected, and his opinion was likely to carry weight where his own would not. He looked out on to the lit-up verandah and was relieved to notice the doctor already there and in deep conversation with Garston.

The clubroom was becoming crowded, the atmosphere heady with cigarette smoke. Chalisi at the bar was inundated with orders. But he took his time. While people like Garston and Manley were there, he was not usually bullied. Peebles and Björnsson reappeared, and the last to arrive, Leslie Farrar, stood half-smiling in the doorway in his bow-tie and tweedy jacket, looking rather like a tough insurance investigator taking stock of a wild west saloon.

"Come in quick, Leslie, we're waiting to start," called Jack Chivers, the Education Officer and retiring president of the Club. Business began and, amid subdued titters and irreverent witticisms, John Fawcett was elected to the presidency; Garston became Sports Member; Diana was voted in as Entertainments Member; the Forestry Officer's wife was made Secretary, and her husband accepted the job of Treasurer, while Reg Blagdon was given a third term at the bar. The new Committee assumed its place at a table in front of the chairs. Expenditure on bar billiards was agreed. Reg volunteered to help on the building of a clubhouse extension with a few bags of cement that he described as being surplus to official requircments. A flat rate of sixpence per caddy per eighteen holes was agreed upon and members were asked not to tip. Fawcett cleared his throat:

"Item no. 5 on your agenda, ladies and gentlemen," he intoned, as though he was reading from a charge sheet. "Mr Freeman, I believe that you have something to say on this."

Peter Freeman stood up, almost paralysed by nerves. Any other issue would have come easily to him but he guessed at the hopelessness of this one. Again, only at the A.G.M. were formalities like 'Mr' employed; and, because the formality existed, members deferred to it and took advantage of it. The more strongly they felt about any matter under discussion, the more formal they would become, at the same time not hesitating to introduce those gratuitous scraps of familiarity, some humorous, some spiteful, that the occasion paradoxically seemed to invite. It seemed to Freeman no accident, either, that he should have been invited by Fawcett to speak on a proposal that would amount to a major change in the Club's constitution with the casual suggestion that he might 'have something to say on this'.

"I think most of you know what I am going to say about Rule Two, so I won't waste much time explaining," Freeman commenced, discouraged in advance. There were loud cries of "Hear, hear!" "Jolly good" and one "Sit down!".

"The point is that here we are in a protectorate rapidly advancing to self-government, and this club denies membership to Africans on principle. Even an African Minister couldn't join…"

"Quite right," interrupted Diana quite audibly, a remark followed by half-repressed sniggers like those to which children succumb in Sunday school prayers.

"It's all very well saying that," Freeman was, by now, flushed and angry, his nerves forgotten and his scheme of attack disorganised, "but if Julius Nyerere came to Romba today, and there's a man who I suppose has dined at Buckingham Palace, he couldn't walk in here for a drink."

"Yes, he could – as your guest," shouted Willie Ives.

"Wouldn't come as mine," added Blagdon, elbowing Peebles.

"What about Kenyatta while you're about it?" put in Farrar amid general laughter.

"There are one or two Africans," Freeman went on, "who could qualify educationally and culturally for membership of this Club…". He was interrupted by cries of "Nonsense!" and "Name them!".

"If you want names," Freeman hesitated for a moment, "what about Morris Mbuya?"

"What! That jumped-up office boy?" asked Chivers, as though he had not heard Freeman correctly. Meanwhile, Chalisi's understanding of English was good enough for him to know what was being discussed; he was leaning across the bar straining to hear what was being said and by whom.

"Mr Chairman," Freeman pleaded. "I can't speak in this racket." Fawcett requested order and there was silence as Freeman went on: "I'm not going to be drawn into an argument as to whether Morris Mbuya or Livingstone Okot, the other African I had in mind…" At the mention of Okot's name, there were several studied groans or cries of shock. "What I am going to say is that it is us with all our talk of civilisation, progress and the effect of two thousand years' history who are the uncivilised ones in being nasty, small-minded and exclusive in persisting with anachronistic attitudes, in…"

"Mr Freeman," interrupted Fawcett with an air of weariness. "May we please have your proposal?"

Halted in his tracks, Freeman swallowed hard. "Yes, Mr President. I know I haven't put all this very well…"

"You certainly haven't," someone said.

"…but we can't afford to behave like this. My proposal is that Rule Two of the Club Regulations be amended so as to allow Africans invited by the Committee to become members."

"Don't let the Asians get a look-in, Peter?" called Peebles.

"Yes, and Asians, Mr President," added Freeman as he sat down hot-faced and trembling slightly.

"Before we try and frame a proper proposal, any seconder?" asked Fawcett. Nobody said 'yes' but Manley rose slowly to his feet. Slightly built, with a well-kept moustache and incisive eyes, he looked very much the country squire on a tropical holiday.

"I'm not seconding this proposal but may I say a few words, please, John?" said Manley. "I think I speak for most of us here tonight when I say that Peter Freeman's sincerity over this matter is obvious and, in its way, admirable. It takes a lot of courage to say what he said." There were some uncomfortable coughs and fidgets in the audience. "But," and he glanced over at Freeman, who was looking up at him apprehensively, "we British have always been a very independent people who enjoy each other's company in our leisure hours…". He was strongly applauded. "If we go to the Continent, nothing delights us more than to fall into conversation, on the train or in the hotel, with the chap who, by coincidence, lives two streets away at home." He was speaking in an authoritative monotone, carefully measuring his sentences. "In my hospital, I work with African Medical Assistants and African nurses all day long. We get on very well. But come the evening, I don't want a busman's holiday trying to make conversation with people who don't really understand me, and whom, let's face it, I don't really understand myself. No, I want to relax with people of my own sort…"

Manley was, again, loudly clapped. "Peter says that we're being nasty and exclusive, at least I think that he used those words but, you know, if a group of people get together in London and decide to form a club, the membership of which is restricted to men with squints and crooked big toes, I wouldn't call that being nasty and exclusive. It so happens that I have very little chance of ever belonging to the Athenaeum but I don't begrudge its existence because of that. On the contrary, I am very grateful that I belong to a Nation that works on the democratic principles that allows clubs of all sorts for people of all sorts. And so it is with Romba here. I have a lot of sympathy with what Peter has said, as I think I told him this morning. But Peter won't change the world in a day. It may be that in fifty years' time there won't be a problem of this sort, although I, for one, hope that there will be the odd corner in every large town in the world where Britishers can get together by themselves over a pint. My view of it, in any case, is that, after Independence, you'll have large numbers of clubs that deny membership to Europeans; then where are you?"

Manley sat down amid general approbation.

John Peebles was now on his feet. "If I may add to what Geoffrey has said, I would like to point out that a lot of us, particularly Reg Blagdon and Jack Chivers here, have worked very hard indeed over the last few years to build this Club and its facilities into what it is today…"

"Hear, hear!" "Hear, hear!", general voices exclaimed.

"Now, I happen to know that they did not do this for the benefit of any Tom, Dick or Harry of an African who talks enough English to impress Peter Freeman…" continued Peebles.

"Hear!" "Hear!"

"…you may as well face it that Africans and Asians live differently from us. It's no good Peter burying his head in the sand," continued Peebles, sitting down. "I believe one has got to be brutally realistic about this thing."

Garston stood up: "I would merely like to associate myself with what Geoffrey Manley has said. I think we should leave this sort of matter to the Committee. If it feels strongly enough about the issue, it can raise it again."

People seemed to agree.

Freeman, convinced that he had made a fool of himself, and resentful of Manley's patronising speech, rose once more:

"Well, Mr Chairman, there can be little doubt about which way the land lies. I just want to answer the point Geoffrey made about Reform Clubs and the like. Personally, I don't care if people with squints or even big moustaches have their own clubs.

What I say is that we are wrong and that it is morally indefensible to draw the qualifications for membership along the lines of a man's colour. That's all."

Heavy and deliberate sighs from the audience accompanied his words and he left the club wondering whether he should resign.

"He'll learn," said someone.

Cedric Hamilton-Gandon had been sitting all this while next to Dorothy Ward, the Nursing Sister. She had come straight from the hospital and was still in her white uniform.

"Geoffrey's quite right you know," said Dorothy, "but you've got to give it to Peter; he had pluck!"

"I don't know," replied Cedric. "He struck me as one of those people who try to attract attention by taking up unpopular causes. I've only been here a week or so but it seems to me from what I've seen in the office that some of these Africans aren't ready for a typewriter let alone self-government."

"You've been talking to Leslie; I can see that," smiled Dorothy. "Be a dear and get me another crème de menthe; here's the money."

OCTOBER 1961

CHAPTER SIX

Building a Bridge

"And remember, Leslie," Garston was saying, "if Okot thinks it can't be done, try to make it clear to him that I shall have some difficulty in putting him forward for that Queen's Medal he's always asking for. He sometimes gets this way, refuses to see sense. Yet he knows more than anyone how useful the road will be."

"But won't his line be that we should get Bulikiki people in on this as well as his own?" queried Leslie. Sitting by him in front of Garston's desk were Cedric and Morris, taking notes.

"He may try that one but I daren't ask the old Sultan. He's so thick with Onyango these days that I'd be accused immediately in the Legislative Council of organising a slave trade if he didn't want his people involved. Then the Provincial Commissioner would get hold of it, jolly the Sultan along with his effete conciliatory talk and tear me to bits while he's about it. As it is, I think that Okot has enough influence on Onyango to keep him quiet. After all, they're the same clan – one of Okot's wives is Onyango's sister, and, in addition, he's helping Reuben to pay for his new car. I happen to know that straight from the horse's mouth: he got drunk in a bar last week. Okot reckons that provided he keeps our Reuben in a state of dependence, he can prevent him from doing too much about the various rackets we think he's up to. For our sake, we must hope that John Fawcett doesn't pin him until we've got the labour. And until we've got anything solid on Okot, I think we can go ahead with a clear conscience."

"That's the road dealt with. You haven't told us about the Koi Bridge yet. Where's the money coming from?" asked Leslie.

"Reg estimates that it would cost him five thousand to build it himself. I think that Dison Apau from the District Council can do it for half. I had him along to the Koi yesterday and he says he'll have a shot."

"Look, Garston," Leslie said with a tired expression. "Dison may be a good hand at building footbridges across streams, he can even lay a culvert but he doesn't know how to build a bridge over the Koi for two and a half thousand or twenty thousand for that matter…"

Moorside interrupted with a gesture of his pipe stem.

"I see it this way, Leslie. They want the bridge; alright, they can build it. It's at the root of all this community development ideology that we hear so much about. On all sides, we're told that we don't give Africans enough responsibility. Well, this is Dison's big chance. Isn't that right, Morris?"

Mbuya was startled from a doodle.

"Yes, at least, well, I should say, yes. But there will have to be much supervision."

"I've been on to the Treasurer," Garston continued, "and we have arranged to switch three thousand from the capital grant for Chief's houses. Yes, don't tell me. I know what you're thinking. Well, the answer is, gentlemen, that the incredible Blagdon has agreed to demolish the abandoned mission church at Ogi and Dison tells me that this will give him enough stone to put up a Chief's house of sorts patched together with a load of wood that he has over from last year. The Archdeacon gives us the stone with his blessing – the letter's on the file – and says that if I wish it, he could arrange for the Bishop himself to open the bridge when it's completed. This invitation, gentlemen, I shall decline with thanks. The last census showed GodiGodi as 90 per cent Catholic."

"And what happens when the Provincial Commissioner comes on his next tour of the GodiGodi Counties?"

"He, Leslie, and not the Archbishop, will be invited to open the bridge. All puzzlement will be lost in convivialities and people will attend funerals and sell cotton happily ever afterwards."

CHAPTER SEVEN

GodiGodi

"It's all about self-aggrandisement," said Leslie, as he drove the office Land Rover wildly up the snaking road to GodiGodi, leaving a pall of orange dust hovering far in his wake. "The silly ass admitted it to me himself one night at a party. He said that he wanted to be remembered for something in Mamba. Well, by God, he will be!"

Cedric felt embarrassment listening to abuse against Garston coming, as it did, from an officer senior to himself but he decided to tread the insecure path between the D.C. and Leslie and avoid taking sides.

"Don't you think it will work?" he asked Leslie, who was restraining himself visibly from becoming altogether apoplectic.

"You just watch, just watch, that's all. Only it's going to be difficult for you, I must say."

"Why?"

"Because Garston's putting you in charge of the project."

Cedric felt an immense elation at this sudden news and at once felt less inclined to sympathise with Leslie.

"Did he give you that old bull about his first District Commissioner sending him out to map a swamp?"

"Yes," Cedric was forced to admit.

"Well, he never forgot that. He thinks up the craziest schemes and sends his cadets out to do the work. If the scheme is not too crazy, the cadet succeeds and receives a good report. If it's impossible, the cadet can look forward to being posted away and how!"

"And you?" ventured Cedric.

"If you really want to know, I like this District. I put up with the schemes for the sake of the sunsets, the fishing, the golf course and even the Africans. Just take a look at those hills!"

The Bulikiki Hills now loomed high on the left, seemingly interminable in their convolutions. Rearing up black and sinister, Mount Buni looked very much like a gigantic slagheap, except that, in the setting of the other hills, it dominated sternly and lent to the whole area an atmosphere of weird unreality.

The Land Rover took a sharp corner with a dry skid and coursed unsteadily along the hot road of the West GodiGodi Plain, from which, in all directions, sprouted borassus palms, their tall blanched trunks reaching up to the umbrella foliage like inverted cigars.

The rest camp at West GodiGodi County headquarters was built in the usual mud, wattle and thatch. The main building was approximately rectangular, its cracked walls bulging ominously in places and elsewhere conceding unaccountable inlets in the architecture of their corners. The thatch had been renewed in honour of the visitors and grass hung over the broad eaves like hair over the eyes of a shaggy dog.

The floor, too, had been recently smeared with cow dung and the imprint of the smoothing hands made little waves in the yellow-grey surfaces. The walls were half whitewashed inside.

As the Land Rover halted, Boaz, the rest camp keeper, emerged from one of the satellite huts used as boys' quarters, interpreters' houses and kitchens. He helped with the luggage and exchanged brief vernacular comments with Timoteo and Kalisto, the two houseboys, who were climbing with difficulty out from the hooded back of the vehicle, where they had been packed among a heap of palliasses, camp beds, pressure lamps and canvas baths. From the same source, the interpreter Semei extracted himself and set to smoothing out his creased trousers.

The party was joined by Boaz's two naked babies, who stood watching, wide-eyed with excitement, their pot-bellies grotesquely assertive.

From the distance came the sound of prolonged hooting. "That'll be Okot," said Leslie.

Livingstone Okot, county Chief of West GodiGodi, was still young. Intensely ambitious, he was known to have his sights levelled on a Junior Ministry in the Post-Independence Parliament. He looked upon his Chieftaincy as an opportunity for doing some of the necessary groundwork. At the same time, he was considered the strongest Chief in the District, was always prompt and thorough with tax collection, encouraged a great deal of communal maintenance of communally-built roads, made sure that his junior chiefs kept a constant eye on the people's kitchens and pit-latrines and carried out periodical drives on soil erosion measures and cotton picking. A true son of Paulo's, he was well feared. And, although Leslie always referred to him as a 'smooth bastard', few additional qualifications could have been wished for by the British Administration. It was small wonder that certain irregularities on the Prison Farm were, if not actually ignored, then at least minimised and conveniently relegated to mature within a closed file. John Fawcett's policeman zeal was becoming some-thing of an embarrassment.

Ever since he had visited England on a local gov-ernment course at Torquay, Fawcett had taken to wearing a gold watch chain, and this, in turn, entailed a waistcoat. He had, therefore, bought a vivid green waistcoat with mother-of-pearl buttons, and always wore it beneath his current suit on any occasion that seemed to him in some way official. But when he attended the District Council, the whole outfit would be covered by his embroidered kanzu, for, by wearing the kanzu occasionally, he hoped to retain the common touch. That afternoon, however, he was dressed only in his suit.

"Good evening, sir," he greeted Leslie with a slight inclination of the head, and turned to address Cedric:

"I understand that you have just come out from England, sir?"

"Yes, that's right."

"I hope that you will be very happy here."

They sat down at a little card table under an acacia tree that drooped rather pitifully onto the dusty space in front of the rest camp. Leslie opened up beer cans, and poured out three glassfuls.

"I... er... had the D.C.'s letter," said Okot. "What he proposes is going to be very difficult." He had a habit of grinning expansively like a Cheshire cat, and never more so than when he had a delicate disagreement with a European with which he had to deal.

"In what way, Livingstone?" asked Leslie sternly.

"Well, the fact is, sir, that I have been making the people work pretty hard on communal projects as it is. The D.C. said we would need a gang of 600 men doing a morning's work for three months."

He hummed and shook his head. "That is going to be difficult, I should even say impossible."

"They'll come, won't they, or are you losing your grip?"

"No, no, no... Mr Farrar, sir, it is not a matter of disobedience... it is merely that I hesitate to make the people discontented..."

"Look, Livingstone, are you trying to tell me that you don't know that being a Chief involves taking the rough with the smooth, carrying out unpopular orders as well as popular ones?" Farrar was becoming less than diplomatic and Okot put out a restraining hand like some orator imploring silence to cope with a special point.

"Sir, as you know, the people want the road and the bridge. They have asked very many D.C.s for it and you gentlemen are the first to listen to their request. It is just that it will be difficult to ask people to leave their fields and join a road gang without food or pay. I have discussed this with the county chief of East GodiGodi who will be at your baraza[1] tomorrow and he agrees."

"Are you afraid of Onyango?" Leslie tried a shot in the dark.

The watch chain caught the sun and dazzled in Cedric's eyes. Okot smiled even more broadly, his faultless white teeth changing the whole aspect of this face.

---

1   Baraza: A market where problems can be discussed

Unsmiling, he had all the gravity of a tribal elder but when those teeth were displayed, one knew that he had only recently been a boy kicking a football over the uneven field at St. Anthony's Senior Secondary College.

"No, sir, I do not fear Onyango. He is my clan brother. Anyway, I will arrange for the people to come and work. I hope that the Sultan of Bulikiki will help too as the road will assist his people."

"We're making this an all-GodiGodi project, Livingstone."

And Leslie opened more beer cans. "The D.C. feels that coffee is too new a thing up there to make it desirable for the people to come long distances to work. You're all on the spot here."

Okot nodded acquiescence. Clearly, the D.C. meant to have his own way. Yet, genuinely, he had been worried recently by reports of disobedience to his sub-Chiefs. Moreover, men had, it seemed, been meeting in small groups in the sacred woods all over GodiGodi. That was always a bad sign. His father had come to him the day before and told him to be careful. Even Paulo knew that people had changed since Gamage's day. Farrar had not understood his hesitation and it was out of the question to be more explicit. He had promised himself that Queen's Medal and, if he received it, he would be the youngest so honoured in the whole Protectorate. And, taking an even larger view, it would be fatal to all his hopes to be posted away at this stage.

"Oh, Livingstone," called Leslie, as the Chief returned to his chauffeur-driven Mercedes. "The D.C. asked me to say that if you make a success of this, he won't forget you at the New Year."

Okot smiled once more. Garston had used this tactic more than once. Okot was certainly being made to work for his honour.

But it would be worth it. Okot remembered the pride with which he had watched the Queen's Medal being pinned to his own father's breast. He had been allowed into Government House as a special concession. His father had bought him a grey flannel suit just like those worn by the European children who went off in cars to take them to schools hundreds of miles away. And there, on the faultless lawn at Government House, three long days' journey by rail and steamer away, he had seen the Governor walk out of his brilliant white home, in his magnificent ceremonial uniform, the plumes on his great helmet fluttering like captured birds and his decorations tinkling quietly. He had walked slowly down the steps one by one and, on a dais set up under a tree that shaded a piece of the perfect lawn, the Chief Justice had stood next to Okot, immutable and awesome. Then someone had called out names and one by one, the honoured people had come forward to receive their medals, some of them Europeans in stiff white colonial uniform, others, the old chief included, in worn-out suits that lived a lifetime in treasured wooden boxes. As each recipient of an honour came before the Governor, it had seemed to the boy that His Excellency had allowed a gentle smile to break through his stern features; and, when the pinning took place, the great man seemed to be whispering something to each recipient of an honour.

Some of the old Africans came with polished medals already shining on their breasts. His father was one of these and the Governor seemed to spend especially long in pinning on his medal.

"Did he say anything to you?" Okot had asked his father when everybody had dispersed over the lawn to drink sherry. But Paulo had not replied, too absorbed in his moment of greatness.

"I have arranged the baraza at the usual tree near the river," he said, and Leslie nodding knowingly.

Timoteo and Kalisto had, by now, set up the beds and mosquito nets. The hut was a home for hornets, their eggs clinging like opaque white frogspawn to the roof poles. Boaz had disappeared when he was needed to fetch wood and water but arrived back in due course with milk and eggs, a gift from the nearest sub-chief who, ill in bed, had apologised for not coming himself.

An intense orange-gold light bronzed the plain. If you looked for them, you could see hundreds of round huts grouped into little households of four and five but they were part of the plain in the same way as the peasants out late in the cotton fields were part of it.

Voices from nearby called out a message and, scarcely audible, came a reply from far away. Leslie, who was practised, could hear several different conversations conducted between people hundreds of yards away from each other.

The light went and the pressure lamp snorted away while Kalisto laid the table and Timoteo did the cooking. Sitting cosily in his canvas bath, Leslie sponged his chest vigorously to the rhythm of tunes that he had learnt from borrowed records. Outside, the frogs and crickets had begun their interminable squawling in reply. He thought of Thelma, her leaden eyes, her flat chest and her silly, pointless remarks. She would be putting Jill to bed about now and Jill would be playing her up. There would be a scene because Jill was too weak with her. It was good to be on safari.

Leslie decided that it was too late to visit the Father Frascati, the oldest priest in the District who, with Brother Pizzi, ran the Agricultural School. He lived in a nearby Mission. Leslie would often drop in on the old man and enjoy a glass of his guava wine produced especially for Brother Pizzi by the Romba nuns.

The Father never touched a drop himself but seemed to take vicarious pleasure in every sip trickling down a stranger's throat. They wouldn't talk very much and Leslie would spend most of his time looking at pictures in "Oggi" under an enormous photograph of the Holy Father. But tonight, Leslie felt too tired to face the old man's broken English and Brother Pizzi's internment anecdotes. Instead, he sat down at the table under the glare of light and looked up a marker in his "Penguin" Agatha Christie.

It was only when Timoteo brought the soup bubbling in a saucepan that Leslie realised that Cedric was not about. He called but received no reply. He looked behind the mud partition wall into Cedric's bedroom. The bathwater was cool and had obviously been used. He shouted into the night but there was again no answer. There seemed to be no sense in letting the soup get cold and he started to eat. But when Timoteo's version of roast chicken was produced, Leslie called out to Boaz, told him to look for Cedric and, less comfortable, went on eating. And he continued through to the coffee stage before seriously imagining that perhaps something was amiss.

The local chief would have men at hand and quickly he drove up the road to the Chief's house.

Leslie's headlights brought out startled wives and children who stood mutely in front of the vehicle like moths trapped in a beam. They too had been in the middle of eating. He entered the compound of round huts and was led into the chief. A dim hurricane lamp hung from the apex of the hut, casting a glow on a merikani sheet that had been strung across the diameter of the room. Behind the sheet lay the Sub-County Chief, Joel, on a wooden bed. He apologised for being in bed. One of his wives, bare to the waist, retreated from the hut with some dirty plates as Leslie came in.

"I'm sorry to bother you, Joel. What is it, malaria?"

Joel nodded. He was old for a Chief and had received no formal education. What English he knew, he had picked up from his sons and three years' experience as a waiter on the steamer service, many years before.

"Can I have your askaris and any porters who live near at once? Bwana A.D.C. Hamilton-Gandon has disappeared."

Joel called for his eldest son and repeated Leslie's instructions. He insisted on getting up himself and, from a long box well hidden under his bed, he drew out his shotgun.

"Bad, very bad, bad," he kept saying as he pulled on some trousers, struggled into his ex-army greatcoat and crammed an oil-stained shapeless old trilby on his head.

The two askaris were soon found at a local beer club. One reluctant porter stood shivering next to them. Like Joel, he had been in bed, but he had no greatcoat.

They all worked back towards the camp in file along the main road – Joel's son leading, Leslie second. Their progress was almost noiseless and the blackness of the night all-enshrouding. They were about to turn off down a path when the leader heard a noise and stopped in his tracks. The others followed suit at once. Joel gripped his shotgun tighter and steadied his trigger finger. Out of the dark, so tentatively that it was almost inaudible, came the frightened words: "It's Boaz, it's Boaz."

The keeper led the party quickly back to the rest camp while Leslie went for his torch. They all grouped round the latrine. Unhappily wedged on a piece of rock three foot from the filthy bottom and about fifteen foot down himself, Cedric Hamilton-Gandon looked up pitifully at the blinding circle of Leslie's torch.

"Just gave way under me," Cedric said weakly. The light exhibited to him, for the first time, the wealth of insect life with which he was sharing the hole; a cockroach three inches long was crawling across his shirt.

"There but for the grace of God," thought Leslie, as he examined the broken wooden stance that was rotten with white ant.

CHAPTER EIGHT

An Old Type of Chief

Okot had made it an offence under customary law to show dilatoriness in obeying a chief's drum summons. It was, in any case, an offence through the whole District to refuse to answer the summons at all but it was typical of Okot to have made that further stipulation even if it was only casually enforced. He had, moreover, issued an impressive judicial instruction to the Sub-County Courts that sat within his jurisdiction:

"Sub-County chiefs and Court Members must remember that everything which a chief orders is customary law because, according to all our cases and traditions, disobedience to a chief is an offence against customary law."

When he saw a copy of this wisdom, Onyango had fulminated all over the District. "These are not our true chiefs! These are not our true customs! We want traditional men we respect, not prostitutes!"

That morning, the drums were beating all along the Koi banks. Large numbers of people were congregating underneath the Tree of Freedom, so named by Onyango because he was in the habit of holding his meetings there, often as soon as chiefs and touring officers had vacated its shade.

Cedric's camp bed suffered from a pronounced sag. It did little to relieve the aches and bruises that he had inherited from his Joseph-like experience in the pit.

The sun was already hot. He could hear people going about their business outside and was, for a moment, overcome with a feeling of nausea combined with homesickness. But Leslie was already shaving and he levered himself slowly out of bed. A disgusting smell of eggs cooking in cottonseed oil wafted in at the door. It mingled with the odour of polish and Brasso that had been used on their shoes and uniform.

By wearing his solar topee at an exceedingly rakish angle, Leslie managed to escape looking absurd. Cedric had no such good fortune. The brim of his topee very nearly touched the uppermost tips of his ears. He had forgotten elastic bands for his long socks that now slipped slowly anklewards.

They motored through the county for another eight miles, past the County Dispensary with its vividly-coloured congregation of women in long dresses with babies strapped to their backs, past the great red Roman Catholic Church which had been built over sixty years back by Father Frascati and one lay brother, past several mud-walled schools standing in green spaces also used for football.

Now and again, a lorry would approach from the opposite direction at frightening speed leaving Leslie guiding his car almost intuitively through the encircling cloud of dust. They turned right into a rough track leading to the river.

From the Tree of Freedom, one could hear the Koi swirling round great rocks in its bed. In the wet season, these boulders were well covered by the swollen current but, during the dry months, people were able to hop from stone to stone with some difficulty. Men were crossing from East GodiGodi that morning.

Akisoferi Adaa, the County Chief of East GodiGodi, was already sitting under the tree with his sub-chiefs, waiting.

Adaa was what the Administration called the "old type of chief". A little addicted to the processes of democratic government, he had no patience with the growing element of boys just out of school who would not decide to knuckle down to cultivation, fondling hopes of being a clerk in the D.C.'s office instead. There were always a few of that sort in his County lock-up, on remand for some unspecified offence. He had noticed with great sorrow that mounting disrespect borne by sons for their fathers, the growing incidence of emigration down-country with its consequent impoverishment of the District. One night at an official sundowner in Romba, he had sighed to Garston that the steamer on the Mamba Great River was like the rain. "It takes away our children as the rain takes away our land." For the rest, he could be more or less relied upon to obey instructions even if he was considered a little stupid. But he cut a dignified figure, and, although he was scarcely capable of writing a letter himself, from the breast pocket of the shiny blue jacket that he wore over his kanzu peeped the caps of six ball pens.

About two hundred men were waiting for the officers by now. There were no women for it was considered a presumption for them to attend barazas. All were sitting around the tree in a great semi-circle. Some were full in the heat of the sun and were complaining in low murmurs. Nearly all were wearing shirts and shorts in various stages of repair and decrepitude; the shirts of a few were torn generously right across the back; various of the shorts had been patched so many times that little remained of the original drill. Not many wore shoes. There were, however, one or two, conversing loudly to each other over the heads of the others, whose tidy white shirts and well-ironed grey flannels marked them out as schoolmasters. But, with that exception, dress signified little or nothing. The economics of a man's life had to be read from his face and not argued from his clothes. For instance, Manuel Fenekhazi, who sat cross legged with a serious, important expression on his long, furrowed face, was dressed in an ancient pair of yellow underpants and a dirty singlet that only crossed one shoulder. Yet he had collected over one hundred and fifty pounds for his cotton in the previous season, enjoyed eight wives and had just opened a small shop in the Koi Trading Centre.

Although there were some in the crowd who, at Onyango's instigation, had vowed that one day they would remain seated when the D.C. or an A.D.C. came to address them, just as in England a few people promise themselves a similar outrage in a cinema during the National Anthem, they all rose as one man as Leslie walked to his chair followed closely by Cedric.

"Ikawa," Leslie greeted them in the local tongue.

"Muruli," replied the two hundred. Many were smiling.

They were immensely pleased when a white man took the trouble to learn their greetings and, if he could say additionally, 'How are you?' and 'I am well' in the vernacular, he would at once be congratulated on his complete fluency in their language.

There was much handshaking with the various chiefs present. A few of the traditional village elders came forward to present their respects. Adaa then rose to introduce the officers. Semei, the interpreter, translated back to Leslie:

"Mr A.D.C. Furry, Mr A.D.C. Hamilt, we are glad to have you with us today. The people of GodiGodi always welcome touring officers for they know that they bring progress. Today, the people of both counties have gathered here to listen to your important news. We shall all obey what you have to say because you bring progress. Before you came there were no dispensaries, no schools, no roads, no buses, no shops, no cotton. We were in very poor condition. But you lifted us up and we have gone forward. Soon, we shall be independent and we shall have to do alone those things that you have done for us. We hope that you will remain to help us."

Okot added a few words, sedulously avoiding the subject of the road. He had decided that Leslie should take first knock on that score. Leslie began with the time-honoured form of address:

"County chiefs, gombolola chiefs, muluka chiefs and council members of each, and people of East and West GodiGodi Counties, I thank you for your greeting. I am pleased to be talking to you today. I want to introduce Mr Hamilton-Gandon to you. He has just come from England and the D.C. is sending him to work with you."

The chiefs clapped this remark. Cedric blushed.

"I know that he will do all he can to promote your wellbeing…"

"Promote?" queried Semei.

"I know he will do all he can to make you happy," paraphrased Leslie. "I have several things to say to you today." With Okot beside him, he now felt bound to give the road emphatic publicity but hoped to weaken the shock by wrapping the news in the standard exhortations in which every District Officer was expected to indulge.

"Your cotton must be properly picked over before you take it to the buyer… latrines at least 15' deep are advisable… tell your wives to wash their hands before going back to prepare the food… it is no good eating plantain by itself, you need meat and eggs and beans as well… give your children some groundnuts to eat at school for lunch… no wonder your cows get thin and weedy if you keep them tethered all day…"

After fifteen minutes of this, eyelids were half-closing on many pairs of eyes. The audience had, over the years, developed a resistance to the gamut of injunctions dutifully ranged over by many generations of touring officers. Ultimately, each man there knew what counted was the degree of intimate control exercised over his affairs by the local chief. A chief with a passion for time and distance tests on pit latrines could make life unbearable. The dropping stone would be heard almost immediately, the chief would issue a warning, and if there were no apparent change a week later, a summons would follow. Perhaps there had been an understandable use of a mildly perjorative term in the process and there one would be in front of a sub-county court charged with showing disrespect to a chief, with disobedience to a chief, and finally with breach of the custom that pit latrines should be at least fifteen feet deep. That could be worth 20/- or one month and, if, in addition, one called the prosecuting chief a lying hound in open court, six months was not too much to expect. But this District Officer standing there giving out the same old stuff on a hot, hot day was relatively harmless.

Leslie was rapidly running out of subjects. If they had grown tobacco in the GodiGodis, he would have talked about moisture content in the leaf but there was no tobacco. Abandoning the idea that they might swallow an academic discussion of the problems of producing this crop in Bulikiki, he took the plunge.

"Now, I want to say something very important." Semei knew what was coming and translated 'important' by such a potent word that all looked up from their torpor and assumed wideawake expressions. Leslie remembered that, after all, Garston would only have himself to blame for the consequences if the scheme misfired. He was damned if he knew why he had been treading so cautiously.

"The D.C. and the officials of the District Council have decided to help you build a bridge and road from West GodiGodi through East GodiGodi to Port Steamer." There was an outbreak of quick clapping.

"They are finding a lot of money to help you make these things but you must do the actual work with the assistance of a few skilled people from the District Council." Now there was absolute silence. Only the rush of the river came muted through the trees ranged along its banks.

"The County Chiefs will arrange to inform you on what days you must come and work." From several mouths came a blunt "ee!", the local enclitic of dismayed surprise. "They will do this very carefully and make sure that nobody does much more than anybody else. I know that you all wish to co-operate with the chiefs in this. You have seen the great trouble you receive at present. Many of you have lost relatives trying to cross the river. With a bridge, you will be able to travel freely. Again, with regard to cotton, those of you who belong to the co-operative society, will not have so long to wait before your cotton is collected and taken to the ginnery. In that way, your stores will not become so full up that you have to keep the cotton on a dirty floor at home and then sell it at a low price. Also, the co-operative society which is still very much in debt will pay for the ginnery much more quickly."

These advantages were evidently not palpable enough for the listeners. Leslie was disturbed to notice that, instead of exchanging angry glances among each other, many of them were smiling unnaturally and joking more or less audibly to each other. Angry looks here and there could mean individual discontents but that was nothing new and could be dealt with; sardonic smiles and jokes in front of a touring officer were more sinister portents. Trials of strength were never pleasant affairs.

Leslie decided not to persevere further with his address but, instead, to attempt to ride the inevitable storm of questions.

Rising to his feet as though a superhuman effort had been necessary to achieve the position, one of the schoolmasters surveyed the sea of heads around and beneath him with a boyish pout intended to denote casual unconcern. He could not have been long out of teacher-training college. As he spoke, he fixed his eyes on an upper branch of the tree and only when he was about to utter the final words of a question did he bring the full benefit of his awful gaze to bear on Leslie.

"We are, as always, pleased to see the officer. We have come a long way to hear him. We came hoping to hear of a reduction in taxation. Instead, we hear that the D.C. has decided to bring slavery back to this country…"

"Who is he?" whispered Leslie to Okot.

"Prominent member of the Freedom Party of this area. Branch Representative for GodiGodi."

"… the D.C., I repeat, has decided to do what his ancestors tried to stop when they drove away the Arabs from this country. He is showing us that he is not interested in going forward, only backwards. But I am not going to take a long time. I want to ask the D.C. three questions. The first one is…," he braced himself. "Why doesn't he kill us all with a rifle at once since he has decided to kill us?"

"I won't answer stupid, insolent questions," said Leslie, on the verge of losing control of himself. Unfortunately, the only word for stupid that Semei knew had an intensity equivalent to that of 'bastard' applied to a Cockney.

"So the D.C. thinks we are stupid!" There were several murmurings in the crowd. "We thought of him as our father and now he tells us we are stupid."

"What father tells his son that he is stupid?" He paused for effect. "My second question is this…" and now he looked so earnestly and angrily at his branch that one might have thought he meant to bore holes through it with his eyes.

"…why does the D.C. not consult us first before telling us we must build a road? If he had consulted us, we should have told him to bring machines from the District Council, bring paid porters and skilled workers and then build the road."

This remark met with much success from the people who clapped it immediately and semi-hysterically.

Leslie countered: "Your country is a poor country. The District Council receives very little in taxes and there is not enough to pay for the machines and porters. That is why we must build the road cheaply. In other parts of this country, people are very willing to contribute to the good of the community in this way. It is only silly persons like you who pretend to represent the good of the people and who, in fact, slow everything up by talking as you have talked."

The schoolteacher, totally unimpressed by this attempt to shame him, gave the appearance of not having listened to it while he continued to bore through the branch.

"The third question which I wish to ask the D.C. is when will he introduce a new crop like tobacco to these counties?"

Leslie was delighted. The questioning had taken one of those illogical twists that sometimes occurred at barazas and a diversion from the main theme had been created. Had opposition at the meeting been strong and organised, the teacher would have been ordered to sit down by the others as soon as he had introduced this irrelevance. As it was, Leslie answered him at some length and he did not rise again except to announce that he was far from satisfied.

An old man was on his feet. He turned out to be a village elder who had walked about ten miles to the baraza. His voice was so weak that Semei could hardly translate what he said.

"Er… Bwana D.C. … you said we are poor here… that is true… we are very poor… your country is rich… bring us the machines that print your money and we too shall be rich."

Leslie turned with a smile to Cedric.

"Would you like to answer that one?"

Cedric braced himself, blushed deeply again and stammered out:

"Well, it's all a matter of inflation. Too few goods being chased by too much money. It would never do, you see, because paper notes arc only symbols…"

Semei turned to Leslie and said that he did not understand a word of this. Leslie asked him to tell the man that the machines were very expensive and that the country could not afford them. The man, highly contented with this reply, sat down laughing at his new-won knowledge.

Another man came forward with a wad of dispensary chits going back to 1927. They were all indecipherable but he laid them gently on the table in front of Leslie.

"He wants tax-exemption on the grounds of sickness," said Semei. "Next safari," replied Leslie tersely and the man went off waving the chits above his head.

More questioners spoke up with requests for dispensaries, boreholes, cattle vaccine, cottonseed, markets and a vernacular programme on the Protectorate broadcasting system. Nobody mentioned the road again. At one point, a tall, emaciated man wearing only an ill-cured goathide round his waist jumped up from the outer fringe of the crowd. His hair was not short and matted but, Medusa-like, sprouting black snakes of dusty wool hopelessly intertwined. His ribs were protruded miserably. With an idiotic smile that revealed long, yellow teeth here and there in his mouth, he trod delicately between the people who separated him from the table. Then he stood silently in front of Adaa who immediately took out an odd piece of scrap paper from his pocket – it turned out to be a bus ticket – and wrote his name upon it. He handed it to the man, who snatched it greedily and retreated uttering wild, unearthly shrieks. Everybody was laughing at him and he himself joined in.

"He comes every day to Adaa for a letter," explained Okot.

CHAPTER NINE

A Tryst

A grassy track curled three times around The Bishop's Pimple like a chute on a fairground tower. It was just wide enough to admit a car and the Fathers' vehicle had carved out well-defined wheel tracks, leaving a high mud ridge, dried rock hard, between them. The weeds sprouting profusely from this ridge concealed its hazards, among them small rocks and incipient anthills. The Romba Fathers alone seemed able to negotiate successfully the "Pimple" while other motorised aspirants were soon discouraged from testing the thickness of their sumps and usually walked up from the bottom. The church, which had been Mamba District's first experience of the Gothic in sun-dried brick, stood to the fore of the Pimple, its west end topped by a large wooden cross set with electric light bulbs. Nearby stood the long tessellated block of the seminary. Flowerbeds had been laid out in profusion around these buildings but there were few flowers to fill them.

Just before one passed through the iron gates of the Mission, a little path forked off to the right and led down gently to a great concrete plateau patterned with manhole covers. This was Romba's reservoir. Just to the side of the plateau was a tiny copse of trees standing on what was known as the European cemetery, a misnomer, as no Europeans outside the missionary population aimed to die or to be buried in Romba and the missionaries made other arrangements within their own grounds. There was, however, one explanatory grave. It belonged to a Nathaniel Stedbury who had died in mysterious circumstances on the slopes of Mount Buni in 1929. He had been digging for gold and, according to the current theory, had started channeling into the traditional resting places of Bulikiki notables when a spear had checked his further research. As always, the Public Works Department had had a coffin ready for such a contingency and an issue voucher had promptly been made out in the name of Nathaniel Stedbury. On his collapsed gravestone sat Leslie and Angela.

"Leslie darling, I don't feel good about meeting here. It seems all wrong so near the church."

"I don't see that distance would make it righter."

"It's all very well for you. You're not a Catholic. You forget that I'm supposed to go up and tell the

Father that I have committed adultery not one hundred yards from the confessional. It's all so sordid. Let's go somewhere else next time."

"And will you tell him?"

"Don't be ridiculous! But just suppose I broke down or something. It happens, you know. Emotional stresses get on top of one and one longs to confide in…"

"You're not a very good security risk, you know."

"I know, Leslie, but couldn't we make other arrangements?"

"I find these surroundings rather delightful and exotic. Nobody dreams of coming here yet we're within five minutes of home. We have trees, birds, a superb view and… I have you."

He reached for another Penguin biscuit.

"You never take your pleasures singly, do you?" said Angela.

He lay on his back in the deep shade watching the patterns made by the leaves and branches against the bright afternoon blue of the sky.

"Has your husband been good to you?"

"Why ask? He is utterly, but utterly, consumed by this new road idea of his. He gets up at three in the morning and draws the seating arrangements for the opening ceremony all over my best writing paper. He said 'cantilever bridge' in his sleep last night. Garston is nothing if not the visionary these days. I can't tell you what a bore he is with it all." She sighed deeply. Angela was not pretty in the unsubtle and obvious way in which Diana was pretty.

But she had those austere good looks associated with certain young English horsewomen, enhanced perhaps because she had been away from horses for a long time. The ten years separating her from Leslie had perhaps been the principal catalyst to form their present involvement. He saw in her the attractive, mature woman with whom he could satisfy the devil-may-care roué that he imagined himself to be, an essential aspect of his nature, hitherto sadly neglected through the exigencies of the service but, since the very service itself was packing up, not to be denied a moment longer.

Thelma, too, was an added incentive towards Angela's slender – and only slightly freckled – arms. She, for her part, felt that she saw in Leslie something of what she had wanted Garston to be years back: acute, unceremonious, slightly disreputable, and passionate. She recognised that Leslie would probably never really get anywhere in his career, while Garston had, after all, been given a District but told herself that she would rather have had Garston selling door-to-door insurance with the sort of offensive apology for a smile that Leslie so often wore than administer the whole Protectorate with that killing earnestness of his. But she was clear on one thing: Leslie could never actually replace Garston. Leslie, after all, was only Garston in another guise, a stand-in. Only, during those long weeks of safari when Garston pushed her casually out of his existence as easily as he closed the verandah door to leave her behind, she had the leisure to lie on her bed and watch images of life as it might have been forming in the beam of blue smoke that curled from the cigarette in her long ivory holder. When those moods arrived, she needed Leslie desperately.

It was while they were preparing to leave their love-nest that the unprecedented happened.

"Listen!" whispered Angela.

A medley of voices seemed to be coming nearer.

"My God! There's someone on the little path," said Leslie, lying down as though under rapid fire from a machine gun.

"Don't stay there, stupid! Let's move down the hill quickly," said Angela.

But it was too late. A babble of voices speaking Urdu heralded a party of four Indians, among whom was the eldest Patel of Messrs. Patel, Patel and Patel, the tycoon grocers. The other three belonged to the ranks of the Romba solvent, if not the wealthy. They were all old men, two of them were wearing dhotis and velvet pill-box hats.

They sat down cross-legged on the concrete plateau.

"Oh Lord!" moaned Leslie, "they're going to play cards."

He had adduced correctly. The pack of cards was produced and the four were soon immersed in one of those marathon meditations that one associates with oriental systems of philosophy and world-championship chess games.

"We dare not break cover, dare we?" asked Angela, after one hour prone in the copse.

"No!" said Leslie.

"Couldn't we say we've been visiting the church or something and decided to come down another way?" she pleaded.

"No, there is no other way."

"What time is it?"

"Five-thirty."

Angela shuddered. Garston would surely be home by now if he was not on the golf course. Usually, she told him that she had been walking but rarely did she take walks lasting more than an hour when he was not on safari.

"What about Thelma?" she asked Leslie.

"It's her raffia class day at the Anglican mission. Won't be back till six. God! How much longer are they going to be?"

Another thirty minutes passed.

"It might not be so bad if I didn't owe Patel three months' groceries," muttered Leslie. "He's already asking me to be generous about his quota of whole-saler licences."

It was getting dark.

Angela started: "Look!"

Garston and Geoffrey Manley were playing off No. 6 tee immediately at the bottom of the pimple. From the hideout, they looked like absurd tin soldiers. The meditations on the plateau continued unabated. Lying immobilised in the copse, the couple began to feel its cool evening dankness.

"Got pins and needles everywhere," said Angela.

But Leslie was asleep.

When it became too dark for cards and not a minute sooner, the four players broke spontaneously into a pent-up babble with Welsh-like intonations, and then they got up.

"Thank God! They're going!" Angela tugged gently at Leslie's jacket. They both watched the retreating party.

Then Patel stooped to pick something up. It was a half-empty cigarette packet that Leslie had forgotten near the tank when he had sat down for a cigarette before Angela's arrival. And it could only be of interest to Patel because Leslie was the one European soul in Romba who smoked that brand. He had to make a special order down-country for it.

Leslie watched in disgust. "Sherlock Patel bloody Holmes!" he muttered.

Angela went first up the path. Then she ran down the hill on the main track. Feeling secure in the darkness, she took a short cut over the golf course instead of following the track down to its junction with the main Port Steamer Road, and, too intent on examining the ground she was treading, bumped abruptly into the corpulent white-cassocked figure of Father Grimaldi from the seminary as he toiled upwards.

"Ah! Mrs Moorside!"

Angela smiled sickly. "Sorry, Father. I wasn't looking where I was going."

"No worry, no worry," said the Father, smiling indulgently.

And he began scrimmaging about in the folds of his robe. Then, he withdrew a number of duplicated pamphlets considerably rucked up by his hasty search.

"Would you be so kind...?"

"Of course," said Angela. She took the letters, invitations to the Romba whites to come to a showing of *Richard III* in the Seminary Hall.

Leslie waited for fifteen minutes after Angela had left. He then stumbled through the grass and boulders to the bottom, avoiding the tracks.

Thelma had just put Jill to bed when he arrived home.

"Where on earth have you been?" she asked, looking at his long socks that were full of burrs.

Their houseboy, Timoteo, stood at one door, looking on impassively.

"Oh, I had to go and investigate some tale that a man on the outskirts of the town was distilling gin."

"Diana's houseboy told Timoteo that he had seen you visiting the Fathers."

Leslie bent down quickly, ostensibly to pick out burrs. "Oh, I dropped in on the way back."

"I don't quite know why but I don't believe you," said Thelma quietly, as she went to look for her sewing bag.

Jill began sobbing noisily as though terrified by some dreadful augury.

"Oh hell!" said Leslie.

Angela entered her house through the kitchen door and immediately began supervising arrangements for the evening meal, which the cook had well in hand.

A sweet smell of tobacco preceded Garston down the corridor leading to the kitchen from the dining room.

Angela braced herself.

"Terribly sorry, darling. I didn't know you were in here. I got down to some paperwork on the old road when I got in from golf."

"That's alright Garston, dear," said Angela, sprinkling paprika into the stew.

CHAPTER TEN

Politics

Reuben Onyango was trying to win the four counties of Bulikiki for his party. He lodged with the area representative of the Freedom Party near the Ogi Trading Centre and only two miles away from the Sultan's compound.

Onyango, a man from GodiGodi, was at a tribal disadvantage here but if it was true that the Wagodi and the Babuliki were traditional enemies, for all practical purposes, Pax Britannica had put an end to the actual fighting. The one point on which Garston and Onyango were absolutely agreed, however, was that the old Sultan's aspirations for Bulikiki to secede from the District and set up on its own had to be proved patently absurd, the mental aberrations of a senile old man, or, if that were not possible, rendered anodine by sterner methods.

For Garston, the problem was one of security but, for Onyango, it was the effect of a direction from his Party. The first representative elections would soon be held and the Freedom Party was looking to Mamba District for a clean sweep of four members returned to the new Legislative Assembly. The only other national party of importance, the Independent People's Group, was weak in the District. But the Sultan of Bulikiki was known to be organising a new group pledged to secure the Bulikiki secession. Bulikiki was to be worth two seats, possibly vital to Freedom Party interests.

Until recently, Onyango and the Sultan had co-operated in the subversion of much that Garston had tried to do in Bulikiki. But now this serious difference had sprung up between them. The time had come to discredit the old man.

The Sultan (who was only a "Sultan" because Captain James Martinsen had decided that this was a suitable translation of the local term for the position of the present chief's father) lived on the slope of a hill in a large settlement of round huts enclosed by a high fence of papyrus. A gap in the fence admitted a drive that was swept daily by prisoners in the Ogi lock-up. Parked just inside the fence and inside a mud garage, was the Sultan's Chevrolet. It had three wheels, no engine and one side was bent in from its last crash ten years previously. The Sultan had long since preferred the mountain to come to Mohammed.

He would spend a large part of his day sitting on a rocking chair at a metal table that was transfixed by the pole of an enormous blue sunshade, which he had spotted in a London shop. He had paid heavy excess baggage on his flight back but the sunshade now lent additional prestige to the sanctum and comforted his old age.

Although he had no official duties to perform, the Sultan took care to supervise those who had.

Effectively, the four county chiefs were his appointees. Many District Commissioners and appointment committees of the African District Council had attempted to provide their own men. A word from the Sultan had ensured the necessity to replace them at once with more suitable candidates.

Onyango's gleaming blue car nosed gently up the drive. His schoolboy interpreter sat beside him. It was one of the illogicalities of his position that he could not speak Kilikiki and was forced to use English. After a few words with the Sultan's private soldier, an old man of eighty dressed in a uniform made for him in Romba eight years before was allowed to park his car at the entrance and accede to the Presence. He left the schoolboy behind. The Sultan, dressed in a kanzu and turban, was fanning himself with a fly-switch. A film he had seen in England had persuaded him that all Sultans worth their salt had to be discovered fanning themselves with a fly-switch.

Onyango, for his part, was wearing his bowler hat. It was known, even to the Sultan, that the politician would only remove the precious article from its cardboard box on very important occasions and the Sultan took the compliment to his heart. He greeted Onyango in English. His father had had him taught, but not converted, by the early Christian missionaries in the District.

From beyond the pallisade came the lowing of the Sultan's three hundred cows as they were driven down the hillside to pasture. The morning air was cool and crisp.

"I hear that you have been telling my people that the D.C. has been bribed by an Indian."

"Yes."

"Well, stop it! Nobody can bribe Bwana Moorside, you know that."

Onyango took some little time to recover.

"But I have only been telling what I know…"

"You know nothing! Stop telling my people lies. You will make trouble."

"I have come to tell you something very important," he looked straight into the Sultan's eyes. "I want to help Bulikiki to become independent at once."

The old man ordered his nearest wife to buy European beer at the Trading Centre.

"Why do you think that I can believe you? Your party is against Bulikiki Independence."

"I have persuaded them that it is better for Bulikiki to leave Mamba District at once. In that way, we shall be able to put all our energies into GodiGodi and Mamba and win those two seats."

This appeared to make some impression on the Sultan who sat in silence for a little time. Onyango then produced a letter that he described as instructions to him from his party executive. He was to make it clear to the Sultan that the Freedom Party would not stand in the way of Bulikiki secession.

"I have verbal instructions," whispered Onyango, "which my Party could not put in a letter. I am ordered to help you organise a protest march to the D.C.'s office. The people will demand Independence. If the D.C. does not give them a satisfactory reply, they must riot. After the riots, the Government will send a Commission of Enquiry and you will be able to put your case to them." Onyango leaned forward in reverence to the information that he was about to impart.

"The report will go to England and the Secretary of State for the Colonies will make a Constitution with Bulikiki separated from the rest of the Country. You know as well as I do that you never achieve anything with the British unless you make trouble. After the trouble, they are always better friends than before it, though it takes time. It is what is known as the empirical method of government. I have studied English constitutional history at the University College, you know."

The Sultan took some home-made snuff from a little cylindrical cow-hide box.

"You make it sound very tempting," the Sultan said. "I think I may agree. Come back in a week and I will let you have my final decision."

Onyango drove off well-pleased with himself. He was due to address a meeting of the Bulikiki Young Farmers' Association, meeting secretly in an isolated bar some miles away. The Association had been formed by Peter Freeman to ensure better cultivation methods with particular attention to coffee. Its members had abandoned coffee and emerged long after Freeman had forgotten them as Onyango's supporters in Bulikiki.

The politician told them what had been planned by the Party. They could count on him for several paid jobs after freedom if the Party was successful.

"How can we believe you?" a cadaverous man with a squint kept on asking. Onyango grew increasingly impatient with these interruptions. "Will you be quiet and allow me to explain matters to the people here?"

"How can we believe you?" the man persisted.

"Shut up, man, will you!"

"I think you talk nonsense to us!"

"*Will* you be quiet?"

"No".

"Wait until you have your freedom! Then I'll make sure that you bloody well *will* be quiet!"

But, for the most part, Onyango convinced his clandestine supporters, one of whom, a minor chief, was taken aside by the politician and asked to warn the dissenter among them that a land case would be brought against him in the local law court if he continued his bickerings.

After four more days of secret meetings, all attended by police informers, Onyango decided to head back for Romba. A new session was about to begin in the Legislative Council and he wanted to prepare a fresh onslaught on 'the unnecessary and wasteful post of District Commissioner', as he called it. He had already drawn up three headings for his speech on the matter:

"District Commissioner":

1.   Has no influence;
2.   Does nothing;
3.   Steals land.

Nonetheless, the morning after he had arrived in Romba, he sought an interview with Garston. Rodrigues poked his head through the D.C.'s office window and cleared his throat.

The pipe was smoking well and Garston was studying a secret report on the meetings in Bulikiki.

"What is it?" said Garston, not looking up.

"I do believe it's that dreadful man Onyango," whispered Diana, who had caught sight of the bowler-hatted figure hovering outside.

"Send him in, Rodrigues," directed Garston. Onyango appeared, grinning. "Been expecting you, Mr Onyango." He greeted the politician cordially. They shook hands.

"Mr Moorside," began Reuben, removing his hat. "I would not trouble you this morning except that I have important news for you, and I know that you are the man with the influence in the District."

"You flatter me."

"No, it is true. I do not always praise the D.C. but you must understand that I have to humour my supporters." He smiled faintly.

"Well, what's the news? That I've been taking bribes from Mr Muljibhai?"

"Sir, you must understand that..."

"I know, you have your supporters to think of. Well, what is it?"

"The Sultan of Bulikiki is planning to make a big march to Romba and to start riots here."

Garston looked through the appropriate paragraph of his report.

"And what else?"

"I thought that you would remove him from Bulikiki so that he cannot cause the District to suffer."

"I shall have to wait for the riots."

"It will be bad if they come," said Onyango, uncomfortably. He had staked much on an idea that Garston had long been looking for good reason to give the old Sultan a holiday somewhere else in the Protectorate.

"Is that all, Mr Onyango? Because, if it is, please leave my office before the office boy helps you to. And be very careful what you say and do during the next few weeks. I have my eye fixed carefully upon you. Now, get out!"

"You are colour-bar![2] You are colour-bar! Yes, colour-bar!" called Onyango, raising his voice as he retreated backwards, brandishing his briefcase.

Garston leant back in his chair and turned to Diana. "I can expect trouble now. I can see it all: "D.C. hinders settled British policy of Democracy". That's how the Freedom Press will put it. He'll get on to the District Council – get them to pass a motion of censure on me which I shall have to delete from their minutes as unconstitutional and then they'll pass a vote of censure on my deletion before dissolving themselves in a fury. What a Country!"

"He'd be in prison if I had my way," said Diana.

During Onyango's interview with Garston, the old Sultan, relaxing his general rule, had also come to

---

2   A much used expression to define colour descrimination.

Romba in a County Chief's car. He decided to visit Father Cincillati before seeing the D.C.

Muslim and Catholic, chief and priest, were nonetheless the best of friends, the Father believing that the Sultan's conversion would be the key to the fall of Islam in the District. They had frequently hunted and eaten together when the Father was living on an out-mission in Bulikiki. Now, recalled to Romba as Education Secretary, Cincillati sometimes needed the old man's advice on place names in a treatise entitled 'Native burying places in Bulikiki' which he was about to publish. He had already written several books on various aspects of the District's history and was now, through a study of the Mount Buni graves, so fatal to Steadman, arriving at some exciting new conclusions on the nature of the Bulikiki area, its former wealth and the likelihood of it having been the centre of a not inconsiderable material civilisation concurrent with the Aztec experience in Mexico. But he was quite sure that neither the Bulikiki, the Wagodi or the Wamamba had been in the vicinity at the time. It was this that grieved the Sultan.

"Look, Father, you say that many graves on Mount Buni do not seem to belong to my people. Do you think that we would adopt the burying place of another people?"

"It certainly seems to have happened. At the time of Bulikiki's greatest wealth, I believe that your ancestors were in Ethiopia or possibly Mauritania. I cannot be sure yet. All the pots indicate one or other of those places. But the older ones in present Bulikiki are quite different."

The Sultan paused for a moment, adjusting his voluminous turban. His sandals tapped impatiently the stone floor of the Father's ante-room and he wiggled his bare toes.

"Is it not possible, Father, that the old tribe you talk about came from the same place as we did? After all, the people of Bululiki might have invented new pots when they decided to drive out the Mamba many hundred years later?"

"I cannot rule it out," said Cincillati, smiling and stroking his grey goatee.

"Good, then it is quite clear to me that Bulikiki has had a great civilisation and, if so, my people cannot for that reason be joined with these Godi and Mamba savages when we are independent."

"That is not my affair," replied the Father firmly. The Sultan persisted.

"And now, I want one more favour from you," he said. "I want you to change the title of the book you are writing about this ancient civilisation. Mr Peebles, when he was digging rocks in Bulikiki, suggested a good title."

He fumbled around in the cavalry drill trousers under his kanzu and took out a wallet crammed with dirty pieces of paper. Laying all these out on a table, he finally selected a piece of graph paper on which Peebles had written: *"Ancient Glories of the Bulikiki Independent Empire"*.

"It is true, Musa, that people say that the pen is mightier than the sword," said the Father, still smiling benignly, "but you cannot fight with my book."

Down in the D.C.'s Office, Garston had been conferring with John Fawcett on the best way to counter the Sultan's protest march. Fawcett, never the sentimentalist, had suggested "mowing them down with Bren guns" but each had, in the end, gone back to his desk to prepare a draft scheme involving more acceptable measures which they would compare later.

The Sultan appeared at the office just as Garston was leaving for lunch. After a long exchange of courtesies in the course of which Garston asked after the ruler's wife, never his wives, the old man leant across Garston's desk and confided that Reuben Onyango should be removed form the District at once. He was trying to persuade Bulikiki people to riot in Romba.

"My people have been civilised for very many centuries. We do not riot. The pen is mightier than the sword, you know."

CHAPTER ELEVEN

Avoiding Snakes

Cedric was accompanied on the Koi Road project by Morris Mbuya. Garston had made it clear that, although Morris was the senior according to the Staff List, it would be easier "in light of the delicate mood of the people" in GodiGodi if Cedric appeared to have the command. Morris realised the strength of the argument and resented it.

Okot and Adaa had put the full force of their authority to the test. Communal labour was ordered throughout the two counties and several minor chiefs were told to keep records of the men who turned up to work and the defaulters. Unfortunately, the main effect of these lists was to focus attention on the casual absence of those who never appeared at all. There was also a market in exemptions granted by certain keepers of the list, sixpence per day or 2/6d. for the whole week being the prevailing rates. When business tailed off, it was merely necessary for the chiefs involved to walk a little further afield and quote their rates, with, of course, a "consideration" for keeping a prosecution for disobedience out of the Courts. Several indictments for attempted corruption of a chief were brought before the Native Courts against unfortunates who had not possessed the ready cash.

The honest chiefs, however, relied on the Courts from the beginning. It was a signal of the decline of their powers that they should have found it necessary to do so. The sub-county chiefs took to convening their Courts at least twice a week. They too had their incentive. Okot had warned them that failure to produce their sub-county labour quota would involve them in a loss of increment.

Cedric and Morris had been instructed to keep an eye on the conduct of these cases whenever they could. But their main task was, as Garston had put it, to "throw the bridge over and push the road through before the rains beat you to it". Dison Apau, the Works Superintendent from the African District Council, had arrived with a lorry-load of worn-out spades, picks and crowbars. He was accompanied by three subordinates who had been on a three months' bridge-building course. In his pocket was a carefully-drawn sketch by Garston of what he wanted the bridge to look like when complete. Two lorries with a large selection of rusty girders and several dozen bags of cement stood at an embryonic works yard near the Tree of Freedom.

A column of porters carried their loads from the Tree of Freedom through the river bed and three miles into East GodiGodi. Dison remained behind with the river and his drawing to occupy him. The terrain through which the projected road was to run was mostly flat and rocky. A proliferation of small trees covered what was otherwise a surface of bald, powdery earth, the victim of vicious sheet erosion. Homesteads followed the sinuous convolutions of the Koi River but, otherwise, East GodiGodi was very sparsely peopled. Now and again, a candelabra euphorbia would raise its imploring arms to heaven as if begging for rain.

As they walked, they became aware of the rhythmic thumping of machinery somewhere ahead. It was an odd noise seventy miles from Romba and in one of the more deserted parts of the District.

"It's the driller's hammer, I think," said Morris, after listening for some time.

The drilling rig was set up in an open, dusty space. A few apathetic Africans supervised the endless plunging of the great steel bolt hundreds of feet into the dry earth. Nearby stood Björnsson's caravan, similar in many respects to a Roma's. It had a diminutive verandah at one end, like the platform on a railway guard's carriage, where a mangy-looking dog of uncertain breed lay sleeping on a red carpet thick with its hairs. At the foot of the steps up to the verandah reclined a pretty African girl of about fourteen. She wore a brilliant mauve sheet that coiled round her body, leaving her shoulders bare. She was biting, sucking and spitting out sugar cane, interrupted only momentarily by the newcomers. As Cedric climbed the stairs, the dog sat up and barked. Björnsson rolled off his bed and came out to see who was there.

"By God! It's hot, eh?" Björnsson was wearing an evil-smelling singlet and an old pair of drill trousers. The sun caught his silky blonde hair and individual spines on his stubbled chin. He was not sure whether he recognised Cedric but asked him in for a bottle of beer. Morris wandered over to the pounding drill.

Inside the caravan, Cedric took in an iron bed-stead, two camp chairs, a trunk full of clothes, an expensive-looking radio, a box with some improvised shelves for a few cups and plates and a battered kerosene refrigerator covered with unwashed plates and saucepans. A metal mirror was nailed to the wall.

"I'm going to Romba tonight. You going?"

"I've only just got here. I don't think Moorside would approve."

"You come to work near here?"

"Yes, I'm supposed to be building a road."

"What about that black?"

"He's helping me."

"You been Africa long time?"

"Just a few weeks. And you?"

"Ten year."

"Have you always been drilling boreholes?"

"Alway."

"Do you like the life?"

A rueful smile played for a moment under the stubble.

"You like the money, you like the life," Björnsson said eventually, going for another bottle. "Come 'ere, I show you something," and he beckoned Cedric to a small slit in one wall of the caravan. Standing beside seven empty beer crates stood an immaculate new estate car.

"She lovely, eh?"

"It certainly is," said Cedric.

"I drove her through the trees and bloody rocks from Port Steamer. Took us three hour," explained Björnsson.

"Hot today, eh?"

There was a pause.

"Yes it is. Don't you ever get lonely here?" asked Cedric.

"I get used."

The porters with the District Officers' baggage were resting from the midday heat under the grudging shade of nearby trees. Cedric ordered them up and the final leg of the walk began. The pulsations of the drill stayed with them for another half an hour. They rejoined the Koi at a point seven miles from Port

Steamer, roughly the halfway point in the road. Adaa was there to meet them. A group of locals had been preparing the site. They worked hard till evening.

The insects came out in battalions with the night: sausage flies, mosquitoes that gave you malaria and mosquitoes that didn't, insects that looked like flying twigs, minute crawling things that covered the inside of the tent, clumsy flying beetles that fell to the ground like bombs, a great range of moths – some tiny, some huge and gawky – and lone ants on safari. The sausage flies were the most irritating. They swirled rapturously round the pressure lamp and then straight into the glass, away again, offended, then straight back at it, and right into the soup. Flicked out by an angry spoon, they came back for more and nestled, wet, buzzing between shirt and skin. Thrown down and trod upon, they continued to wriggle. They had no concept of dying decently.

The lamp with its white hot mantle dazzling at the centre lit up a tiny section of the light around the tent and emphasised the outer blackness. Frogs drowned the noise of flowing water nearby.

"I think I'll swim," said Cedric, abruptly terminating the silence in which they had eaten their evening meal.

"You may catch bilhartzia, if you are not careful," said Morris, his flat nose shining gently in the light.

"Oh damn bilhartzia!" Cedric was trying desperately to escape the insects by now. He took a towel and left. Garston had warned him of the risk – it didn't sound too terrible: "they stick long needles in your bum". Kalisto cleared the camp table. From an unknown distance came a noise of drums.

The water gave delicious relief. Swimming alone in the ink-black river, his body and mind seemed to fuse into an assertion of existence at once aggressive and dominated. The swirling, chattering water coursing round smooth boulders spelled out to him the irrelevance of everything else outside the river. But then he felt himself being carried away too fast by the current. He hit his ankle sharply on a submerged rock and, by the time he managed to struggle to the shore, he was well down from the campsite. He groped naked along the steep bank with its thick encumbrances of thorny bushes and small trees that leaned drunkenly towards the water and drank it with stray branches. Then he stopped. Something was moving in a tree ahead of him. Against the dark sky, he saw a blacker thing dangling and swaying like a length of hosepipe strung over a branch.

"Morris! Morris! For God's sake, Morris!"

Mbuya heard him and came running through the trees.

"Watch it! It's a snake!"

The African froze in his tracks and then slowly looked around for a weapon. With a desperate wrench, he tore off a small branch from the nearest bush and advanced on the snake. Then he swung his stick at what he thought was the snake's head. The hosepipe winced and then, quite unseen in that light, slipped in one movement along its branch and disappeared. The two men waited uncomfortably for a moment before Morris whispered, "Run!"

"That was bloody good of you," said Cedric, as he dried himself, sitting on his camp bed. His stomach was still reacting to the shock. "What sort of snake was it?"

"It was impossible to see. A big one I should say," said Morris, who was examining a great tear in his trousers that had caught a thorn on the dash back.

"Big like this tear," he said, "which please explain to my wife!"

It was the first time that Cedric had realised that Morris had a wife, still less a wife to whom one explained tears in trousers.

CHAPTER TWELVE

Parties

On most evenings in Romba, dinner-party lights burned late in a few of the European houses. Now and again, somebody threw an all-station party; or perhaps it would be an approximately all-station party, and Diana, for one, would greedily make a mental note of the significant absentees. Some of the wives were guided in their invitations by a methodical and comprehensive roster, amending it as necessary when the invitation was not returned within one month. A few restricted themselves to inviting people whom they liked, while a still smaller group only accepted invitations and never extended them. In this last category were the Mbuyas, who had recently moved on to the New Circle. They never dared to entertain their neighbours and were severely criticised as a result. In the end, they were left to themselves.

Diana Manley was one of the more prominent climbers of a social ladder that was as meaningful to her as its rungs were few. She suffered agonies whenever she heard of a dinner party to which she had not been invited, and would spend long unhappy hours rationalising her omission from the invitation until she discovered a more or less anaesthetic solution to the painful fact. Once, through an accident in the distribution of invitations to an all station-party given by the Harrimans, she found herself excluded while the rest of white Romba made merry. Not only would she not speak to Mavis at coffee parties for several weeks but she began to spin a web of complex calumnies about her which, to their credit, everybody disbelieved. When the missing invitation finally turned up in her houseboy's pocket, too much damage had been done to effect a genuine reconciliation. She was a dedicated campaigner in such matters. Within months of arriving in Romba, she had made it clear that she did not believe that Angela carried the position of first lady of the station at all satisfactorily. Naturally, she herself was unable to do the amount of official entertaining which inevitably fell to Angela's lot but, even if deprived of the odd Minister on tour, she attempted to redress the balance by asserting herself within the very organism of white Romba itself. It was a consuming battle and involved many fronts. For instance, Garston could not be unalive to the interest that she took in every detail of his work. She would demonstrate involvement with such things as bush-fuel reserves, protein fish-ponds or sub-grade schools in Mamba, and she did this both in and out of the office. It was a skilful ploy in her well-conceived war, for she knew that Angela showed little such interest and that Garston resented it. She knew too that Angela remained indifferent to her intrigues and this made her redouble her energies to secure Angela's abdication. Never had she been more sympathetic to Garston than in his planning of the road. What she conceived secretly as nonsense, she affected to see as the fruit of a pioneer intellect. In all this, she had split successfully the station into two rival factions and, to that extent, complicated the dinner-party rosters. Her husband, Geoffrey, kept his peace and enjoyed popularity throughout Romba.

Not in the slightest concerned in the cat-fighting, Björnsson was never invited anywhere. Some voices had even been raised in protest when he was put up for the club by Blagdon and Peebles. But, once admitted, he spent most of his off-time on a high stool at the club bar. When it was closed, he would sit at a table in the Happy Events and tap his dirty, bitten fingernails to the rhythm of the jukebox high-life that always blared through the establishment. Shariff used to let him have a squalid room to sleep off what was left of Saturday nights. Sometimes, he would go for three months without coming into Romba; but, recently, the weekends in the bush had been too much for him. And when, on the day he met Cedric, his radio had cut out on the No. 103 site in East GodiGodi, he had decided to make the tedious run back to Romba for the two days, even though he would again have to risk damaging his new car on a native track to Port Steamer. He had judged that he would not be welcome at Cedric's camp and, in any case, found himself recoiling at the too obvious decency and untouchedness of the English cadet.

Björnsson had changed. Five years before, he had written plaintively home to the only person in the world left whom he really knew and who wanted to know him:

"My dear mother, it is a very hard life here. Loneliness is the big enemy. The money is good and I am so happy to help you a little. Sometimes I am saddened by remembering about the things you said I would be, like a lawyer, a surgeon or even a big actor. This is, in many ways, so different. It's difficult to explain to one's own mother…"

Björnsson had made a superhuman effort to be honest in letters to his mother, at that time wanting nothing more than the embrace given to the prodigal son. But, in a moment filled with the sort of pathos that he had only experienced in films and never believed happened in real life, he opened his post-office box one day to find that three letters had been returned to him unopened. With it was a letter from his mother's landlord telling him of her death.

He passed Saturday afternoon in Shariff's. Black faces glanced round at him from the counter, then met each others' looks and winked knowingly. Marciano, the Military Affairs Clerk, came in and asked Shariff's son quietly for a bottle of methylated spirits. The Arab looked round the tables and, noticing one of Fawcett's men sipping Pepsi Cola, made a great show of shaking his head in pious refusal. A laughing and excited group of Africans was crowding a fruit machine on the wall. Reuben Onyango came in with the chairman of the District Council, looked round, and left.

The streets and shops werc milling with black and brown people for whom Saturday afternoon was a weekly, if sometimes penniless, carnival. Here and there, an African shambled along aimlessly, children stood and stared inside shops, bicycles wobbled precariously as husband carried wife, swaying side-saddle on his trailer with their baby on her back, rolls of Japanese cloth came down from jammed shelves in shops tortured by the sun beating on their iron roofs, trinkets were examined expertly by African women who had collected a few shillings from their beer brewing and the machinists on the pavements laughed and joked to each other without for one moment relaxing their attack on the endless seams and hems. In one shop, a vast Indian matron counted out ball bearings with podgy fingers. Next door, her neighbour, with sunken eye-sockets, hollow cheeks and a look of death about her, measured out lentils from a sack. Miniature bars of soap, miniature packets of tea and miniature sachets of instant coffee, looking more like amusing samples than goods seriously on sale, tempted out the odd few cents left jangling in passing pockets. A loudspeaker van was making circuits round the bazaar, blasting out the merits of something that sounded like "Jooble" with a recorded song that said that pain was old-fashioned with "Jooble". Compact pharmacopoeia in dusty glass cabinets within a dozen shops carried further the whole cheerful speculation in African credulity and competed with the dead birds, bundles of twigs and bats' skeletons carefully laid out on sacks by an old man who sat daily under the market wall next to the crouching corps of bicycle mechanics as they, in turn, went about their particular but vital attempts at professionalism with hammers and ill-fitting spanners.

Eleanor Mbuya had walked up from the New Circle with her "boy", Joseph. Morris had left the Volkswagen behind but she could not drive: she had crossed the golf course and narrowly escaped being hit by one of Reg Blagdon's better drivers in the 'Monthly Mug' competition.

She took a pair of shoes to the repairer, a cross-legged Indian cobbler who had a habit of rolling his tongue round his cheeks as he concentrated on a shoe held in a tight combination of his bare toes. He took the shoes from her in silence, muttered something, scratched himself and went back to his sewing.

Then she met a friend of hers, the wife of the Assistant Education Officer whose rank had not yet qualified him for assimilation onto the New Circle. Neither woman was a native of Mamba District and this had encouraged their friendship. Eleanor Mbuya came from Lunduland where she had worked as a schoolmistress in a Catholic Mission. She had accompanied Morris on his year's course at Oxford and learnt a little English and adopted European clothes. Her children had all been born in hospital and not in the secret confines of a dark hut haunted by the incantations of toothless grannies. Morris always told her that they were both people of two worlds but she had never felt more than a guilty refugee from one world living now in the wasting emptiness of another. Tea and cakes on Angela's lawn scarcely constituted a new world.

Eleanor looked at her wristwatch. Her baby would be crying for his feed and she should return quickly. But Joseph insisted on his Pepsi Cola. She pushed him impatiently into the Happy Events where Björnsson looked up and saw her. When she had left, he asked the Arab who she was.

The Mbuyas were not great gardeners but they kept their lawn cut and their houseboy often worked on his day off to turn over the flowerbeds. Morris could not afford a gardener, a deficiency in his domestic arrangements that did not pass unnoticed by his neighbours. "I had to pay too much to be married to Eleanor," he would explain apologetically, knowing that he was not being really understood but merely inviting his listeners to turn themselves into amateur anthropologists. And they forgot that they earned a special expatriates' allowance for doing the same work as him.

"I dare not go home too often in case I am asked to pay for yet another relative's school fees."

"But why don't you tell them to go to hell?" would come the regular answer. Explanation made everything worse.

Eleanor had been right and the baby was yelling loudly when she reached home. His great moon eyes were pearled with unbroken tears, and his thick shock of fuzzy hair gave him an adult expression in his misery. Eleanor's schoolgirl sister was helping out with the baby during her holidays: she unburdened herself quickly of her comfortless bundle as Eleanor brought out a breast and calmed the baby at once.

The sister played with the dials on the saucepan radio and, having tuned into a close-harmony group singing a rhythmic piece about a faithless sweetheart, gyrated slowly round the room jerking her hips and bosom to the thumps in the music. Little Joseph left his chair and partnered her, edging round her swaying figure with snatchy little paces of his white-socked feet while his head nodded up and down with a deliberate expression of idiocy on his face.

Willie Ives had won the Mug and there was some hard drinking going on in the club. All the talk was about the tournament, except that Mavis Harriman who didn't play golf was thumbing through some *Vogue* back numbers. Chalisi, who had acquired an assistant, was making some important notes on a bar chit. His was a job that, with care, could be made to pay quite well.

But soon, the bar was deserted. Diana Manley was throwing an all-station party that evening. Chalisi settled down to a lurid South African magazine full of boxers, political rights and cheesecake. He knew that it would be only a matter of time before Björnsson pitched up. His new assistant had seen him drive in that afternoon. But Björnsson stayed much longer than usual in the Happy Events and kept away from the golfers at the club. Instead, he wandered round the New Circle in the fading light, read 'M. F. Mbuya' on a sign outside one of the houses and thought out confusedly what he would say if the husband was in. Then he walked slowly but without hesitation up the gravel drive. He was drunk in the way that a man accustomed to excessive alcohol becomes drunk, with no stumbling and falling about but only a special mood to show for the drink.

Björnsson went round to the kitchen at the back of the house and asked the houseboy to fetch his master. The boy wanted to usher him in at once, but, noticing a wild look in the European's eyes, decided to confer with Eleanor first. She went to the door and Björnsson beckoned her out. He gripped her wrist and she tried to snatch her arm back.

"I don't make trouble. Come and dance at Shariff," he said, with a grotesque pretence at a smile.

"What do you want?" she asked with her fingers still in the vice. She was trembling violently. The houseboy and the schoolgirl stood nearby watching, as confused as they were frightened.

Suddenly, Björnsson relaxed his grip; he took her arm gently and stroked it for a moment. His eyes looked at her with a weird tenderness without savagery. Then he let her go and ran quickly down the drive to his car.

It had been an easy night for Chalisi; even Björnsson didn't arrive. "It must be a good party," thought the barman, as he cycled home past midnight and heard a great outbreak of laughs coming from the Manley garden.

CHAPTER THIRTEEN

Trouble Ahead

Archdeacon Grantham read the letter back to himself. It sounded exactly right:

Dear Mr Moorside,

I am grieved to have to bring to your attention the conduct of one of your clerks whose name I could supply to you in due course. It has been reported to me by one of my fellow workers that this clerk, who regularly patronises the Happy Events Bar, has recently been prevailing upon several of our girl students to accompany him to a place which is a source of lively temptation to them.

I would earnestly request you, if you cannot see your way clear to withholding a licence from the bar in question, as we in this Mission would wish, to address your clerk on the matter. I would add that it has always been my view that the District

Commissioner is able, if he so chooses, to give excellent executive force to ordinary standards of a morality that native customs and vices habitually offend. I have generally found your predecessors sympathetic to that view. I could call to discuss this matter at your convenience.

Yours faithfully,
Cuthbert Grantham
Archdeacon, Romba, Protestant Mission.

When he received this letter, Garston did not need to ask the Archdeacon to come and reveal the culprit's identity as Grantham had hoped he would. He taxed Marciano immediately with his conduct and, showing little conviction in his voice, instructed the clerk to ensure that he confined his immoralities to Non-Protestant girls in future since he was answerable to the Catholic priest for his private sins and not to the Archdeacon. At the same time, he replied to Grantham:

Dear Archdeacon,

I have long been aware of, and, in many ways, sympathised with your views on certain bars in Romba and I have now spoken with the clerk to whom you refer. You will, doubtless, not be unaware that at least two of your girl students act as waitresses in the establishment that you mention – after school hours, of course. All this is deplorable in the extreme and is a source of lively temptation to my clerks. I could let you have the names of the girls in due course.

I am, I confess, slightly puzzled by your suggestion that I should give executive force to what you call 'ordinary standards of morality'. If you mean that I should prevent European ladies shopping in the bazaar wearing bikinis, I could perhaps agree. But with certain other matters that your Mission has regarded traditionally as a breach of the ordinary standards, I cannot begin to interfere, nor would I wish to. I refer to the evergreen topic of polygamy, the dance known as the 'ibi ibi', the exposure of the bosom (and of the buttocks in the case of ladies in South Mamba) and the practice of male circumcision among the Wamamba.

You may, as I have no doubt you will, quote me to your Bishop.

Yours faithfully,
Garston Moorside.

And, following the usual sequence, the letter had gone to the Bishop who had passed it indignantly to the Provincial Commissioner for action. Garston received his customary brief admonishment.

Confidential

From: P.C.
To: D.C. Mamba

Be a good chap and don't write silly letters to old
Grantham. I spend all my sundowners explaining
you away to the bish.

P.C.

Grantham had been in the District just before
Gamage. He had, as was the case with all missionaries of his generation, walked up from the coast,
canoed up to what was now Port Steamer and taken
the Bible to Bulikiki. There, he found the sway of
Islam a little overpowering and was asked to leave.
He did so just in time to escape a party sent out by
the Sultan with what corresponded to a warrant for
his arrest. Retreating to GodiGodi, he found Father
Frascati at work on his church and, deciding that
popery was preferable to paganism, did not compete at the time. Instead, he moved down to the most
backward part of the present District, to the land
of the much put-upon Wamamba. There, he established a whole network of very successful schools
and, before the Protectorate Medical Department
took over, ran a system of dispensaries staffed by

lady missionaries living in pairs and not seeing other white people for months on end.

A hospital was put up during the thirties in the extreme south of the District and one of its doctors had discovered the cure to a local virus disease. Another had written a Mamba dictionary before translating the Bible into Kilikiki. But the Archdeacon's own forte was building. A man of little education, he left intellectual matters to what he called 'the academic workers'. He was always quoting Corinthians on 'talents'. Issuing sharp orders in Mamba slightly suffused with Devonshire, he had produced building upon building up and down the District. In the early days, Africans flocked to help his few paid porters but recently, they had become more grudging. He blamed this, quite unjustifiably, on his own faithlessness. If the original magnetism of his preaching had weakened over the years, he remained, at seventy, the most active person in the mission. Wherever Grantham-trained lay preachers were to be found, there would be a bush-church congregation that had a crystal clear idea of what its faith should mean in daily life. And the Archdeacon was the first to regret that some of the converts, notably the Blessed Ones Holy Group, overdid things.

The mission at Romba was organised on a feudal basis. All the workers and schoolchildren took part in a closely supervised system of obligations and privileges. Grantham had never been sentimental about Africans and would always discourage his brighter charges from involving themselves in 'this nationalist rubbish'. Without finding it necessary to enlarge on the different careers pursued by the sons of Noah, he believed that Africans had an appointed place in the cosmos. He would never attempt to define that place; his theory a direct result of the spiritual nature of the message he propagated. If events changed the situation of Africans, that was as may be. Only it was not for him nor for his students to participate in the process. Annually, he would watch with understandable pride the parade of schoolchildren round the Muljibhai Community Games Ground that took place on District Council Opening Day. The children would march singing from the mission led by a drum and fife band; first the secondary school boys in their white shirts and shorts, then the secondary girls in yellow blouses and green skirts, then the primary boys and girls all in green. They joined up with the red Catholics and the blue Muslims at the field and their three bands would compete ferociously. The newly-elected Chairman of the District Council would say how pleased he was to see the hopes of the District lined up in front of him and the District Commissioner would congratu-late the children on the very fine show they had put up. "But you know, Leslie," Garston once said after an opening, "it never occurs to the Archdeacon that generating before his very eyes is a fantastic amount of energy that demands to be expended in all sorts of odd ways that half-literacy suggests to young minds." But Grantham and his staff would pray that once they had left school, the children would hold fast to the tenets of the Message. Ambitions were left well alone.

And yet the evidence was there. When Leslie or Garston or Geoffrey Manley came down to the mission to give a talk on current affairs, as they frequently did, boys would get up and ask for the vote.

"No, not yet, young man. The government believes that twenty-one is a better age."

"But why? We have education and many people who are allowed to vote cannot read and write."

"Education isn't everything. And being able to read and write isn't education," came the reply.

"We have education and the government must be chosen by educated people."

And the fourteen-year-olds would not budge from that position.

Grantham was fortunate in his helpers from Britain. He had fifteen of them in all. Except for the hospital staff, they were all centred on Romba, and, except for Dennis Hillman and Gordon Rice, these were all female.

"I wonder if we do the right thing, all living here as we do," he sometimes asked Gordon Rice soul-searchingly. "After all, the Catholics pepper the

District with white priests who must, in the nature of things, be more influential than our African preachers and lay teachers." He had a strong practical streak running through his theology and had long learnt that the Provider helps only those who help themselves. But in the end, worrying questions like this were put aside by an urgent building problem that had to be solved before tea, leaving Gordon alone with the cuckoo clock in the front room of the original thatched cottage on station.

Gordon Rice was becoming less interested in the Mission; he found himself wrestling with the agony of being inextricably integral with a way of life that rested on a faith which was becoming unreal to him. The process had begun slowly. Certain phrases used by other workers irritated him. He no longer prefaced every project with "God willing". He defected from his daily Bible reading. He saw no sense in praying for good weather in the dry season and once shocked a woman teacher by asking her why she didn't ask for rain instead. He wished too that he could be made subject to the absolute prohibition on marriage that bound the Catholic priests. As it was, he felt that marriage could perhaps save his faith; but his tour had two more years to run and the women on the Mission were not only unattractive but had long since rationalised sex out of their lives.

Every Sunday morning, the Mission held four consecutive services, each in a different language. At eleven, the Europeans came and the Archdeacon usually officiated. And, for Garston, church on Sunday was a necessity, just as hoisting the flag in his garden on the Queen's birthday or calling the P.C. 'Sir' were necessities. These things did not brook argument, and Garston never analysed them. He knew the jokes that people made about colonials and laughed at them but that did not mean one could depart from the established forms.

Leslie was also involved.

"How's my hat?" Thelma asked, unable to make up her mind at which angle to tilt her white toque.

Leslie approved its position without looking up from his copy of *Life*. Richly comfortable on his long easy chair, he recoiled at the reminder of church. Garston expected him to go and, while he was the last man to do what Garston considered consistent with the code, he could not afford to displease him these days. Angela would be back from early morning Mass and he could, in theory, pack Thelma off to the service with Garston and have coffee with his D.C.'s wife. Perhaps he could develop a weekly headache, or recurrent bouts of scepticism and so found a new Sunday morning institution.

Unfortunately, none of these things would convince Garston, for whom religion existed without faith and headaches were cured by willpower.

The dust of several cars appeared above their hedge from the road outside.

"We're terribly late, Leslie! Do come on. Jill! Will you leave mummy's tonic water alone! And go and tell Timoteo to polish the dining room table while we're away."

Thelma was trying, damn her, to introduce into his household the same heavy atmosphere that had pervaded his parents' house in Ealing on Sabbath mornings when he was a child.

Boredom and frustration like twin guillotine blades bissected his Sunday, while a combination of drinks at the club and vast curried lunches often kept him on his bed until seven at night when he awoke in the dark with a foul taste in his mouth and the remembrance that the next day was Monday.

The Mission grounds were crowded with the outpourings of the service in Kilikiki that ministered to the needs of the large Babuliki colony in Romba. A dozen shiny cars drew up in the yard in front of the church and, chatting around them, the miniature congregation for the service in English waited for the Africans to leave the church. Black pastors were circulating joyfully about, shaking hands enthusiastically. The wild colours in the dresses of the African women shouted hosannas to the sky as they greeted, laughed and joked, and their babies cried. The secondary boys and girls in their spotless uniforms grouped together and mimicked Europeans. Somebody rubbed against the tiny jacaranda tree that supported a thicket of leaning bicycles, which tumbled noisily in a heap on the ground. Everybody laughed.

"We're pathetic and excluded," thought Peter Freeman, as the tiny group of whites in lightweight suits and cotton dresses passed through the crowds to the porch of the church, many of them still discussing Willie Ive's achievement of the day before.

"Sufficient unto the day is the conversation thereof," whispered Freeman to the Nursing Sister, Dorothy Ward, who shushed him and giggled. Garston was the last to enter. Whenever he saw large groups of Africans, he would distinguish himself by plunging into the crowd, finding a familiar face and engaging them in warm conversation. This time he had found the Township Chief and they had discussed a threatened strike by the night soil porters who looked after the shops in the bazaar.

"Mustn't happen, Silvester, mustn't happen," Garston had said. "You see that it doesn't happen." And the Chief had said weakly, "yes, of course."

The blistering heat outside gave way to the immediate coolness of the interior of the open-walled church. Three rows of tubular chairs were ranged in front of the altar rails and behind these, long stone boulders did duty as additional pews. The Archdeacon climbed into the pulpit that he had built himself out of firewood you know and hung a hymn board on the cement-block pier behind him. He nodded to the congregation and took them through the first hymn to the piano accompaniment of his niece, Rose Grantham. "Praise, my soul, the King of Heaven" swelled powerfully through the hollow building and out through the arches that formed the walls. John Fawcett, normally quiet, let forth with a complicated and not very happy experiment in descant.

The Archdeacon often delegated the sermons in English to members of the mission. But within a few months, it was easy to guess what line each of the regulars would take when his turn came up. Grantham himself restricted his usual didactic approach to African congregations and, for the Europeans, usually did some suspect expository work on a text. Denis Billman gave painfully diffident performances as he strung together some of his own inner experiences. One doctor from the Mamba Hospital occasionally delivered a rousing exercise in blood and hellfire, while his colleague had, on his sole appearance, made a gallant attempt to explain the divine purpose of pain. Only Gordon was unpredictable.

"Gordon, I'd like you to preach on Sunday," the Archdeacon had said. "But I hope you will feel led to say what you will say," he had added awkwardly. The more troubled the waters of his faith, the more desperately Gordon tried to deliver his sermons with the conviction he so badly needed.

"This Sunday," he was saying, "I would like to talk about Job." He was looked upon as the best preacher on the station, if an incurable orator. But this Sunday, there was something new and deeply personal in the way he traced Job's story. He never departed from the meaning of the text but contrived so to involve himself and his congregation that, when they left after the service, they barely talked to each other just as people come away silently and reverently from a film or a play that has made devastating inroads on their emotional reserves.

A few days later, one of the mission runners brought a notice round the Circles.

"ROMBA PROTESTANT MISSION

Mr Rice will begin a new Bible Study series beginning next Tuesday evening at 8pm. Subject of series: 'Discipleship. All welcome. Carol Practice under Mr Billman on Wednesdays as usual."

And Thelma Farrar, patiently loyal to the Archdeacon during his recent Biblical pilgrimage through Old Testament Egypt, very much looked forward to Gordon's classes.

CHAPTER FOURTEEN

Secrets

Eleanor Mbuya told nobody about Björnsson. Three days had passed and she dared not make a move. Morris was still on safari. If only he had been there, he would have taken the matter to the D.C. Meanwhile, she lived in terror that Björnsson would return. Joseph, however, did not feel so inhibited. Seeing that his mother was not prepared to take action, he presented himself at the D.C.'s office one morning.

"I want to see the D.C.," he told a clerk.

"What about?"

"I cannot tell you."

"If you cannot tell me, you cannot see the D.C."

"I must see him."

"If you don't tell me your business, how can I find the proper file to give him?"

By this time, Rodrigues, who was already in a temper about a solicitor's letter in the morning's post, intervened crossly.

"Why are you arguing and arguing with the people all the time, Oboo? Anyway, you are not having the work of interviewing clerk. Interviewing clerk is Marciano, isn't it?" Marciano, who was polishing on his sleeve a medal just received from Military Records, looked up startled and pretended to be looking at a letter in the stack of files in front of him.

"What is the use? Nobody is being prepared to co-operate," fumed Rodrigues. "Now, what do you want, boy?"

"I want to see the D.C."

"You tell me what is matter and if I cannot deal, then I am taking you to see D.C."

"I cannot tell you."

Rodrigues shrugged his shoulders.

"Then I must ask you leave," and he pointed to the door. Joseph hung around Leslie's door hoping to be seen. When he was noticed, Leslie ordered him so loudly to address himself to the chief clerk before coming to see an officer that his patience failed him and he walked sadly home.

In the middle of the morning, Leslie drove into the bazaar for a quick small beer at Patel's. He found Manley there before him.

"What you had out this morning, Geoffrey?"

"Only an appendix."

On every station in the Protectorate, there was always one European who befriended and was accepted by the Asians more effectively than any of the rest. With his Indian Army background and a smattering of Urdu, Manley was that person in Romba. He enjoyed immediate access to Patel's back room where they would talk about India over beer. He was a constant caller on old Muljibhai whom, in any case, he looked after professionally. "You make me eternal," Muljibhai once told him.

Patel ushered them into the back room. They sat down on a gigantic sofa upholstered in deep blue velvet, and sank onto its plushy red cushions that were decorated with golden tassels and silver birds in flight. From the ceiling hung a cluster of electric candles. A shaggy nylon carpet had been abstracted from stock and sprawled over the lino floor like the remains of a sequestered polar bear. Occasional Arab pouffes weighed it down. On the cream walls hung pictures about Lord Krishna from the hagiographers round the corner. They were accompanied by several trade calendars, one for soft drinks, another for timber, a third for Patel and a fourth for sports cars. The sports-car calendar displayed a different nude frying herself on various parts of a car for each sultry blue-skied English month. Leslie fell naturally into the category of people who never conceal their fascination for provocative pictures on strangers' walls.

"By Jove, Patel, you certainly have taste," Leslie said, reviewing the year. "Last time I came, the calendars you had were full of brass couplings and English fieldfowl."

In a lacquered vase on a contemporary table, a joss stick consumed itself patiently and loaded the room with its vigorous fumes. Across one corner stretched an enormous radiogram incorporating a tape recorder, a drinks cabinet and an illuminated aquarium in which angelfish flipped disdainfully round.

Patel explained the knobs to Leslie. There were sixteen controls.

"Where's the earth, Patel?"

"Earth I did not put. The Man say earth not necessary."

"I wouldn't trust him. You just can't begin to get good reception without an earth."

They switched the set on and some modern Radio India hits came chanting through in faultless reproduction.

"See what I mean, Patel. It's all whuzzed up. You need an earth."

Patel nodded anxiously and tried to drown Leslie's dissatisfaction with his radio in mugs of beer. He shouted an order into the kitchen, and presently Mrs Patel floated in solemnly bearing a tray of Indian sweetmeats.

"My God!" whispered Leslie to Geoffrey as they sank further into the sofa, as he muttered "the original fat and wide bride."

Mrs Patel retreated to where she had come from, trailing diaphanous pieces of her complex robes behind her like the insubstantial aquarium fish. Her swathings attached to themselves while Mr Patel offered round cigarettes and lit them with a silver dragon lighter that belched out controllable flame.

"Good man, Patel, my favourites," said Leslie, too late.

"Ah, Mr Farrar, there is something I am wanting to give you for very long time." He went to a wall cupboard and brought out the half-smoked packet that Leslie had left on the Pimple.

"I am finding this on the Catholic mission hill near water tank. So I am thinking they must be Mr Farrar's, isn't it?"

Leslie played for a moment with the idea of refusing to recognise the miserable packet but, noticing some notes of his at the back, accepted them as naturally as he could.

"I can't imagine what he was doing up there on the water tank, Manibhai," said Manley, winking. "Probably running about with a woman." And they all laughed. After three beers all round Manley said that he had to be off and Leslie trailed after him. Patel renewed the joss stick and went back to his counter.

The two Europeans drove off and halted in front of Muljibhai. The old man had just flown to India on holiday but his son was worth another two beers before lunch.

In his youth, Manley had rowed. Diana had travelled up to Cambridge on scores of occasions to watch her fiancé stroking his crew to victorious conclusions. He had earned a Trial Cap before taking up skulling with a Club. The trophies then accumulated at an alarming rate. Manley pretended not to care about them but Diana saw status gleaming out of the humblest spoon and ensured that every house they occupied set the prizes off to advantage. It was like rubbing salt into a wound when Angela had mentioned quite ingenuously that her eldest brother had nearly killed himself pulling an oar between Putney and Mortlake on two successive years and that his mother thought he should give it a miss for his third year. But Diana's house was cluttered up with little cupboards: cups, mugs and vases glinting out of dark corners. They had two standard lamps made out of oars, a rudder in their bedroom and a long line of commemorative photographs showing what Geoffrey Manley could do before he started drinking even more than rowing men should. Geoffrey was content to let her indulge her hobby. And in their special way, they had contrived to make their marriage one of the most successful on the station.

"Did you have a good morning, darling?"

"Just an appendix, and some beers," Manley replied, sprinkling a ferocious amount of chilli sauce into his soup.

Diana rang the table bell.

"Don't be home late tonight, sweet. People coming."

"Who?" Manley struggled with a piece of market meat full of gristle.

"Well, the Fawcetts are coming, Harrimans, Ian Peebles, Dorothy and Peter Freeman."

"I thought Freeman never accepted an invitation which didn't include his houseboy?"

"He's agreed to relinquish that principle. Dorothy tells me that she's been getting to work on him. They see quite a lot of each other."

"Garston thought anything new up?"

"No, but he dictated a letter to Cedric saying that he was going on an inspection of the works next week. It appears that the politicians are getting busy up there."

Sanseverino brought in the fruit salad in the only silver bowl they possessed that had nothing to do with rowing boats. It was a gift from Romba Express Motors whose manager Geoffrey had once treated for a crushed finger.

It was inscribed: 'To Dr Manley, For services to humanity.'

They had coffee on their closed-in verandah.

"Oh, I knew there was something, Leslie. Do you want to go to see the film of *Richard III* at the Seminary on Friday?"

Manley frowned for a moment.

"Sounds a good idea. The trouble is, old Cincillati always asks me to explain English jokes to him. Last time, he wanted to know why we all laughed when Tarzan told the girl to come into the jungle with him."

Diana went on, tapping the end of a cigarette on the coffee tray. "Anyway, Father Grimaldi came in for a gun permit or something this morning and asked me if I knew about the film. Apparently, three weeks ago he gave Angela a pile of circulars about it and, in her usual fashion, she forgot to send them round."

"Errare humanum est," put in Geoffrey, looking through the newspaper for unit trust prices.

"At first, I thought that she was getting at me but Christine hasn't heard nor has Garston even."

"He'd be the last one to hear," intoned Geoffrey, deep in an account of a railway accident in China.

"Father Grimaldi said that it was a pity because he thought at the time how lucky he was to meet her. Angela bumped into him in the dark apparently, running down from the mission at one hell of a rate. He said he scared her out of her wits. It's all rather peculiar."

Manley had, by this time, moved on to the less absorbing topic of Geneva talks and Diana was coming through strength three.

"That's odd," he said, looking up. "Patel found some cigarettes of Leslie's up on the pimple three weeks ago. The place seems to be exercising a novel attraction all of a sudden." Diana's jaw dropped. She narrowed her eyes, trying to remember.

"Sanseverino!" Diana called and, when he stood in front her, she said: "Sanseverino, did you tell me that you saw Bwana Farrar going up to the Catholic Mission about three weeks ago?"

"Yes, memsaab."

"Was he alone?"

"Yes, memsaab."

"Where was he going?"

"I think he was going to the Fathers, memsaab."

"Then why, Leslie, why didn't the Fathers give him the circulars?"

Geoffrey had listened to the cross-examination intently but he pretended to be detached and indifferent.

"Look, Diana, it's quite simple. Angela was going to confession – she had so many sins to tell the Father that she was late home. Leslie had some business with Grimaldi, was told he was out and dawdled leisurely down having a smoke en route. The only reason he didn't get the circulars was because Grimaldi had them with him."

Geoffrey and Diana looked at each other in silence. Excitements were not easily come by in white Romba.

"No, my dear Geoffrey, Angela was not going to confession at all. Her confessor happens to be Father Grimaldi."

CHAPTER FIFTEEN

Progress

The member for Mamba had been active in the capital.

The Freedom Party Press reported him as having delivered a "deadly and effective attack on all branches of government activity." The official record ran: "Mr Onyango (Mamba) rose to say that he would not keep the House long. What he had to say did not require big phrases and long-winded explanation such as the House was accustomed to hear from the Chief Secretary. He would let the facts speak eloquently. The Hon. Member asked if the House knew that the theft of bicycles was increasing daily in the Protectorate. The Hon. Member did not know what the police were paid for. He would like an undertaking from the Chief Secretary that police would bear the cost of such thefts since they did not prevent them. Turning to the District Administration, the Hon. Member believed that District Officers were a waste of time and money. There was a serious situation developing in parts of the Protectorate of which the District Commissioners were not even aware. He would like to see good people in government jobs, not what the Hon. Member would call highly gin-soaked imperialists of old guard ancient game politics. The time for sending gunboats was over (cries of 'shame!' from Government Front Bench). The Government could make fun but they should never forget that the man who laughs first laughs last. The Hon. Member was laughing first (cheers from Government side). The Hon. Member invited the Minister for Agriculture to explain the decrease in the cotton subsidy. And he did not wish to hear more nonsense about world markets. The House was tired of that sort of excuse that was merely a cover for inefficient Civil Service Ministers. The Hon. Member would further require to know why leasehold titles were being given to certain schools in his District. He must assume, in the absence of better evidence, that the land was required for development as farms for retired expatriate civil servants (extremely loud cheers from Government side). The Hon. Member had several more points but he thought he would give the Government a chance to answer what he had said so far."

The Chief Secretary said that if the Hon. Member would put his points into the form of written questions, he was sure that they could be dealt with rather more satisfactorily.

Mr Onyango said: "I am bound to construe this as yet another example of official deceit. The Government is like an ostrich with its head in the mud."

Mr Wilkinson (Parliamentary Secretary, Ministry of Commerce) commented loudly: "You can't blame us for your climate as well."

Mr Onyango replied: "I would blame the government for everything." (This attracted applause from both sides). "The Government had its head in the mud, and the Hon. Member opposite could not see the wood for trees."

Mr Wilkinson: "Naturally."

Onyango had, however, held his fire on the subject of the Koi to Port Steamer Road. If he raised the matter prematurely, the Government would merely make its usual enquiries and Moorside would find a way of wriggling out. The Chief Secretary would tell him that this was yet another example of enlightened self-help. As it was, if he agitated effectively enough, Moorside would hang himself with his own rope. All was ready for the offensive. He had just sold a lot of his own cotton and paid Okot another instalment on his car. The County Chief would have to sing for the rest in gaol. Slightly afraid but deeply committed, he declared war in earnest and began his tour of GodiGodi, enlisting support and organising secret meetings.

Meanwhile, Okot, whose sensitive intelligence tendrils warned him that Onyango was out for blood and votes, restricted irregularities on the Prison Farm, and ensured that the justice meted out by his chiefs was more substantial than it had been latterly. He no longer employed thirty prisoners fully occupied on his own holding. He told the warders that he would not accept a third of their pay in return for the right to dispose of Prison Farm tools: that practice was suspended sine die. Prison sentences would no longer be commuted to personal payment of cattle to the County Chief. District Council licences would be sold at face value. In short, he put his house in order. It was, moreover, high time: Fawcett had been over-curious latterly but he had only seen the prisoners in his plot and they were under orders to be imaginative about the boundaries of the Prison Farm.

The road was taking shape after only six weeks. And Dison Apau, working every available minute of daylight, had almost completed the bridge. The pier had been erected on a massive boulder in the river bed and he was now working on the transverse girders and timbers. He hoped to have the whole bridge ready for the D.C.'s inspection. Garston now made it no secret that he wanted the road opened on New Year's Day. Cedric had written to say that he thought it would be March before they would have it all finished. Garston exhorted him to a final spurt before the rains.

The road ran for four miles in West GodiGodi and for eight in the East GodiGodi; men were now working along the whole line. Until the Freedom Party agents had received the green light from Onyango, people had come to work with a grudging goodwill and, during the earliest days on the road, they sang loudly as they hacked at the soil, cracked boulders with fire and chopped down the trees. It was mostly easy work and there were no deep cuttings to carve out. The campaign against absentees seemed to be successful and the chiefs were jubilant. They even took advantage of having their people on the spot to harry tax defaulters and any judgment debtors from the native courts whom they could find. One minor chief was overzealous with his cane but Okot allowed a case to be brought against him and his sentence of a 50/- fine with a goat in compensation made the men working on his stretch happy for a week.

Cedric and Morris patrolled the road constantly discussing difficulties with chiefs, joking with the labour, sticking plaster on cuts and planning the work for the next day. When the men went home at midday, they would confer with a road inspector from the District Council and extract as much technical

advice from him as they could without appearing
not to actually be giving it to him. Often, sometimes together, sometimes separately, they walked the
whole line of the road in a day and did not return to
camp until dark.

Cedric and Morris would pass little heaps of red
embers glowing in the night underneath granite rocks
that had not yet cracked terribly apart. Trees lay in
their way like slaughtered men after a battle. The
smell of the freshly dug earth assured them that the
road was going through and wresting a life of its own
from the bush from which it came. During the day,
they often looked in at the Port Steamer ginnery. It
was exciting to walk along the new road to the point
where it joined the established route a few hundred
yards before reaching the ginnery. The Manager,
Ahmed Hussein, would have a curry ready for them
if they happened to call around lunchtime, which
increasingly they did.

The first obvious signs of trouble came on one
of the days when Cedric and Morris had decided
to walk through to the ginnery. It was very hot and
the nearer they approached the Mamba Great River,
the more clinging became the humidity in the still
air. They emerged into a swampy area from a plain
of little trees and could see the corrugated-iron
roofing of the ginnery miles away reflecting the sun
like some grotesque headlight. They greeted the men

they passed working on the road but received mumbles for replies. Only the minor chiefs and their minions greeted the two officers with enthusiasm. Once, Morris stopped to ask one of them whether everything was quite alright. The man at once replied that things had never been better and that all the people were pleased to be associated with a task that would bring so much good to the community. Morris followed this up by asking a particularly disgruntled-looking man standing nearby whether anything was trouble him. This man took on a pained expression and said that he wished to take his wife to the dispensary that morning as she was complaining of stomach pains. He also pointed to a small cut on his finger that had turned slightly septic. When Cedric told the chief to excuse him, the man threw his pick into the air and did a little dance round it when it fell to the ground. His companions laughed so much at this display that the two District Officers forgot their anxiety and turned to thinking of the curry ahead.

"I must say, old Hussein is very generous," said Cedric as they walked.

"The Asians are naturally hospitable people," replied Morris, "but they often choose very carefully to whom they extend hospitality."

"How do you mean?"

"Well, put it this way. One year ago, before I was made a District Officer, not one of them would have invited me to his house. And before the London Talks, very few of them were interested in seeing Onyango. Now, he has to turn down their invitations."

A party of baboons loped across their path, piggy-backing their young that were earning their keep by removing the fleas from their parents' bodies.

"Yes, but what would somebody like Hussein stand to gain from you or me?"

"Not much in the short run perhaps. But for an Asian like him, to be well thought of by a white officer before Independence and a black one after Independence, is worth quite a lot. All most of them want to do is to carry on and trade in the same old way. But they've got a lot of ground to catch up on with the Africans and some of them will never learn. Apart from all that, they really are hospitable people."

Cedric and Morris found Hussein with his headman in the ginning room. The machine minders crouched precariously on a ledge above the stomach of the gin they kept fed constantly with fistfuls of cotton from the downy mass behind them. Some were masked like bandits; others tolerated the sneezing but prevented the tiny flecks floating thickly in the air from settling in the mesh of their hair by wearing knotted handkerchiefs; all their eyelashes looked snowed upon.

In the baling box, careless of all protection, two men were treading down ginned cotton that men at the top showered upon them in great armfuls. They became as one with the lint as wine-treaders became one with the grapes. When the long box was full, the couple hopped out, pathetic away from their element, and the press below began its inexorable upward journey until the whole white mass had been reduced to a dense oblong inside a hessian covering gripped by steel bands. All the machines combined to give out a sound composed of a continuous roar and a tremendous rattling. Cottonseeds tumbled from the gins into their tunnel under the floor and scurried like thousands of harassed mice up through fat tin pipes, out of the building through a wall and into a shed where two bored workers held a sack to catch them. And, all the time, the gins dribbled out long meshes of cotton wool which accumulated in heaps on the spotless wooden floor, and the engine room vibrated fearfully as the driving bands were sent convulsing through the wall to a main shaft from which, in turn, revolved a nightmare of smaller bands like washing lines in a gale.

"I am glad to see you gentlemen," shouted Hussein above the thunder. "Please come with me."

When they had composed themselves over a cold drink in Hussein's office away from the noise, he called his headman over.

"Tell Mr Hamilton-Gordon what you know about last night."

The headman, an aging African with pierced ears and a face framed within three parallel lines of beads picked out on his skin, told the interpreter, Semei, in an excited and hushed voice. He continued for five minutes before Cedric asked for a translation.

"The man says that he heard about a meeting last night at a place near the river. Some men decided that they would kill Okot and Adaa and some of the minor chiefs. The leader of the meeting is the man who made trouble at our baraza with Mr Farrar."

"Why do they want to kill them?" asked Cedric.

"Firstly, because the cotton price is too low. They think that this will show that they are not satisfied with it. Secondly, because of taxes, which they say are too high, and, thirdly, because of communal work. They say the chiefs are being very severe with them and..."

"Yes, and what does he say about the ginnery?" Hussein interrupted.

"The man says," Semei continued, "that they are going to burn down the house of anybody who works at the ginnery until the cotton price is put up."

While the men were talking, Garston and Fawcett drove into the ginnery compound. They had received similar reports from other sources. There was a brief consultation with Hussein. Fawcett went off to warn his substation N.C.O. (non-commissioned officer) to expect reinforcements. Hussein excused himself and went home to give his wife similar instructions.

After the curry, Garston drove bumpily up the new road to the camp with his two subordinates. Then he went forward to the bridge. He waved to Björnsson as he passed the rig that was being packed on its lorry. The new pump was already attracting a queue of women with water-pots and the Swede shouted that water had been reached at 300 feet.

At the river, Dison Apau promised to have the bridge usable within a week. "The Koi will soon to be conquered," he said.

"Well done!" said Garston, as he watched the water passing gently each side of the pier.

"You've both of you done bloody well," he told Cedric and Morris back at the camp as they all sipped hot tea out of mugs. "Carry on just as before but try to pick up any odd scraps of information you can. Above all, let me know what the people are thinking."

Through the trees from the new road, they heard the frantic revving and coughing of Björnsson's lorry pulling out.

"He's having it easier than when he came," said Cedric.

"In a week's time, I'm sending the cotton lorries down here, as soon as the bridge is over," said Garston.

Cedric looked up stupefied.

"What I want to do is to demonstrate to the locals the practical fruit of their work. They're cutting up a bit now, so we should be able to mollify them with the sight of a few dozen lorries rumbling up and down."

"The road's still very ropy, Sir," dared Cedric, remembering what Farrar had once said to him about Garston.

"Well, a few hundred wheels will help to stabilise it. As soon as the bridge is up, I shall get the lorries down here."

There was no further discussion. Cedric, who had hoped to hand over a completed road, felt numbed. Morris said that he thought the people would be calmed if they saw the lorries.

"Oh, I was forgetting," said Garston as he prepared to leave in his car. He handed a letter to Morris. Eleanor had finally written to say that she would like to see him as soon as possible. She gave no reason.

CHAPTER SIXTEEN

A Trial

The next day, the two officers decided to leave the camp very early for a quick shopping expedition in Romba. They needed fresh fruit and vegetables. They could buy neither at the Koi and Port Steamer Trading Centres and the mysterious letter from Eleanor was worrying Morris. At first, he had tried to dismiss the whole thing as some foolishness on her part but the night before he had eventually confided his anxiety to Cedric.

"She has never written a letter like this to me. What do you think has happened?"

"I expect she's mad with missing you, Morris, and just wants to smother you with kisses the whole length of Romba High Street."

Morris laughed. "It's not quite like that."

Soon after dawn, they walked to the Koi. Dison's men were already at work.

"The communal labour's late," said Cedric.

Dison replied that the sky had been overcast that morning which always made people late for work. The officers nodded and walked across the unfinished bridge. Cedric's estate car was waiting inside a grass garage on the other side.

After so many weeks away in a tent, Romba was almost a city to Cedric and its official designation of 'township' no longer seemed absurd. Miles away from its boundary, people seemed to be converging upon it: women balancing baskets of grain on their heads; cyclists with huge bunches of green plantains strapped to their trailers with thongs made out of old inner tubes; old men with sticks walking there quietly, some of them wearing sandals cut out of car tyres. They passed the ancient car with spoked wheels. It was carrying fish from Port Steamer and belonged to an early D.C.

Cedric dropped Morris off at his house. Eleanor heard the car and walked down the drive. She took Morris' briefcase and carried it ahead of him into the house without saying a word.

"Well, he said it wasn't quite like that," thought Cedric, driving away.

Only six men appeared for work on the road that morning and they, seeing themselves in a substantial minority and fearing for their thatches, slunk off quickly. Little groups of chiefs down the line of the road organised themselves into parleys. They were all agreed that they too would be better off at home with their families. Only Dison and his paid gang carried on relentlessly.

Okot had not been dilatory. A few known ring-leaders had been rounded up and put on remand in sub-county lock-ups. At Koi, the sub-county court convened a special session on the chief's orders. The Court Members had been summoned to attend at one hour's notice. This measure was part of Okot's plan for nipping in the bud what could be a serious threat to his position, his medal, even his life. Meanwhile, Adaa was, if not equally active, just as worried. He decided to sit at his headquarters in Port Steamer with a loaded shotgun at the ready and await devel-opments. He was wondering how long it would take the Protectorate Police to cover the half-mile from the post to his house in an emergency.

Four peasant farmers stood accused before the Koi Court. Chief Joel took his seat flanked by two minor chiefs and two lay members. The little mud-and-thatch hall was packed with men sitting cross-legged on the ground. Through the open sides peered another hundred faces with drawn expres-sions. The public was entirely made up of defaulting labour.

The criminal casebook was brought out by the court clerk, a boy taken on after his father had not been able to find fees to keep him at secondary school. He opened it at a blank page. Adjacent to a case record headed "Adultery in the R.C. Chapel", and, after thinking for a moment, wrote painfully at the top of the new page "Refusal to build a Road and Attempted Arson". Then, he prepared to take down the evidence.

The accused were called forward and stood with folded arms in front of the president's table that had been raised on a solid mud platform. The prosecution evidence was called. A minor chief deposed that he had been visited at his home the night before by the accused men who had told him that they were not coming to work any more and that they were going to tell everybody else to stay away. The men had, he said, threatened him with the burning of his house if he still made the people come to work on the road.

One of the accused, a young man dressed in a blue shirt and patched red shorts, cross-examined the chief:

"Did I tell you that it was bad to make people come for work?"

"Yes."

"If I told you that, why did you not arrest me last night when I came instead of coming with askaris this morning?"

The chief hesitated and looked meekly at Joel.

"Because there were four of you and you were threatening me."

The chief's wife was called up and asked to confirm her husband's evidence. She said that she had heard nothing and was busy cooking in the house at the time. Then, the three District Council police askaris who had arrested the accused that same morning each gave an account of the arrests. Another of the accused men cross-examined:

"Did we resist you?"

"No."

"Does a guilty man run away or does he wait to be arrested?"

"He waits to be arrested so that he will not get too big a sentence."

There were jeers from the peasants on the floor and the two askaris in attendance at the back of the hall took a firm grasp of their sticks. The case for the prosecution had ended and the court asked no questions. The accused men said that they wished one of their number, the man in the red shorts, to speak for them. The young man looked round at the faces behind him and smiled as though assimilating the great surge of support that was silently going out to him.

"The first thing is this. We are being tried by the same chiefs who caused our arrest this morning." A murmur of assent rippled through the crowd. "In that way, we cannot have a fair trial. Therefore, we ask you transfer the case to another Court.

Secondly, we cannot tell a chief that we will burn his house. Such things are bad. This chief is angry with me because I defeated him in a land case concerning my ancestral holding which he wanted to steal from me."

The man rested momentarily for his labours and noted that Joel had put on his wire-rimmed spectacles and was making a note of what he had just said.

"Thirdly, we never went to the chief to tell him that we would not work on the road. Even his wife has said that she did not hear us coming. This chief is bringing bad blood to the country and we ask you to get rid of him!"

This was too much for the watchers who exploded into a burst of quick clapping. The askaris barked out for silence but the peasants took their own time to quieten themselves.

Joel conferred nervously with his Court Members. They all nodded assent at a suggestion he seemed to be making.

"It is not necessary for you to continue. The Court finds that there is not enough evidence to support a conviction. You are all acquitted."

A cacophony of whoops and cheers ensured and the dignity of the court crumbled into a noisy confusion. The Court Members retreated almost surreptitiously. The released men were hemmed in by laughing men; women appeared from nowhere and joined the crowd; Joel cycled off to report to Okot, who called him a "cowardly idiot", and wrote a letter asking Garston to transfer him to a sub-county "more suited to his weakness".

Garston was displeased to see Cedric and Morris at his office.

"You certainly choose your convenient time to come shopping. I've just had a wireless message from the Police Post at Port Steamer that none of your men are at work and there's talk of a mob going round Koi Trading Centre! Now, bloody well get out there at once! You camp at Koi, Hamilton-Gordon, and you at Port Steamer, Mbuya." Garston's reversion to surnames was always a sign of deep disapproval. "I shall be out again with the police today and we'll visit you both with detailed instructions." As they were leaving, he shouted after them: "And remember, the work on the road goes on!"

Morris, like Joseph before him, had steeled himself to tell Eleanor's story to Garston, and, like his son, went away silent: time was not propitious. "You were a bit hard on them, weren't you?" said Diana from her typewriter after they had gone, "and, in any case, don't you think it wrong to tick a white officer off in front of a black one?"

Garston mumbled something, bit a hole in the mouthpiece of his pipe that had gone out and stormed off to see Fawcett.

Old Father Frascati was shopping in the Trading Centre at Koi when the mob from the court appeared shouting and waving sticks. Their grievances had become generalised and they were talking of looting one of the shops. The Father was able to take a few of the leading hotheads by the arm.

"Remember that you are Catholics and not savages!" he shouted. And once the fight had drained out of their leaders, the crowd fell part. The Father went on with his shopping.

CHAPTER SEVENTEEN

The Bridge Opens

Dison Apau was true to his word. Within a week of his promise to Garston, the last timber had been nailed down on the bridge. There was an unofficial opening when hundreds of the locals who had been waiting for this moment rushed from side to side of the bridge, the crowd becoming so dense in the end that there was a jam in the middle. Apau had no money for rails on his bridges and a man was forced off the side into the stream. At this time of year, the water was too shallow to cushion the man's fall appreciably: he sat in the river with the water up to his chest unable to get up and painfully bruised. The crowd, precarious above, seemed to be going mad with laughter but, in the end, a few schoolboys waded into the river and helped him out.

No work had been done on the road after the disturbances at the Koi Trading Centre on the first day of organised defiance. But otherwise, everything appeared peaceful. Leslie, who had been recalled from a joint safari with Freeman, the Agricultural Officer, in the Wamamba flats, was able to go back. Fawcett put a few extra men at Port Steamer but recalled them in order to mount a guard of honour for the Commissioner of Police who had come up for an Annual Inspection, having refused to be put off by Fawcett's suggestion that there seemed to be some possibility of trouble in the District. "If," the Commissioner had written, "your surmise turns out to be correct, presumably I shall have a first-hand opportunity for seeing your force in action." It was, after all, not often that the Commissioner could get away from the capital for a spot of shooting and be able to play a round of golf that did not resolve itself into an extremely irritating queue.

Meanwhile, the District Council was meeting for its final session before Christmas. The Romba bars were flooded with members in dark suits and stiff white collars discussing tactics. In the Council Chamber, Onyango, for the first time in his life, said nothing. The usual motions of censure were passed on to the Secretary and Treasurer of the Council but the expected attack on Garston was not forthcoming.

Two days after the bridge was finished, the first heavy cotton lorry edged slowly onto its planks and rolled carefully across. Two more followed. Within one hour, they were at the ginnery. They were forced to tip at frightening angles to pass uneven stretches in the road, their sumps sometimes scraping unremoved rocks; and, at times, the turn-boys perched unsafely high on the camel-humped tarpaulin had to climb down the sides of the lorry and clear tree trunks that barred the way. But they got through. The people were plainly impressed and some sections started thinking of defying the party line. Nobody felt happy about disobeying a chief. It was better, after all, to fall in with what was ordered.

But on the morning when about two hundred men had intended to obey the drums, it started to rain. A full month premature, the storm lashed the new road into a morass, trapping two lorries on their way down to the ginnery. Both drivers attempted to push through but were constantly stuck in the mud up to the axels. One lorry, top heavy with cotton sacks, was unable because of the wet, to take an absurdly banked corner at sufficient speed and it toppled over into the sludge. One of the turn-boys could not jump clear in time and was crushed by the side of the lorry. A crowd gathered from nowhere in the downpour; men started chasing the driver who had extricated himself through a window and was floundering in the mud in a desperate bid to escape the wrath that ensued the turn-boy's death. In the end, he stumbled badly and, shiny with filth, cringed to accept the stones and the sticks hammered upon him by the insensate group.

Most of the cotton from that lorry was spoilt but the mob that took what they could from the other vehicle while its driver looked on helplessly and tried to remember faces. "The riots began quite literally by accident," Garston was to tell the Commission of Enquiry.

Small groups of men broke away from the mob round the lorries and went off into the two Counties, attracting large numbers of followers as they went. Women marched with the columns screaming curses; men on bicycles cycled round the advancing masses like sheepdogs; leaders blew whistles and horns; others beat drums with fanatic precision; schoolboys shouted slogans. The rain had stopped but the countryside was drenched and the crowds trampled through long wet elephant grass that soaked the women's dresses. The imprint of hundreds of feet was left in the steaming mud of house compounds as the mobs moved to the nearest chiefs' houses.

In Koi sub-county, the column made for the house of the minor chief who had given evidence against the four peasant farmers. When they were still half a mile away, he could hear them promising to tear him apart. With his wife and children, he quickly made a pile of their most precious household possessions: a radio, a gramophone, a small suitcase full of cloth and a bag of cotton, which he secreted in their banana plot near the huts, covering them with soaked mulch. The crowd, led by a screaming man on a bicycle, was only a hundred yards away by now. The family dispersed quickly in different directions through the banana plantation; the wife, with her two children, towards her mother's home, and the chief to a nearby papyrus swamp where he left the path and waded in up to his knees. Then he lay completely down in the slime bed, quite still, breathing through a papyrus stem. The mob had reached his compound and was firing at the butts. He had forgotten about his cows and these were herded together inside a hut and were nearly burnt alive. They found his possessions in the banana plot and smashed what they could with sticks. A white-haired granny from a neighbour's house stood shouting and waving her fist ineffectually at the hysterics. Someone shouted that the chief was probably hiding in the swamp and the mob veered round with one will just as the great flame torches of burning thatch were swept around with a change in the wind.

The mob splashed excitedly through the papyrus probing their way with spears and sticks, hacking pathways in the sudd. The Chief lay absolutely still below the surface. He could hear voices approaching. The water had settled above him and a triangle of sky filtered through the papyrus to his eyes. Suddenly, he heard loud splashing noises and the next moment a spear zipped bubbling through the water and embedded itself in the mud between his arm and his ribs. Immediately afterwards, a naked foot obscuring the triangle of sky, came heavily to rest on his chest kicking the breathing tube away. Still he lay quiet, his lungs pleading terribly for air. Mud swirled all about him; the foot was driving him further into the slime. And then it left him. The spear was withdrawn and the splashing continued behind him. But now there could be no hesitation, no further reasoning with his body. He climbed up and broke the surface, gasping to relieve his tortured lungs. Behind him, the splashing continued dreadfully near. He waited for a spear thrust but it never came, and for the entire day he made his bed in the bottom of the swamp only leaving it to renew his stems. At night, he slept in the water with his head on solid ground, ready to slip in at a moment's notice.

Other chiefs in the Koi had run to Father Frascati for sanctuary. The mob appeared in front of the Father's long bungalow house near the church, gesticulating and screaming. Brother Pitti came out on the verandah with the white-haired priest. A man in the crowd vaulted a low parapet separating the missionaries from the crowd and tried to shout in Father Frascati's face that it was imperative to give up on the chiefs unless he wanted to see the mob tear into the Church. The priest looked horrified: the man was one of his catechists. Brother Pitti, a huge man, pushed him into the flowerbed on the other side of the verandah and then crossed himself as he got up. This had an unexpectedly calming effect on the people, some of whom started to laugh. The priest was able to tell them to go away and behave like Christians. This time, however, they did not disperse but moved quickly away towards the County Chief's house. Meanwhile, Brother Pitti fetched his elephant gun and the priest went to prepare tea and bread for the eight chiefs and their families locked in his bedroom.

Okot had prudently driven to Cedric's camp, ostensibly to warn him about the mobs. His family was crowded in the car with him.

"There are at least four groups in this County. They are going from house to house burning chiefs' property. The people in East GodiGodi have already destroyed my private house there."

Cedric quickly left a report on the road that he was writing at the time and fumbled in his suitcase for a little booklet that explained to magistrates what they should do in front of large crowds that threatened violence. He had daily tried to imagine a situation like this and now that it had happened, he was sick with fear; he had heard the shouting coming from the distant crowds in the direction of the Trading Centre and the mission but both Semei and Boaz seemed to think that it was probably a funeral. He had preferred to think that too.

The mob had done as much damage as it desired to the County Chief's official house, tearing away corrugated iron from the roof, spearing the water butts, axing his furniture. They made a bonfire of his collection of school textbooks, ripped down and stole his curtains; a schoolboy jumped on the wireless. And then, one grievance allied to another, they surged on to the Indian Trading Centre where they joined up with a much larger mob that had crossed the river by the new bridge.

All the traders had pulled down their shutters and were sitting terrified in the squalid backrooms of their metal hutches, roasting from the heat that now blanketed down on them from the scorched tin roof. But there was one trader who remained impassive, almost inviting the mob to come and do business as usual. This was Bimji Virji, a dwarf of a man with a grotesque hunchback and a disturbing cataract in one eye. He was perched on his counter gently humming a tune and absorbed in twiddling nuts from one little box onto screws from another box. His toes protruded from his dirty cotton trousers and twitched along with the tune. Affecting not to have heard the drumming, whistling and screaming outside, he looked slowly up and confronted the bloodshot eyes of one of the leaders who had entered the shop and was exhorting the people behind him to start looting.

"What do you want?" asked Bimji Virji in his most businesslike voice, never once ceasing the twiddling of the nuts. But as the first hand grasped the first bale of cloth, the noise of a police tender driving up to the door deterred it. A dozen constables jumped out and elbowed their way through the crowd to the shop. Fawcett and Cedric followed. The police officer had a hand on his revolver.

"Well, give them the speech," said Fawcett. Cedric fumbled with the book and realised that he had not yet been sworn in as a Magistrate.

"Do it all the same!" snapped out Fawcett impatiently. And Cedric read the Riot Act.

"Now give them some oratory," said Fawcett, relaxing slightly. The cadet, sufficiently terrified not to be nervous, began to address the inattentive crowd which was by now about six hundred strong.

"People of West GodiGodi, what you are doing today will take many months to undo. You are going backwards not forwards. I know that you don't want that…"

"Pep it up with some humour, for God's sake!" whispered Fawcett.

"He's asking the impossible," thought Cedric, unsteady at the knees. The crowd stood before them with not a smile to be seen among them. He wondered weakly whether they would understand shaggy dog stories. In the end, rather more apprehensive of

Fawcett's frown than the crowd, he told them that if they stopped rioting at once, he would order the Chiefs not to take action on their absences from the road labour gangs.

"There are no Chief!" someone shouted.

"Here! Translate this!" said Fawcett to Okot, who was standing nearby, almost holding onto an armed constable. The policeman suddenly scorned translated into a Regimental Sergeant Major addressing a battalion on the evils of slovenly turnout.

"I don't know why you want to loot from poor old Bimji here! Bimji only sells nuts and bolts and old tins for you to brew banana firewater in!" There was a reluctant tittering in the crowd that the leaders tried to repress.

"That's the only reason that Bimji hasn't locked anything up! Now, you should go two doors down to Shah. There's a man who sells so many cigarettes that you could steal enough for a month and be so sick you wouldn't come back for a year! My men here might shoot a few of you but it's worth trying, isn't it?"

By now, laughter came through unequivocally. The fury had subsided and the picture that Fawcett began to paint to them of the joys of their domestic hearts relative to the colder comforts of half a lifetime in a Protectorate Prison had its effect. An hour later, the shops had opened and were doing good business.

The police patrolled conspicuously and took down scores of contradictory accounts of what had happened and who was responsible. But the bush whip was still firmly on and they learnt very little.

In East GodiGodi, events had taken a more serious turn. The injured lorry driver had been so badly beaten up that he had died as he was dragged along between the driver and turnboy of the other lorry who were hopelessly trying to move him to the Port Steamer Dispensary. His murderers now thought of Adaa.

Adaa had made an unsuccessful application for permanent police protection ever since trouble had seemed imminent. Now a crowd was converging on his house so rapidly from the west that he had only just enough time to send his eldest son to warn the Police Post. They were already fully engaged with a mob threatening the ginnery. He sat in an old wicker chair on his porch. Between his knees rested his double-bore shotgun. He was an old man, he reflected, and the end might as well come then as ever. But it was a pity; it was a great pity.

When, however, the crowd pressed insolently into his compound demolishing the neat papyrus fence that enclosed it, his fury at the impropriety knew no bounds. The people drew up in a solid phalanx before him. The nervous eyes of his two youngest sons peered round the door. Their father was advancing slowly towards the people, his long kanzu blowing gently in the wind. All was quiet in the eye of the storm.

Adaa stopped five yards short of the crowd and drew a line in the earth with the butt of his gun. He noticed the schoolteacher from the baraza in the front line but said nothing. Then he turned to the crowd, retreating as he spoke. He would shoot down any man who crossed his line.

For a moment, the people strained to look at the line as though it were a river that could be jumped. Adaa pointed his gun at them from the hip. Then, with a great shout, the schoolteacher rushed over the line. The shot that punctured his stomach barely stopped him from reaching the chief and he fell head-long like a man checked in a flying tackle, throwing his panga wildly into the air. The weapon clattered onto the tin roof of the house, slid slowly down and fell a few inches from the dead man's hand that was almost touching the chief's foot.

The sight of the young man in his muddied white shirt, blood beginning to ooze out from beneath him, could easily have deterred any other challengers. But the crowd stayed where it was, murmuring at the outrage. A spear was quickly levelled at the chief from the right and, as he stepped to avoid it and pulled his second trigger into the crowd, he was pierced from the left and soon engulfed by a multitude of assassins, each of whom, long after he was dead, slashed at him with a panga. The family was allowed to escape. Inside the house, the rioters found Adaa's Queen's Medal for Chiefs in silver and started squabbling over it.

Garston had by now reached the ginnery. Outside the gates, he found Morris already addressing the mob there, with police at the ready. African that he was, they were the more prone to interrupt and abuse him but the sight of the police rifles deterred them from any overt attempt at violence. But they were achieving their main object, the picketing of the ginnery. Only the foreman and the night watchman were inside the ginnery compound. Hussein sat trembling with his wife and ten children in their quarters opposite, looking out occasionally to see if Morris was making progress. Some of the cheerleaders were shouting for his blood. The foreman, also in demand, kept on slanging the crowd through the fence as loudly as he could whenever Morris stopped speaking.

On Garston's arrival, the crowd parted to make room for him, and Hussein ran gratefully out of his house to recount the full story of the siege. At that moment, too, Adaa's son arrived to tell of the crowd round his father's house; three constables were detailed off to the house with Morris, who was to find nothing but the two bodies and a pile of commemorative photographs ripped from the walls inside.

Garston, meanwhile, read the riot act and suggested that he should meet three of the people's leaders in Hussein's office to discuss their grievances. This was answered by wild catcalls and fierce spear-raising cries of "Freedom!". And when Morris returned with his news, Garston wrote a note quickly on a slip of paper and told him to look for Onyango whose home village was only three miles away; there was chance that he could be found. Then, he ordered the police to return to their post until further notice in deference to one or two vocalists who were shouting to the effect that any representations that they could make were likely to be inhibited by a spray of bullets.

Morris drove with his escort to Onyango's house. The politician, in common with many people involved in the violence of that day, was sitting at home quietly awaiting developments. Morris found him stretched on a deckchair in front of his white plastered house. As though to make the scene idyllic, a hired peasant was guiding an ox plough through a nearby field in preparation for potatoes. Onyango was dressed in American drill trousers and an open-necked cream shirt with a paisley neckerchief. He was reading the autobiography of Dr Nkrumah.

"Yes?" Onyango asked Morris, looking up at the District Officer at the last possible moment.

"I have a note from the D.C. He would like to see you at Port Steamer," said Morris, handing him the scrap of paper Garston had hurriedly scrawled. It read:

'Don't ask questions. Come to the ginnery at once. You'll be sorry if you don't.' Signed: Moorside, District Commissioner.

"Tell me, Mr Mbuya, have you read this note?"

"No."

"Well, I consider it most offensive." Onyango paused. "What, by the way, is happening at the ginnery?"

Morris told him quickly. Onyango tried hard to maintain an attitude of reflective unconcern but the thought of possible repercussions now pressed upon him with such force that, with considerable restraint, he put his book to one side, yawned at some length and climbed into his sports jacket which was draped over the back of the deckchair.

"Well, under the greatest possible protest at this treatment backed up by threats, I will come. I haven't, as you see, got much option." And he pointed to the escort of constables waiting in Morris' car. "And incidentally, Mbuya," he said, climbing into the car, "I consider someone like you doing a job like this to be an enemy of the people."

Garston was joking with the crowd when they returned. He had not, however, succeeded in dispersing them. Morris and Mbuya pushed through the crowd to where the D.C. was standing alone on a chair in front of the ginnery gates.

"Ah, good morning, Mr Onyango," said Garston, bending down to proffer his hand which the politician shook coolly.

"Mr Onyango, I have a problem. These good people won't go away. Mr Hussein and his labour want to start work and these fellows are rather anxious that he should not do so; I'm rather sorry to say that some of them have even threatened their friends with house-burning if they come to work here. A few of their companions, whose names I possess, have also murdered Mr Adaa. Now, two sessions ago, you advocated two things in the Legislative Council, if I remember correctly. First, you announced yourself in favour of rapid non-violent progress to Independence, if necessary by unconstitutional means but nonetheless non-violent. Secondly, you wanted the Government to do more to encourage cotton productivity. You referred to the slow handling of the crop by ginneries. Do I make myself clear?"

"I hope, Mr Moorside, that you are not suggesting that I have had anything to do with this morning's events?" said Onyango steadily.

"On the contrary, Mr Onyango, I leave that for others to decide. My contention is that you could very well dissociate yourself in public." And he pointed to an empty chair. "Mount if you please, Mr Onyango!"

"Are you obliging me to do so?"

"No. Do as you please."

Onyango climbed on the chair and put out his hand for silence. He began to talk excitedly.

"He's calling them 'heroes of the revolution'," said Garston's interpreter, trying to catch Onyango's gabbled phrases. "He says that they must lay down their arms and enjoy their victory... the D.C. will arrange to give them what they want... they must let men work at the ginnery... they must not kill chiefs... they must..."

At this juncture, the murmuring against Onyango became so intense that he could not be heard. Fists shook in the air, sticks were waved and there were a few blasts from a whistle in the crowd.

"I think that that will do nicely, Mr Onyango," said Garston, and, addressing the crowd, he said that now both he, the D.C., and the local representative of the Freedom Party had condemned what they were doing as bad. If they did not disperse within five minutes, he would call in the police again.

"Will you want a lift back, Mr Onyango?" asked Garston, removing his topee and wiping his forehead, as the crowd fell apart.

"No," said Onyango, striding off. But seeing that a few questioners were standing in his path, he returned and took up the offer.

"I'm sure Mr Mbuya will oblige," Garston smiled, indicating Morris's Volkswagen.

NOVEMBER 1961

CHAPTER EIGHTEEN

A Commission of Enquiry

Garston learned some days later that the Governor had appointed a Commission of Enquiry into the disturbances. It consisted of one High Court Judge, Sir Mortimer Butterworth, who could begin work in January. The D.C. had Christmas in which to recover from one crisis in order to face the next.

For weeks, Patel had been receiving large deliveries of European toys that now sprawled over the top of half his showcases. His own features being a little odd in character, he cut a grotesque figure as he kneeled down to demonstrate to some embarrassed child the prowess of a clockwork-articulated King Kong gorilla done in tin with green eyes that lit up. But he was never quite sure of what Europeans wanted him to stock and would frequently ask them what he should order, a tragic look in his eye, as he recognised that business was not ideally done in this way.

"Well, Patel, if you really want to know what we English like round Christmas time, it's nice, seasonal snow." Patel ordered snow in packets.

"It's nice of you to ask, Mr Patel... let me see. I know that some people are very fond of plum pudding." Patel wrote for twenty dozen tins.

"Mummy, has Mr Patel got some of those sweets that change colour as they get smaller?" Mr Patel hadn't but he said that he would receive a large consignment of them on Boxing Day.

"Wifes love perfume, Mr Patel. Oh, you know, Dior, Schiaparelli, Chanel, Lanvin, any of those names will do. Wives love the stuff."

Patel obliged but the liquid evaporated and he recorded a turnover of one bottle in a year.

But he did sell scores of paper chains. And Freddie Carr, the Forestry Officer, took orders for trees approximating in appearance to conifers. The District Council temporarily replaced its sign reading "Welcome" over the Council Chamber with one that said "Welcome Christmas". Leslie came to the office on Christmas Eve with a piece of plastic mistletoe that he hung on Garston's office lampshade. Diana and her boss were discovered by Johnson Ezekiel in an unseemly clinch refereed by Bwana District Officer No. 2.

"Break!" Leslie had shouted but he was too late.

The Indian Government Controlled Public School, as it was styled in exaggerated deference to the official grant, laid on what their programme called a Sing-song of highly traditional English songs. Garston was invited to open the entertainment with a half-yearly distribution of prizes contributed by the parents.

The headmaster, Mr Hansraj, was also the sole master, though he teacher-trained a few of his older pupils to relieve the effect of his constant darting from Class One to Class Two and back again.

It was difficult to understand how much English Mr Hansraj really possessed as he deprived of their consonantal force all words of which he was unsure. But he had immense admiration for anything British, a sentiment passed on to him almost as an article of faith by his father who had died a schoolmaster in India. His classrooms both exhibited loyal photographs, in addition to large posters depicting the manifold activities of the City of Bristol, the City of Manchester and the rivers of Scotland. Neither had he been proof against a quiet indulgence in moral propaganda that combined an insight into the profundities of the accumulated wisdom of the East with a sensible appraisal of the more practical things in life. After any marking that he had to do, he would spend his lonely bachelor evenings in the drafting and painting of his maxims. In Class One, appeared the words: Even wisdom of Solomon does not equal brain of little child' side by side with Clean your Teeth. Class Two had a more worldly flavour, advising: Never ask for credit, never be refused and Twelve Pennies always make Shilling.

On the day of the carols, it was full service marching order for the Europeans who turned up; the women in hats and long gloves, the men uncomfortably in suits. The afternoon sun made no concession to the Christmas card ideal of Christmas. Outside the school, Hindus and Muslims waited together in a sort of reception committee and each arriving European was made to run the gauntlet of a dozen warm welcomes.

Garston unburdened himself of his prizes which, following the headmaster's cultural predilections, were all books in a series that described the feathered friends, man's best friends and reptiles of the British Isles.

Muljibhai, back from India, emaciated and skinny in his loose dhoti, looking as though he had just emerged from a hunger strike to turn the hearts of zamindars, rose as Chairman of the Parents' Association to thank Garston for his munificence in presenting the prizes, and to welcome honoured guests.

The choir then marched onto a specially constructed platform. The girls wore blue dresses with red sashes; the dots on their foreheads had been touched up, their eyelashes were heavy with kohl and their shiny pigtails were tied in uniform red silk bands. The boys suffered in plain grey flannels, for which Mr Hansraj had, for him, a conclusive if climatically inappropriate precedent.

While the children were delivering their unaccompanied rendering of John Peel and Vicar of Bray, Diana's eyes darted constantly in the direction of Leslie and Angela, who had been placed next to each other. She had long convinced herself that her suspicions about them were valid and had often hinted at them in coffee parties. All she now required was a discovery of the two in what Geoffrey vulgarly translated 'flagrant delight'. When the performance was concluded and, as they all filed out onto the verandah to the choir-hummed tune of *My Darling Clementine*, she was almost sure that she saw the couple touch hands in a highly significant manner. Then they were dispersed among the platefuls of spicy cakes and teapots full of strong tea.

Leslie and Thelma threw an all-station Christmas Eve party that night. Nearly everyone from the Protestant Mission was due to come except Rose Grantham who had a cold. Leslie had had the grass scythed to a respectable length especially for the occasion, and a collection of hurricane lamps with their glasses painted red, blue and green were placed at strategic points in the garden. All over the two Circles, children were kissed goodnight, ayahs installed in position and stockings quietly attached to the ends of beds.

This party had had a precarious history and even when the invitations had been delivered, its future course had been highly uncertain. As he watched the changing expression on his guests' faces when they were told by Timoteo that there were no spirits, Leslie cursed the moment he had agreed to compromise with Thelma's new madness. Four weeks before, she had come home from her Bible Study and announced that, if they were to have a party, they should not compromise with principles as they had done so many times in the past.

"What do you mean by that, for heaven's sake?" Leslie had asked.

"I mean this, that we are always giving parties and are invited to parties that turn into little more than drinking orgies."

"I'm sorry, Thelma, maybe I've had too hard a day at the office but I don't begin to understand you."

Thelma had taken his hands in a gesture quite unfamiliar to him and which almost, inexplicably, endeared her to him.

"Look, Leslie, we don't live a very… it's difficult to know how to put it… a very good life, I mean we're so selfish in what we do and think…"

"What's that got to do with the party?" he had asked.

Thelma's expression had changed again, not into the spineless, feeble look that she usually wore but to one less yielding and less trivial. She had suddenly ceased to be the little woman.

"Leslie, I haven't told you this before but a lot of things have happened to me in the last month. I suppose it's since I started going to the Mission more and more. I've seen a lot of things I never saw before. I think I know now what being a Christian can mean."

Leslie had never seen Thelma like this. He had always recognised a deep religious streak in her nature and had long accepted that she relied upon it to compensate for weaknesses and shortcomings in her own life, just as he himself adopted private make-shifts, Angela among the latest. But the change in her suddenly seemed so profound, and because it was change in Thelma, almost attractive.

"Thelma, I don't know what to make of you. Here we are sitting down planning a party and you come at me with principles, experiences, overnight changes. It's hardly fair."

She put her arm round his shoulder.

"Would you come to the Mission too... Bible studies and things?"

That was, of course, too much. A nauseous picture of women with Adam's apples and dresses out of 1920 Wimbledon flashed in upon him compellingly. But, undeniably, after another hour's solid brain-washing, she had managed to extract from him the fantastic concession that the alcoholic content of the party would be restricted to low proof wine and beer.

"Then we'll be able to invite the Archdeacon and people!" she had said jubilantly, almost clapping her hands in triumph, as Leslie winced in satanic repentance. He himself could see only one advantage in the projected purity of this jolly roistering: it would be cheaper that way.

Thelma had not carried through this major victory without a very definite reinforcement and reappraisal of her deepest conscious beliefs. The weekly Bible readings and carol practices had become opportunities for listening to Gordon with all his quiet and utterly convincing explanations of spiritual realities. She had never met anyone with such inward strength, so completely reliant on his faith and so strong because of it but his Bible classes had not been well attended. While Romba was fundamentally pagan (of this, both he and Thelma were convinced), one night, she had arrived at the Mission to find herself quite alone with Gordon.

"Not much of a crowd tonight, Mrs Farrar," he had said, turning up the oil lamp with its tall, slender glass.

"No," she replied quietly, troubled. Then she had uttered those words that threatened immediately their whole spiritual relationship and came straight from the guilt-ridden ambivalence with which she thought of him in secret moments.

"You tell me to call you Gordon. You may as well call me Thelma... after all... I mean..."

Gordon had looked at her with a nervous smile from which all indication of strength had drained, the same smile that she remembered as he had stepped into the pulpit to preach about Job and which had dissipated as his sermon mounted from strength to strength. And so, mercifully, it had been in that Bible reading. He had set the edifice of faith back in its place, struggled and pleaded with her until she saw the way of salvation, pointed wonderfully through the texts at God's wishes for men. He had shown her how to overcome her misery at Leslie's indifference to her, how to make a better mother to Jill, how to pray, how to live, and, if need be, how to die. It was a discovery that could not be contained within herself. Had not Gordon said that the great injunction was to go out into all the world to preach the Gospel? For his part, Gordon often wondered whether she knew of his daily struggles and doubts. From his mission cottage he could just see the hedge of Thelma's front garden through a gap in the surrounding eucalyptus trees. And he would strain his eyes to see it as he sat in front of his great floppy Bible open on his desk for his morning reading. He knew he was wrong to look and dreaded failure in the day of his testing. And yet he could be thankful that, through Thelma's very need, he had found renewed faith and conviction. Would his faith last for only as long as she required it? And how, oh God!, could he forever try and deny that she was woman, forever attempting to see her as a soul unto the harvest. In the bare sterility of his Mission House, she came with warmth and admiration, a woman with a woman's body. And the Bible said that he was committing adultery in his own heart.

But Gordon had smiled spiritually when Thelma told him of her victory over the alcohol. And Leslie, the reputed hearty of the station, watched himself throwing an almost dry Christmas Eve Party. The Romba carrollers came to sing carols accompanied by the gesticulations of Denis Billman, whose frenzied shadow danced from the pressure lamps over half the garden like a soul in torment. Leslie looked furtively at his watch. Thank God, the singers were taking a great deal longer than he had expected and his guests were able to take their minds off Thelma's two percent proof wine cup that swayed like medicine in their glasses. The Archdeacon at least seemed to be enjoying himself hugely but that was a fair indication that a most extraordinary flop was being enacted.

"I can't think what's happened," whispered Diana, looking into her full glass. Reg Blagdon became puzzled, as a fish must be on first feeling the unendearing deck of a trawler, and then, more forthright, he turned to anger and left early.

And, in the end, only a small caucus of Mission people remained grouped around the desecrated toasties table. The rest of the party had slunk off to the club where Chalisi was roused from a profound slumbering lying against the deep freezer. Leslie, in his shame, went with them. And there he was able to extract a teasing sympathy from Angela, while Thelma, tearful at home, derived strength from an understanding glance that Gordon had given her earlier that evening. Nobody had promised her that the Way would be easy.

Few heads were clear on Christmas morning. The sun greeted Romba hotly. Odd cars floated quickly about the station to and from Church Services. Meanwhile, the Asian traders were mounting their annual assault. Bumping slowly down from the bazaar, past the government offices and towards the Circles, like tanks in the desert, the vans appeared, relentless. The first to wheel into Garston's drive was Muljibhai's son, followed by two African servants carrying cardboard boxes full of bottles of spirit, topped by a tinselled greetings card and presentation Parker pen sets. The boxes were dumped on the front doorstep and the party left as silently as it had arrived. Then came the senior of the grocer Patels in person. "I am wishing you very many happy pictures," he said, smiling as he handed a camera to Angela while his assistants placed three crates of groceries gently on the carpet. Muljibhai himself cruised down in his

vast Plymouth and greeted select Europeans while
his son's gift waggon prepared the way, unburdening
itself of whiskey and more expensive fountain pens.
Romba Express Motors alone, among those who
gave at all, gave indifferently: a trade calendar and
a box of chocolates was all that could be expected
and not everybody received that.

It was of little use remonstrating. Standing Orders
were lucid enough but a steady body of unofficial case
law and practice had been built up over the years. It
was accepted in Mamba that if you could eat it, you
would keep it. After that, it was a matter for the individual conscience. On Boxing Day morning, Garston
went to the bazaar on his annual protest march.

"Look, Muljibhai, I can't possibly accept this."

Garston fingered his fountain pen, already regret-
ting the loss of its rolled-gold cap.

"Mr Moorside," said Muljibhai in his deep voice,
speaking like a rich uncle who quite understands his
poor nephew's desire to get on in life unaided, "this
is merely an unsatisfactory token of my esteem and
good wishes. I would be greatly hurt by any suggestion that you should return it to me."

The two men prevaricated over a beer and the
inner struggle was decided finally for Garston when
Leslie drew up outside in a spectacular dust.

"Dorothy and Freeman," said Leslie, "they went
up Buni yesterday morning, said they'd be back last

night. Cedric went round to Freeman's house and he's still out, so's Dorothy. A few of us thought we might go up and look. Coming?"

The search party set out within an hour. The men who stayed behind with the golfing women couldn't keep their minds fully on the game. Mount Buni, with its unrelieved greyness that turned black in a storm, had that effect. But nobody really believed that anything serious had happened to the couple. They were fools to go up there, that was all.

Peter Freeman had always known that, in the end, some family would inevitably take a lonely bachelor under its wing over the Christmas period but he felt that annually people took him in as a tiresome duty: a man like Ian Peebles was actually competed for. Reg Blagdon usually spent Christmas with the Fawcett's; even Cedric, new as he was, had become something of a station darling. But Freeman had become conscious of boring the station and decided to spend this Christmas away somewhere, alone.

"It'll be nice to get away from the madding crowd," Freeman said, unconvinced, one Saturday lunchtime in the Club.

"That's a selfish and altogether typical bachelor attitude," Dorothy Ward had replied. And Peter reddened.

"I'll tell you what," the nursing sister continued, "I'll come with you and give you something else to think about apart from your dear self." And they had been lost to Romba from early Christmas morning.

Mount Buni offered a stiff scramble with few major difficulties. But a formidable degree of persistency and stamina was required to achieve the return journey in a day. Halfway up, a thick belt of bamboo coincided with a severe steepening of the gradient. Dorothy had needed to rest at frequent intervals and had become discouraged. They had seemed to be forever sliding down into the ravines of mountain torrents, gaining height in painful hours on the other side and plunging once more into the green depth of another stream's profound valley.

It was becoming clear that Dorothy would not reach the top and that they should turn back when she had stumbled badly on a rock and sprained her ankle. Peter had tried to guide her down with one of her arms slung over his shoulder but the pain of supporting herself on her bad foot grew fiercely. In the end, he had carried her down for short stretches at a time. She was surprisingly light: he had the time to notice the way in which the shafts of sun that shot through the overhead bamboo canopy caught her auburn hair. For once, her hair was not enclosed in the discipline of her sister's cap but fell excitingly away from her face.

Gradually, the pain had eased and there had seemed less point in hurrying. And when the rescue party arrived by eleven the next morning, it found two circumspect little igloos made out of bamboo, Dorothy in one, Peter in the other, each asleep and smiling, presumably dreaming of the station wedding they had planned late into the night. Nearby, the remnants of a large bonfire were still smoking.

JANUARY 1962

CHAPTER NINETEEN

A Safari Lodge and A Learned Report

Garston opened his confidential file on the Koi-Port Steamer road. It was all there – right from the first tentative communications with the Treasurer of the District Council to the final warning order from Judge Butterworth, the one-man Commission of Inquiry. There had been unpleasant little darts from the Provincial Commissioner all along but the broadside he expected had somehow never come. The Judge's report would be the acid test.

Garston sighed heavily. The rain had wiped out most of the road. Had the riots not happened when they did, Cedric could have finished it during snatches of dry weather. As it was, the cotton lorries were going round the old way once more. And yet, splendid in its assertion, the new Koi bridge remained as a sturdy example of his desire to help the people. Surely the Commission would understand that he had meant well.

Then Garston thought of Adaa. Poor old Adaa, due for retirement within a year; stupid but utterly brave and loyal Adaa, who had defied them all and lost. Were all the fine people like him going to disappear overnight? Perhaps it was bound to be. The taint of "colonialism" would sit too heavily upon their memory and they would go to the wall. And what would the Onyangos do with what was left?

At best, one could only "hope". Meanwhile, the actuaries in London were drawing up a compensation scheme for expatriates for the loss of their careers. But it would be a loss of something much more than a career, he reflected. For all his mistakes and his apparent failure to go all the way to understand the Africans, he had dug roots among them – not the roots of a settler with disputed land to care for and fight for but those of… of a teacher, maybe, with children for whom he had to care. It was a politically unfashionable view but it coincided with the facts as he saw them.

And suddenly Garston envied them, these Mamba Africans. Their nationhood was something new and fresh; the issues they would face were not old, tired problems about atom bombs and spheres of ideological influence. No, they would have to deal with the God-given struggle against poor soil, disease, mosquitoes, ignorance, squalor, hunger or thirst. They could still run through a gamut of Rights of Man Charters without beginning to suspect that an inexhaustible weariness would be the end result when one day they decided that civilisation is incapable of perfection.

Yet Mamba was so poor, poorer than any other District in the Protectorate. How would they manage alongside richer areas? Would the careful system of Central Government subventions continue, or would the big tribes build up pressure groups in the Legislature and gobble up the grants? He found himself worrying in a close, involved way. Another solution was surely needed. Tobacco was still in its infancy in Mamba. Coffee and cotton were generally produced in amounts gauged to the individual's liability to tax and his payment of school fees. A regressive system of customary land tenure inhibited the ambitious farmer. No – something quite different was required now. He had long been flirting with the possibilities of tourism. If he could pilot through a scheme, he might get the Government interested. He had once written a report on touristic prospects in Mamba and received the reply that Government agreed that tourism was a good thing. Then silence.

"All the same, we do get our Yanks looking for Africans in their natural state, stopping off on the way to New Lunduland," Garston mused, addressing himself to himself more than to Diana, who looked up wondering where the remark would lead.

"Quite a lot of Americans, yes ... that silly art dealer Cornelius H. Silverstone for one; the Danish Hunter, Knut Christiansen and Mr and Mrs Van Goldstone from some mine in South Africa ... still, mostly government people for all that... but they'd use it, they'd certainly use it..."

"Use what, Garston?" Diana queried.

Garston paused for a moment before replying, puffing out little blips of smoke from the corner of his mouth. Then he bit the mouthpiece decisively, causing the bowl to jump suddenly and release a shower of loose ash onto his desk. "I have decided to build a safari lodge, Diana," he said.

"A safari lodge?"

"Yes, by the waters of Lake Menehiya."

Judge Butterworth subvened two days later and caused a worrying, if brief, diversion. He was accompanied by the Provincial Commissioner, and a pimply Crown Counsel. They were installed together in the Rest House and Stanislaus, the Keeper, once again prepared himself for two profitless days. Worse, Butterworth's appetite was so formidable that, in one day, he could wipe out the effect of all the little economies that Stanislaus had been able to make on the cheese, butter, meat and eggs during the whole of the previous fortnight. The P.C. mercifully was known as a modest eater: he normally stayed with Garston but on this particular occasion felt this unwise. Mamba was, after all, in his Province and the Judge would have to be humoured if the riots were to be passed off as little more than an unfortunate administrative bore.

There was one consolation, however. Butterworth always enjoyed his visits to Mamba. The golf course in Romba was his Protectorate favourite. Certainly, he always played better on it.

But Brice knew quite well that the Governor, in appointing Butterworth, was trying to spite his most unamenable Provincial Commissioner. Long chains of letters between the Chief Secretary and himself bore the mark of acrimony – contempt on his side, exasperation on the other. He had never budged from his position that, after twenty-odd years in the Province, he knew what was good for it better than the ordinary puppet Ministries could do. His power and reputation was such that no Governor wished to cross swords with him too often. But the Mamba riots had provided His Excellency with his moment. For Butterworth, like his father, a Colonial Judge before him, was a noted government-baiter. His judgments were proverbially laced with biting sarcasm directed at the Administration. If he was trying an embezzler, he would attack what he called Government's total lack of concern for the necessary re-education of the native population in western concepts of property ownership. If a Romba wife murderer stood

convicted before him, he might offer him the cold
comfort of the Court's belief that he would have
escaped the gallows if only the Government had been
more alive to the tensions of detribalised family life
in a town. He was even on record as having allowed
a rapist to plead provocation because the unfortunate
schoolgirl in question had, as he said, been wearing
"the insanely seductive uniform issued to gymnastic
mistresses at government secondary schools." And he
would make short shrift of any miserable government
employee who fell between his talons. As a Resident
Magistrate, he had once sent a Post Office official to
prison for sending bogus telegrams, with the remark
that never in his long experience of such cases had he
come across a case of such staggering "bureaucratic
turpitude."

The Commission was to sit in the building known
as the Old Courthouse that was, in fact, the only
Courthouse. But the Judge's first day was planned
as a round tour of the area of the riots. Angela personally prepared an extravagant picnic lunch for the
party.

If anyone but a Judge had attempted to wear
a Judge's wig and gown in Romba, he would have
become the butt of several uncomplimentary jokes,
just as Butterworth failed to escape such remarks as
he strode out in a mighty bush jacket and yard upon
yard of drill trouser. The picture was completed by

his white hunter's washable trilby bonded by a strip of imitation leopard skin. The stern and crushing look that normally focussed terribly – through the double-lens black-rimmed spectacles that he was in the habit of wiping and adjusting carefully before delivering a sentence of death, was now replaced by something approaching geniality.

"Are you taking a gun, judge?" asked Brice, as they waited for their Land Rover to be packed up. Butterworth had his Achilles' heel. It seemed a pity not to take a gun. The party visited Port Steamer first. Hussein was excellent and praised the government officers to the sky before showing the judge over the ginnery. Then they saw Adaa's house and talked for a moment with his widows and children.

The rain started and a dark grey bank of thunderclouds moved perceptibly nearer. By the time the party had turned back on the way to Koi, the small convoy of vehicles was skidding wildly on the muddied roads, the steep camber always tempting them towards overflowing ditches.

"If you'd just care to get out in this stinking weather, Judge, I'll show you the bridge," shouted a soaked Garston through Butterworth's car window. The recession of the prospect of a shoot was slowly beginning to tell and the Judge nodded assent with a stormy frown entirely conversant with the weather.

Okot was waiting for them in his car at Koi and, having also saturated himself while the Judge held him in growling conversation at his window, the column moved off to the river.

The spectacle that confronted the party at the bridge had widely divergent effects on each of its members.

Garston saw it as one of those crushing ironies of Fate that happened with such alarming frequency to the heroes of classical tragedy, leaving them numbed and important before the cruel and complicated will of the gods. The judge looked on with a grimace of satisfaction mixed with deep moral disapproval, as though some long cherished suspicion had been amply confirmed by the most blatant evidence. Brice merely frowned, his features frozen into the expression that he assumed whenever some particularly awkward administrative problem cropped up in his Province, an expression that only left him after office hours or upon the solution of the problem. He often solved his problems, however, by heavy delegation or, failing this, by the use of pithy remarks that at once summarised the situation and pointed the way to necessary action.

"Good Lord, Moorside!" Brice said, "You can sack the man who built this straight away!"

The bridge had collapsed drunkenly into the stream. Great jagged edges of torn concrete bared their teeth as the muddy water swirled furiously round them and round what remained of the pier which projected unlovely above the surface like a great decayed tooth. Even as they watched, a solitary girder projecting from the far bank dipped gently like a regimental colour before wrenching off the lump of concrete which held it and plunging with some dignity into the river, marking the final curtain in the story of the Koi-Port Steamer road.

"Bad luck, that," said the Provincial Commissioner distractedly, as Butterworth turned round in escape to the cover of his car and grunted something inaudible. Although the sky was clearing and the downpour letting off, nobody now dared suggest a quick hunt. And, all the way on the drive back to Romba, Brice kept on discussing what exactly could have been wrong with the bridge and requiring the D.C.'s comments, not realising that the memory of the crumbled structure was practically reducing Garston to tears.

Any hopes that Butterworth would approach his task with unaccustomed geniality were cruelly wrecked by a succession of minor accidents which, though trifling at any other time, had a savage effect on the Judge. The omen of the collapsed bridge was followed by a series of ill-cooked meals produced by Stanislaus, who was almost paralysed by a nervous tension induced by his learned guest's bull-like remonstrations. The police Guard of Honour turned up late on the first morning of the Commission and only succeeded in covering the Judge in a fine red dust from its screeching lorried arrival as the Judge emerged from his own car. Garston, who had worked late into several nights to discipline facts from files, gave his evidence with no signs of regarding the Judge as in any way a superior being and, on being recalled, let loose the ambivalent words: "Your Lordship will appreciate that progress must sometimes be measured in terms other than those dictated by the narrow requirements of an imported legal system," at which the pimply Crown Counsel blenched and rose to confirm with this D.C. bent on suicide that, in fact, nothing remotely savouring of the irregular took place in the official transactions connected with the riots. But the most unfortunate incident of all occurred during a sundowner given for the judge by Brice and held in Garston's house. Angela was talking to Leslie and Diana in the deep evening shade of a cypress. She did not notice the lonely bulk of the Judge behind the tree trunk, absorbed as he was in unruffling himself from the effect of another day's grappling with the perfidiousness of Man.

"Of course," said Angela, "Garston knows that he has very little to hope for from that old ox. His mentality is as thick as his outlook is limited."

"We must live in hope, Madam," said Butterworth audibly from behind his tree, and then left the party.

The Judge took his seat in the Old Court promptly at nine the next day. The pimply Crown Counsel was fidgeting to one side, not sure whether a look of confidence or diffidence would suit the presence on the Bench. Sitting in front and below him were the Indian shorthand typist and Secretary to the Commission. Garston appeared, impeccable in a grey suit. He took the oath holding the Bible in his hand and repeating the words of the Court Clerk: "I swear by Almighty God that the evidence I shall give is the truth, the whole truth and nothing but the truth".

The Courthouse was packed daily with men and women from GodiGodi and Romba. Babies peered wide-eyed over their mother's shoulders at nothing in particular. A group of witnesses waiting to give evidence sat at the back of the hall, flanked by two sleepy-looking warders.

Fawcett, Cedric and Morris were among the witnesses following Garston. Then it was Onyango's turn.

"What do you know about all this?" asked Butterworth.

"What I know is the truth," said Onyango.

"Quite," commented the Judge dryly.

"I know that these riots were caused by the District Commissioner and his stooges in their imperialistic attempts to sabotage this District." The public humiliation of himself in front of the Ginnery remained an unhealed sore.

Garston sighed with relief as Onyango continued with a spate of hopeless allegations that were readily mangled by the Crown Counsel, now flushed with triumph. Far more damaging, because much less contrived, was the evidence of the minor chief whose task it had been to keep the people at work on the road. Butterworth took copious notes on his testimonies and the chief was considerably discomfited. But hopes were revived when evidence was adduced by the Police of such Freedom Party contributions to the disturbances as they felt able to produce.

After a week, all witnesses had been heard and Butterworth packed his bags. There was nothing to do but wait on his learned report.

FEBRUARY 1962

CHAPTER TWENTY

A Meeting

Garston was now free to devote all his time and energy to the Safari Lodge. He decided that attached to the Lodge would be a small zoo to give failed hunters a vicarious thrill of some sort, while a fleet of motorised dugout canoes would be used on the lake for fishing. The question of finance would be solved by pursuading old Charlie Burns to form a company with him.

Burns lived on a sort of tropical hacienda in the middle of swampy Mamba County. He had been poaching elephant in Africa before Gamage was thought of, and was the only white to receive a title to land in Mamba. Even that had been a mistake; a directive to the Governor of the time from the Colonial Secretary to the effect that no more land was to be alienated to Europeans in the Protectorate had come just too late to prevent the acquisition. A half-hearted attempt had been made to dispossess Burns on the grounds that he had not gone through all the necessary formalities but Butterworth's father had crushed it with memorable intensity in a High Court action brought by the poacher.

For many years, Burns had considered himself retired. He ran a small limestone quarry that kept him in pocket money and, for the rest, relied on the well-invested fruit of his earlier labours. He had not been left unscathed by the elephants and a glass eye commemorated a story he rarely told. It seemed that he had encountered a bull elephant that had just kept on coming at him with two bullets in its head. One of his gun bearers had flung his spear just as his master was facing the prospect of a tramping by a monumental foot. The spear had missed the elephant's eye, nearly hitting one of Charlie's in its flight instead. At that point, the story descended into apocrypha. Burns had sworn so loudly with the pain that the elephant had backed away conveniently to a position at which even a blindfold hunter, let alone a one-eyed Burns, could fell him.

When Burns came in to Romba, which he very rarely, he was at once feted from bazaar to club to private drinks party. Although he never himself touched alcohol anymore, his mere reputation as a retired drinker was enough to encourage others to organise some very concentrated sessions in his name. His prowess at Scottish Country Dancing was such that an ad hoc evening of it was often called when he was seen at the wheel of his old Chevrolet estate car.

Garston had long since planned this ambassade as he turned his car into a side road signalled by two buffalo skulls. He knew that he would have to weather a few long stories, some funny, others calling for sympathy, before he could begin. Burns could hardly write his own name and had certainly never read a book but, in the way of people with an oral tradition, possessed an inexhaustible supply of these stories. Nobody dreamed that it was his hobby to make them all up as he sat on his verandah in the warm quiet of the evening.

"Hallo, Garston, hallo old boy, how are you?"

Garston had discovered Burns near his quarry, wearing a battered straw hat, sweat streaming down his seventy-year-old face as he attempted to regulate some labour dispute that had just arisen.

"You know, these are funny people, don't you think?" said Burns. "They quarrel at you for the slightest reason." The dissenting workers gathered round and listened in, thinking that perhaps Garston would tell the old man that they should not have a day's pay stopped for arriving three hours late.

"Look, I'll tell you what," said Burns, turning to face his foreman, "tell all those who came late that I shan't stop a day's pay at all but that they will have to work one day extra this month." This proposal was seriously studied until its disadvantages became apparent. But Burns won the contest by threatening to sack them all and his labour went back to work joking at the devilries of their obstinate old employer.

"You know, Garston, a funny thing happened the other day. Two of the porters I'd just got rid of for selling stolen lime to Muljibhai broke into my house at night." The two were walking back to the Burns residence, a ramshackle stone building copied from one he had once seen on a holiday in Spain. "They got in through the fanlight in the kitchen although I never lock the back door. Then they came into my bedroom – carrying knives." He poured out a whisky and handed it to Garston. They were sitting on a piece of garden furniture which Patel had stocked for eight years in despair before deciding to curry favour with the second richest man in Mamba.

"Anyway, I didn't say a thing. I just got up like I was a ghost or something, put my hands in front of me like a sleepwalker and went into the dining room. It was a very moonlit night. I knew enough Kimamba to hear them say that I was possessed or something.

In any case, they decided against cutting me up and went through my cufflinks and the little knick-knacks I keep in my bedside table drawer instead. They kept an eye on me alright but I nipped round the door quickly, bumped into the cat and kicked it such a one in the belly that it let out a great scream and sent these fellows running out through my bedroom window. The Chief picked them up next day but they were too ill to be locked up. Bewitched or something. I let it go at that, although the Chief is going to charge them in his court."

Burns' living room was vast. Arched recesses gave way to surprising new alcoves. He had hung spears, native pipes and arrows on those parts of the white-washed walls not already taken up with hunting trophies. The mournful skulls of oribi, dik-dik[3], gazelle and waterbuck shot out graceful horns that bristled from the wall in untidy profusion. Two vast elephant tusks bowed gracefully at each other as they stood on their wooden mounting in one of the alcoves. The floors were half covered with rather mangy lion and leopard skins. The furniture was of the simplest wicker and local mahogany. There was a distinct mustiness about the place.

"I don't know what these people will do when we go, do you, old Garston?" Burns took some snuff and

---

3   A small antelope.

handed his tobacco pouch to Garston before filling his own pipe.

"No, Uncle," said Garston. Burns had been a pawnbroker before he became a poacher. "We can only hope that they will get the feel of the confusing new world they live in and make good."

"I always said it was wrong of us to come, bar poachers of course. When I first came here, they were naked as nature and the most oral people you could find. They'd knock the morality of that little old Archdeacon fellow into a cocked hat."

Garston smoked thoughtfully while the old man warmed to one of his favourite topics.

"I mean, what have we done for them except turn out a nation of houseboys and thieves?"

Garston interrupted dutifully, although he distrusted his own arguments.

"You musn't forget the hospitals, the roads, the schools, the cash crops and a hundred and one different social services, Uncle."

"I knew you'd say something like that. Your administration chaps always do, otherwise your job wouldn't begin to make sense to you, same as it doesn't make sense to me. Leave them alone and they'd've made out but don't come along, spoil them and then leave them in the mire. That's like crippling a man and pinching his crutches."

The noise of the drill stopped and a profound stillness ensued outside except for the almost imperceptible whining of a whistling thorn bush[4] in the garden.

"Uncle, you can't tell me that they're not better off now than before we came…"

"No, Garston, old boy, no. Of course they're better-off materially-speaking. They don't starve as much as they did, though God knows I would have thought that the big, rich countries could have finished the job and stop half the tots dying before they can walk. Of course, they're better off in a way of speaking. But what about in here… in here… eh, Garston?"

It was odd to see old Burns pointing to the physiological location of his soul, like a preacher enjoining a clear-out of the cobwebs of the heart.

"You've destroyed their guts, Garston. You've bust up their society. You've turned them into a lot

---

4   The whistling thorn is an acacia tree commonly seen on the savannas of equatorial East Africa, particularly the Serengeti plain. This acacia can grow about 18 feet tall, but is often stunted in its growth. The whistling thorn acacia protects itself with pairs of long thorns up to 3 inches long. Interspersed with these are modified thorns, called stipular spines, which are joined at the base by hollow bulbous swellings about 1 inch in diameter. These are home to four different kinds of stinging ants who pierce these swollen thorns with tiny holes. When the wind blows it turns old and abandoned spines into tiny whistling flutes, which gives the tree its name.

of shouting jackasses. Look at that Onyango chap: he's not interested in the sort of things you've given your working life to – of course he isn't, he's interested in number one. Good luck to him, so was I! But that's no future for a country Garston, that's no future at all."

With a little grunt of self-satisfaction, Burns fell back in his easy chair and listened to Garston, like some oracle awaiting the reaction to a mysterious pronouncement.

How often Garston had come upon these points, how severely they had tested the indefinable springs at the very root of his work in Africa! He had never, like Grantham, condemned the Burnses of Africa from any professional pulpit – good luck to them, as the poacher had himself said – but he had always flattered himself upon a superior insight into the day-to-day problems of the emergent Africa. If that insight were to prove a withered tree, he would wither as part of it.

"It's no use, Uncle," Garston said at length, "you and I are poles apart over this and always will be. For the last fifty years, people like myself have been working to make ourselves redundant, to let these chaps have an innings too. We haven't always seen it that way and have only recently started giving way to nationalist pressures but the sum effect has been just that, to give them a place in the sun."

"The only difference, Garston, is that with you life is a game of cricket, while these people will never understand the rules. God knows what will happen, I don't! And I don't reckon I'll like what will happen."

Burns suddenly called for lunch and asked Garston how hot he liked his curry.

"It's bushbuck curry. I got him last week. They're such beautiful beasts I hate pressing the trigger. Still, we can't live by bread alone, old Garston, particularly that muck of Shariff's."

If ever a glass eye winked, it winked then and acted as a cue-line to Garston who had temporarily forgotten the purpose of his mission. In the circumstances, the subject of their discussion had not been propitious but Burns was an extraordinary man and was capable of finding extraordinary reasons for making a business decision. Garston would have to strike now. The curry would kill the project if he didn't.

"Uncle, I didn't come to see you just socially today for a change," Garston began. "What I really came for…"

"I know what you've come for. You want me to buy a bloody zoo."

Garston recoiled. "Who told you?" he asked, not sure whether to be pleased or sorry that the way ahead did not seem to demand more preliminaries.

"Manley. His wife works for you, doesn't she?"

"That was a bum's trick if you like."

"No, don't be sore on them. It was last week, he told me when I went in about one of those corns or mine – it was playing me up like fury. I told Manley that if he could fix my corn, I'd fix the zoo."

There was little point in laughing. Burns was in earnest.

"And the corn?"

"Gone, Garston, gone. I can't tell you how much I suffered with that corn. I'd get up of a morning after the corn and I had had a good night's rest and then the bastard would remind me he was still there while I had a shave. How much do you want?"

The details of the Bulikiki Safari Lodge Ltd. were discussed over lunch. Slowly, it emerged that the prospect of going out to catch the animals for the zoo had attracted Burns even more than the pain- less obliteration of his corn. Charlie's thousands had long been lying idle and although he off-loaded large anonymous sums to various charities and local African families, arguing that they had had a first claim on the elephants anyway and the acci- dental invention of the elephant gun scarcely gave him priority. He had for some time contemplated turning his fortune to commercial development in Mamba but, as the years passed by, his world had become more closely restricted, until the thin wire fence round his leasehold constituted its definitive boundary with the exotic exceptions of the odd hunting trip and the rare visit to Romba.

"Well, Garston," said Burns, "if you look upon me as the Sleeping Beauty, you're the bloody Prince Charming."

The Prince looked at his watch and took his leave, promising to call back soon. He had to return to Romba for the Bishop's sundowner.

CHAPTER TWENTY-ONE

Interrupting a Party

"What does one call an R.C. bishop anyway?" Thelma had at last reached and passed the climax of the struggle with her conscience and decided that her attendance at the Fathers' sundowner would not be a betrayal of but an actual witness to her new-won faith. Gordon had made it quite clear that she should make her stand very obvious and yet remain free from the charge of pharasaism.

"Highness," said Leslie, doing up his shoelaces on a coffee table. From a distant bedroom, Jill yelled.

Annually, the Roman Catholic Bishop of New Lunduland-with-Mamba ordained a social gathering of the Romba whites, seasoned with a few respectable Goans and one or two African notables whose influence was valuable. The occasion provided the many nuns in the District with a great opportunity for recalling what they had once learnt as girls in their native Italian kitchens and, as though they

wished to assert their very womanhood through their
cuisine, afraid perhaps that it would steam away with
the weather if they did not now and again do something in an utterly feminine way, they had quietly
and with infinite care, prepared their contributions
in primitive mission kitchens throughout the District.
Then, in one great gastronomic conclave, they had
met together each with their own excellent witness
to the good things of the earth, hoping hard to please
the Bishop and the Fathers and not unalive to the
reactions of the other guests.

On the night itself, the nuns' artistically-conceived
savouries and desserts were joined by a great company of bottles of Asti and Marsala, although Reg
Blagdon, who asked a delighted Father for a little
spot of whiskey, was not disappointed. Thelma even
managed, though with rather more difficulty, to
obtain a straight lemonade.

Priests and lay brothers in white cassocks were
bobbing up from everywhere and, for some time,
the pimple had been wreathed in a hole of dust
churned up by the speeding of their motorcycles up
the twisting track. Rarely were so many of them seen
together in Mamba: their gathering emphasised the
different kinds of District life which they represented,
not assimilable like the centralised Protestant missionaries and the civil servants into the category of
mere expatriates but closer to the earth, nearer the

people, and because of it, separate. Paradoxically, their off-duty fraternisation with Romba officials was also closer than the forced chumminess of their Protestant counterparts: some of them came in for golf once a week and stayed for an evening in the Club. One Father had a habit of attending club dances at which, perched high on a stool with a glass of brandy and soda in his hand, he would watch the dancers with an air of quiet benevolence.

While the Fathers waited for their Bishop to appear, priest vied with priest, brother with brother in a meticulous handing round of the toasties and a generous outpouring of their good wine. The atmosphere of the seminary hall became suffused with the delicate odour of the Fathers' best imported cigars: they made a rough brand of their own on some of the mission stations but when they really wished to entertain in style, never cared to do more than press a hundred of the home-made variety upon you "for future reference", as Father Grimaldi put it. But for special occasions, the Havana cigars were brought out.

A breeze of urgent, slightly worried, expectation communicated itself from cassock to cassock as the approaching presence made itself felt behind the door at the end of the hall. There were moments in the District ceremonial life when Garston, a sort of Lord Temporal, caused everyone to rise to their feet in a conventional deference. It was thus on

Remembrance Sunday when he arrived at his place on the Sports Field or when he presented prizes at the Indian Public School or when he opened the District Council. It mattered not to what race you belonged; on those occasions you stood up for Garston. But it was different with the Bishop. You would have stood up for him anyway on each and every occasion.

When the door opened, the Bishop paused for a moment with a quiet smile playing on his face, as though he were saying, "yes, I am well content with what you priests have done for me today". The women did not exactly curtsey as he moved in amongst the guests, talking earnestly and intelligently, or trivially and unassumingly as occasion demanded but they deferred to him with a whole range of gestures varying from a slightly ridiculous inclination of the head assumed by Diana, to a sort of marked stoop adopted by Mavis Harriman and a more or less continuous giggle affected by Christine Fawcett. Even Thelma, who had come into the opposite camp to proselytise, found herself, if not overwhelmed, then uncomfortably impressed by his close involvement with people. The machinations of Rome were truly subtle. What, after all, could she do in the face of a Bishop who appeared to be concerned about the latest litter of their mongrel dog? Sue? The Bishop's demeanour was the more remarkable for negating the fact of his physical smallness.

His face was everything and one hardly noticed the rest of him. The face subsumed the man: it was symbolic, like lecterns in the shape of eagles. His iron grey hair meant sternness and inflexibility in matters of the Church and his piercing small eyes meant an acute intelligence well blended with a worldly aptitude for cunning. His well-lobed ears marked him out as magnanimous and his chin, had it been visible and not "goateed", would have been added as confirmation of a formidable will. His lips were neither fat nor sensuous nor thin and cruel; he had a very ordinary mouth, a perfect touch to remind others that he was after all only a man. But his was the tempered authority that regulated the lives of hundreds of priests and brothers this side of the grave. That also added to their feeling of separation.

A nun cast a furtive glance round one of the many doors leading on to the hall and tasted a fleeting pleasure as she witnessed the effect of her sisters' labours. Then she retreated hurriedly to report back to the kitchens, just as Hussein's wife or any one of Aada's five widows might have done.

Cincillati was in close argument with a newcomer to the District, an anthropologist named Nigel Kent, who was camped down in Mamba and doing a study of Wamamba political structure. He was very new to Africa and the Protectorate University College where he held a Research Fellowship had not been too happy about his appointment. He had been a leading light in his University Communist Club in England. Kent had a peculiar habit of edging closer into people the more anxious he was to make a point and so Cincillati found himself reversing slowly in the direction of a group dominated by the Bishop.

"You see, what people don't understand," Kent was saying, "is that to get to know my tribe you have to live among them and, better still, live *with* them. That's why I approve of your safari priests so much, the way they go out and stay out in some village eating native food and getting to talk the language fluently."

Cincillati nodded sympathetically but not unaware that he was being urged by Kent's glass into an undignified collision with one against whom it behoved him not to collide.

Peter Freeman, who was with Dorothy, listening without enthusiasm to this conversation, suddenly found himself incensed by the anthropologist whose sentiments on race seemed to approximate so closely to what his had been some months before. It was only then, that he realised the extent of the change brought about in him by Dorothy.

"It's all very well you saying that," interrupted Freeman, "but to gain the African's respect, you have to maintain a certain remoteness. I'm all for social contacts in the home and at places like this but as for stomaching their food, well..." and he looked rather sheepishly at Dorothy who squeezed his hand. "I've had it before and I'd rather have hers."

Cincillati, who still beamed politely, interceded with a question about Kent's work, thus putting a temporary end to his making of the pregnant points and the concomitant backward march.

"My main concern is to establish the true nature of the principal hinges in which the exercise of political power swings... the clan heads... the chiefs..."

"Well, it's not the County Chief, I can tell you that," said Peebles, who had joined the group. "He's the idlest devil, with apologies to you Father, this side of the Equator."

Kent looked round disdainfully at Peebles and decided that it would be fatuous to try and explain to such a man that a County Chief appointed by the imperialists did not concern his purist investigations.

"I must say, Father, I've found the people most helpful informants," the anthropologist continued. His exceptional shave that morning had not been entirely successful and he looked pathetically dirty. "Probably because they realise that I'm not against them, as it were." And here he eyed Freeman who now secretly desired the young weed's death.

"Who is that obnoxious-looking fellow?" Garston asked Leslie, nodding at Kent.

"Just that student of animal life, who as I told you, came in two weeks ago when you were out. The anthropologist who works in Mamba."

"It's strange, Leslie, isn't it, how many different sorts of people come to Africa for a many different reasons. It's the Foreign Legion on a continental scale."

"Garston, you're getting maudlin," interrupted Angela. "Is he always like this in the office, Diana?"

Diana, disarmed, said, "no, he isn't".

The Bishop had finally turned round and, having excused himself from a conversation about the necessity of taking salt tablets before a hot afternoon's golf, he joined the anthropologist's outraged group. But Kent had long since told himself that he was afraid of neither man nor beast, and the Bishop did not deter him.

"After all, in the West, the good citizen is the man who lets everyone else get to the top and rule him, whereas down in Mamba, there is no need for any poses by authority, traditionally, that is. Everything is governed by a complex system of checks and balances that ensures, or did ensure complete social harmony."

It was not quite clear whom Kent was addressing – himself and the presence of the Bishop, who was not being allowed to insert the tiniest of dictums – made Peebles want to punch him hard. The problem was resolved as Kent caught a sight of Onyango arriving late with Silvanus Apau, the District Council Chairman.

"Excuse me – will you...? I must go and talk to Reuben over there."

"Reuben? Who's Reuben?" asked Peebles, frustrated. The Bishop smiled and said something quietly in Italian to Cincillati.

"You know, Mr Peebles," the Bishop added, turning to the geologist, "we priests often have to listen to young people who do not realise that we have been here since before they were born. That gives us some right to think that perhaps we know about what is best for the Africans better than even Mr Kent does, don't you think?"

It did not take Onyango long to appreciate the pleasant effects of the Fathers' wine although he had never tasted these varieties before. When he had finally achieved a state of delicious euphoria, he abandoned Kent solitary in a corner and made a beeline for Garston.

"You know Mr Moorside... I've been wanting to tell you... for some er... time that I think I made a mistake by being rude to that Judge! Yes, I made a mistake."

Garston wondered whether it would be fun to run him in for being drunk in charge after the party was over.

"Oh, I don't know, Onyango. It's your job these days to make yourself generally unpleasant. Personally, I think you do it very well."

There was nothing vindictive in Garston's voice. This type of conversation was becoming a standard form of address for off-duty officials dealing with the Freedom Party.

"Yes, I know all that, old boy," said Onyango, swaying slightly, "but I think… I think… that if I'd been more polite… the Judge would have given me a chance to… er… say what a good all-round job you do in this District… now excuse me, I must sit down." And the politician retired from the field, hurt.

"Are you coming to our next film?" Father Grimaldi asked Geoffrey. "We were very pleased to see you at the Shakespeare one." Dr Manley was so happy with life that he would have sat through four sessions of *Gone with the Wind* run backwards for the Father's benefit.

"Certainly I shall come," he said effusively.

"This one is called…" said Grimaldi puckering up his forehead as he tried to remember and finally announced with solemnity "…*Don't tell Nina*, and we have decided not to show it to the seminarists, so it will be a private showing".

Diana, who had recently been drawing a blank in her researches on the Angela-Leslie situation and was half beginning to suspect that she may have been wrong about them, wondered how she could tactfully draw Grimaldi into making an inadvertent breach of confidence over her rival's latest confessed sins. She was interrupted by a dull but steady drumming which had started to make itself heard over the loudest conversations. And just as the distant boom of cannons interrupted the ball in Brussels and announced Waterloo, so the drums, which were joined by loud trumpetings that sounded like agonised elephants, seemed to approach with pregnant tidings.

The first stone smashed a pane just above Harold Harriman who dropped his wine glass in the act of performing an untidy ducking movement. Several other missiles followed in rapid succession and the assembly retreated instinctively to the walls while a few of the younger priests with Garston, Fawcett and some others marched to the the verandah to investigate.

A strong party of the Holy Blessed Ones had gathered outside to register their strong disapproval of the Bishop's carousel. Men and women, they stood in the moonlit night like a weird gathering of departed spirits. The stone-throwers among them had retreated and were one with the others. Great trumpets made out of paraffin tins carried by the women clinked gently as they laid them on the ground. Then the whole congregation began a subdued and eerie chanting punctuated with wild cries from one of the women. As soon as Fawcett walked up to them, they began to scream and shout and when he took out his little book, they ran off down the hill only to climb up again and reappear on the other side of the Mission, drumming and trumpeting as loudly as ever.

"They are quite mad," Morris explained to Cedric as both joined in the chase round the mission to prevent further damage. Their usual activity is to make such a noise that the Catholic services cannot continue. But this is the first time that this particular group has used violence."

The Blessed Ones were shouting hallelujahs embroidered with long trilling screams from the women and exactly-timed percussion from the drummers. Then they started a different chant which a Father explained meant "Persecution is holy" and moved off slowly down the hill, this time for good.

"This is what happens when you try and be a good Protestant, a good nationalist and a good polygamist all at the same time," said the Bishop sadly, shaking his head as the screams receded into the night.

MARCH 1962

CHAPTER TWENTY-TWO

Cedric in Court

It was always the same. Whenever Fawcett brought a prisoner before him, Cedric felt bullied by the policeman's unexpressed contempt and his unjudicial insinuations. One day, Cedric would tell him to shut up. He could manage the polite African Inspector alright. He didn't call him "Your Honour" in the same tone of voice as a career sergeant says "Sir" to a brand-new subaltern with pips refulgent on his khaki-clad shoulder. It was bad enough to be called "Your Honour" in the first place without having to suffer the indignity of that sarcastic under-tone in Fawcett's voice. Often at sundowners, the policeman would wax strong about his early days. He had started his working life apprenticed to a bak-er's roundsman in Wales. Then the war had come and, with it, some welcome stripes on his arms. After the War, he had joined the Palestine Police and had finally come out to the Protectorate. Cedric had often, because of an unfortunate inability to be rude, failed to puncture Fawcett's ambition with the suggestion that he should next apply for a job with the Corps of Commissionaires. As it was, one had to admit that Fawcett had made a good Officer i/c Police. If only he himself was not such a bad Magistrate, Cedric could have offered to forgive the policeman his dog-like efficiency, his unimaginative mastery of the Penal Code and his blinkered ideas on the fundamental criminality of so many Africans. Instead, he seethingly took comfort from something that Onyango had once enunciated, flattering Cedric's university background and middle-class origins.

"Mr Hamilton-Gordon... take the police" – Onyango was always "taking" the Police or being taken by them – "take the Police," he reiterated. "The Police, Mr Hamilton-Gordon, are a closed book. There are hundreds of African constables about who should be Inspectors, hundred of African Inspectors who should be Superintendents. But because of the closed book policy, you bring out here a useless number of under-educated men and immediately make them Assistant Superintendents. Those same men would be mere Constables in England."

Having just that day received a peculiarly humiliating lecture on his own magisterial powers from Fawcett, Cedric had not been indisposed to nurse the implication of Onyango's argument but he recalled with distaste that if the Officer i/c Police, Mamba District, would only make a "Constable" in Britain, he himself would certainly not be a Magistrate.

Cedric had just been about to leave for Mamba County on a tobacco safari with Peter Freeman when an unfortunate impulse to look in at the office and take a last leave of his in-tray led him into Fawcett's hands once again. "I can't find Leslie or Garston," the policeman said kindly, striding into the office, "and I don't want to give this to Mbuya." Morris was outside the office supervising the weighing-in of elephant tusks.

"You'll have to do it. It's a quicky. He'll plead guilty, I'm pretty sure of that."

"But I'm off on safari!" pleaded Cedric.

It was too late. "Corporal!" shouted Fawcett, "Bring the prisoner in! Mr Rodrigues! Where's the Interpreter?"

The "prisoner" seemed at first to be one of the Holy Blessed Ones charged with malicious damage and creating a disturbance in the Catholic Mission precincts until Fawcett explained that the three men and four women who stood before Cedric's desk were a mere formality to be got over before the real prisoner appeared. The members of the sect all pleaded guilty to the interpreter, Semei, and, with the doggedness of martyrs, averred that God would strike Cedric with lightning and plague.

"Oh, throw them back in the sea," suggested Fawcett. "They're nuts anyway. Give them all three months on each count – consecutively."

Cedric, hating himself, did as Fawcett said. The warrants were signed and the seven prisoners filed out in the ecstasy of persecution singing a hymn of their own devising.

The real prisoner was finally brought in. He wore only a blanket, cut in half and held by safety pins across each shoulder.

"The others were mildly nuts but this one is stark bonkers," commented Fawcett. "In any civilised country we'd have him for indecent exposure but what can you do here? Gawd!"

Cedric pretended to sympathise with Fawcett over the paucity of legal sanctions against naked natives, and listened to the Constable's evidence that was painfully extracted in the effort to establish a nuisance offence. Cedric now thought that he recognised the prisoner who was smiling at his Judge in a toothy, inane manner. It came to him suddenly that he was trying the character who claimed a daily letter from Adaa.

The constable related how the accused was in the habit of begging sugar in shops not wearing a stitch of clothing and how, when he was given some old trousers by an Asian, he had almost immediately discarded them. At that point, Cedric thought he would

have to say something about admissible evidence but
he had forgotten so much of what he had ever known
on the subject that he hardly dared. Fawcett would
doubtless crush him with some spurious but completely plausible argument.

"Anyway, on receiving a complaint from the
trader Shariff," the African constable continued,
"I proceeded to follow the accused and found him
begging sugar from many shops in the bazaar. He
would not leave until he received sugar."

"Was he wearing any clothes, constable?" Fawcett
asked.

Cedric had had enough. He interrupted as the constable shook his head.

"I can't see that that has anything to do with
it. I mean ... nudity may be less of the accepted
thing these days but there's no law against it." The
policeman looked dumbfounded at the Magistrate
who had dared interrupt his prosecution.

"With respect, your Honour," stormed Fawcett,
showing no respect, "it's got everything to do with
it. It happens that the accused's nudity annoyed the
shopkeepers concerned and that is part of my case!"

"We are not concerned, Superintendent, with the
annoyance caused by the nudity but by the begging..."

"If you'll beg my pardon, we are most definitely
concerned with the nudity. Section 234 sub-section c.
paragraph six of the Penal Code makes that clear."

Cedric tremblingly consulted the work referred to and still could not see how nudity offended against it. At the same time, he dared not lay himself so obviously open to another of Fawcett's coups by relying on his own interpretation. He tried a different tack.

"Anyway, I happen to know that this man is not fit to plead."

Fawcett won the next trick.

"I know, your Honour."

"Well, then, we must commit him for a medical examination by the District Medical Officer with a view to his detention in a Mental Hospital."

Fawcett looked almost sympathetically at Cedric.

"Look, your Honour," he said, trying to make it clear that he was endeavouring to explain in simple words for simple minds, "If you accept his plea, convict him and send him away for one day's cooling off to satisfy the Asians, you can at the same time make an order under S. 183 of the Criminal Procedure Code whereby he undertakes not to do it again but to go home and live happily with his unfortunate relatives in GodiGodi." Fawcett took a deep breath. "If, on the other hand, you make me go through all the palaver of getting him committed to hospital, you'll make the accused miserable miles away from his family and all possibility of eating sugar in the nude ever again."

Cedric heard the rest of the evidence in a deep depression. He had not expected Fawcett, of all people, to make an appeal to his sense of humanity. In the end, desperate to do something just a little different from the policeman's useful suggestions, he delivered a stern telling off to the man and told him he could go home provided he promised never to do it again. An even toothier smile crossed the uncomprehending face of the acquitted man. Fawcett also failed to comprehend, and looked heavenwards praying for understanding. And, before he left, the lunatic asked Cedric to write him a letter.

CHAPTER TWENTY-THREE

An Evening Adventure

African Tobacco Enterprises Ltd. operated without competition in Mamba District and the crop was still in the experimental stage. It was all of the air-cured variety and the Company maintained one of its clean-shaven, failed-Advanced-Level ex-public school employees to supervise the planting out of seedlings, prevent the spread of mosaic, give advice on the curing and eventually to buy the crop. The current Mamba County incumbent was the altogether too handsome Jeremy Lacey. He lived in an undistinguished wedding-cake of a house immeasurably larger than he required. At great cost, the Company had cleared three acres of garden for their representative and an incongruously well-kept lawn had been established. The house itself was furnished by the Company down to the five mustard pots in the dining room and "ducks-in-flight" reproductions in Jeremy's bedroom. Like the old man, Burns, he was only too pleased to keep an open house for visitors. When they were on safari in this area, Government officers were often put up in his house in preference to the local rest camps.

"I think you'll be comfy enough in here," said Jeremy, showing Peter Freeman and Cedric to their rooms. "Get settled in and we'll have lunch."

Cedric was only now beginning to recover from Fawcett's savaging earlier that day. As he unpacked, he heard the strains of Beethoven's Pastoral Symphony coming from the drawing room and for all its overtime on the gramophones of Europe, this music in the middle of Mamba appealed to a whole range of melancholy nostalgias inside him. He had grown more accustomed to the sound of drumming by night and was thrown oddly off balance by thoughts of English woods with black branches dripping rain.

After one of his cook's less inspired attempts at cottage pie that represented one quarter of the entire repertoire, Jeremy brought out a moisture-gauge.

"As you know, our main trouble is that the leaf they market is sopping wet. The grower gets paid less for it in consequence. What we have to do this year is to ensure that it comes in with the correct moisture content. Last year's crop was hardly an economic proposition and the factory spent far too much time extracting the wet." He demonstrated the use of the gauge and they went off to the first baraza of the tour. A large number of Africans was assembled inside a long grass hut. Cedric soon became involved with the crowd in an ardent discussion of supply and demand just as at the River Koi with Gordon. Answering a man who demanded a shilling increase in the price paid for a pound of tobacco, he replied: "It's a bit like this… suppose you have a shop and you want to sell people matches… well, you can only buy matches from the Indian at a price that will enable you to sell them to the people at a profit. In the same way, if the Tobacco Company wants to sell its cigarettes, it can only do so by buying the tobacco from you at a price that will make it possible for them to produce cigarettes at an attractive price. That's why you don't get more for your tobacco."

The questioner persevered undaunted by the good-humoured laughs that came from his fellows who imagined him beaten by the District Officer with all the answers.

"If I sell matches, I sell them to the people at a price that they can afford. I cannot afford to buy cigarettes, but I sell my tobacco for nothing."

Cedric looked despairingly at Lacey who obliged with a long peroration about production costs, all of which was treated with bored contempt and condemned as hedging.

"What's the use of showing us how much water our cured leaf should have if you don't give us each one of those machines?"

Cedric remembered the request for money-printing presses. "These machines cost a lot of money. We have only brought one to show you what the leaf should feel like before you take it off the racks in your houses and bring it for sale."

"But if you who are knowledgeable in these matters we need a machine to know the moisture – how can we who are ignorant know it without a machine? You are our father and you expect your children to learn without teaching them."

Yet, for the most part, the officers made their points and Cedric weathered surprisingly well the people's accusation that he was a District Officer in the pay of the Company. Many of the growers appeared genuinely interested in a way to ensure high grades for their leaf while most of the objectors did not grow tobacco in any case.

On the way to the final meeting at the end of an exhausting and concentrated week of such barazas, they stuck in the mud. From nowhere in particular about fifteen Africans came to watch. One of them appointed himself as leader, bade the Europeans step out of the way and organised the lifting of the whole car until Freeman was able to churn out of the morass. It was one of those spontaneous acts of generosity that had begun to rivet in Cedric a deep feeling of attachment for the local people. A rush of sin-conscious guilt took a hold of him.

"You know, Peter, when I heard you get up in the Club and talk about membership that night, I thought you were putting on a pose. But I think I know how you feel, and I think that, provided one controls the entry, I agree with you." He felt his words sounding hollow and inappropriate as though he were advertising a brand of soap. And Freeman had become almost indifferent to the issue: "I look at it this way now. Whatever happens, the big drinkers who hold the Club together won't give in on a point like this. After Independence, the problem will find its own level. So why bother now? I'd rather give my time to getting rid of the berry-borer in coffee than continue to make an ass of myself about Rule Two."

This pronouncement came as a disturbed revelation to Cedric who was by now thinking about making his own stand on the matter. Freeman explained: "Hasn't it occurred to you that perhaps the Africans don't care one way or the other whether they join the Club, just as the shibboleth about letting your daughter marry a black man overlooks the basic fact that most Africans don't really want white wives. The fact is that Africa has the unfortunate effect of bringing out all that's bad in some Europeans. They're given power and they don't know how to use it. They've got an artificially inflated status and haven't the grace to carry it. They've got leisure and drink it away. They insult the black man and yet sleep with his women. And not one of us in Romba is free from the taint of patronising Africans; they're becoming very sensitive to that these days."

Freeman, having once begun to recite his racial testament, was impelled on as though he felt bound to explain the slightest modulations in his attitudes, conscious that Dorothy with her down-to-earth rationalisations had perhaps robbed him of some precious, if inarticulate, idealism.

"Well, if that proves anything," Freeman went on, "it proves that we've got to wait for something much more radical than the repeal of Rule Two before we see sense about Africans. It means that we've got to have what the missionaries call 'a change of heart' about race, although they don't use the phrase that way."

The car swung into the path leading up to the baraza hall. It was lined with whitewashed stones set there by a chief who had once been a sergeant in the Protectorate Rifles.

"So all we can do is wait," Freeman sighed pregnantly. The baraza hall seemed especially crowded and Cedric wondered why, the more particularly as people tended not to come to meetings late in an officer's programme once they had discovered from friends what he had said on earlier occasions elsewhere. Here, they were on the edge of the real flats where tobacco would not grow but a slight escarpment marked the boundary of the production area. From the hall, one could look into the blinding haze across to the dimly-perceptible peaks of Ora District which revealed their mantle of snow on the rarest of occasions.

Freeman took the first knock at this baraza and added a whole deal of technical advice about food crops. Cedric, who was musing at the crowd, suddenly appeared so startled that Freeman stopped what he was saying and looked at his fellow target.

"Look! ... about the tenth row back!" whispered Cedric.

"My God!" said Freeman audibly.

Sitting amongst the peasants, unshaven, barefoot and more or less ragged, was Kent. He was making no effort to conceal himself which, in itself, was a tribute to the effective manner in which he appeared to have Africanised his dress. His face was in shadow and his dark beard made it even more difficult to pick him out at once. He just sat there on the mud floor smiling in a rather nasty way. A group of questioners put their queries, which Freeman and Cedric answered as best they could, while, with much disgust, they watched Kent who appeared to be taking meticulous notes and discussing what was being said with a close group of Africans huddled round him. Finally, the anthropologist drew himself smartly to his feet. The officers noticed that his kneecaps were showing through torn trousers.

"On behalf of the Wamamba Freedom Group Association, may I please be informed just exactly whom do you two government officers think you are fooling?" He spoke first in English and then gave the Mamba version to the immense appreciation of the audience.

Cedric went red and hot, not knowing whether he was more angry than embarrassed.

"Since, Kent, you choose to start being rude, I too will be rude. You're a … a damned disgrace to …"

Kent butted in sharply. "Yes, it is a damned disgrace to my race, my colour, that's what you were going to say, wasn't it? Well, listen to me! Until Mamba rids itself of such bigots as you, and, my God! the day is near, these people will never get fair government and will continue to be cheated by syndicates, companies, cartels, monopolies, the whole shoot! What the Freedom Group says to you is get out now while there's time to take your trousers with you!"

"Advice that you have signally failed to accept yourself, Kent!" shouted Cedric, now beside himself with true-blue fury.

Then, on a suggestion from Freeman, the trio marched out amid the boos of the little group round Kent.

Over dinner that night, the two government officers and Stacey laid their plans like three undergraduates out of College after hours. Cedric had long since abandoned the idea of merely handing a report to Garston who would have had the man shipped out of the Protectorate within forty-eight hours. Kent had, after all, offered him personal insult at one of his own barazas.

Freeman secretly and uncomfortably recognised in the anthropologist something of the obsession that had gripped his own mind so recently, but there was in addition an overweening arrogance about the man that his North Country temperament would not stomach. And Jeremy was uncritically delighted at the prospect of trouble.

"He camps by a river about thirteen miles down the road when he's not in one of the huts eating native pog," Jeremy elucidated. They were increasing their bank of courage with the help of several stiff brandies.

"If we assume that he's in camp, how many people are likely to be around at, say, two in the morning?" asked Cedric.

"Nobody at all, really. He refuses to employ a houseboy, he says. He says it upsets the balance of nature."

"And if he's sleeping out somewhere, we're not likely to find him anyway?"

"Correct. Even if we looked, some idiot would raise a thief alarm and we'd be stuck by a spear-happy mob of the sleepy Wamamba."

"We shall just have to hope," said Freeman, indisputably intoxicated, "that he's in camp!"

At two in the morning, an alarm clock woke them from their untidy dozing on the settee and armchairs. The radio had not been turned off and a programme was coming through from the other side of the world.

"I feel bloody awful," said Jeremy, rubbing his eyes.

"Not original," murmured Freeman, pulling on his socks and tucking his drill trousers into them. They smeared their faces with charcoal.

The air outside was cold and damp in an all-pervasive way that made them shiver almost convulsively. Away in a shed, Jeremy's generator coughed on with the same lonely devotion as the beacons on a zebra crossing in a London night.

But once they had become accustomed to the rush of wind that came at them as they drove fast down the road in Jeremy's open Land Rover, their awakening was complete and a new nervous exhilaration took hold of them. The headlights caught a frightened dik-dik that ran for several hundred yards ahead of the vehicle. As they wheeled round corners, the light picked out hut compounds and inside the huts, naked children cocooned in sere blankets on the cold mud floors were momentarily troubled in their sleep by the idea of a great light and great noise in the silence of the continual high chatter of the crickets. Whenever the car crossed a bridge or a culvert, the metallic croaking of whole families of frogs celebrating the night from their patches of marsh drowned the noise of the engine for a moment.

At about half a mile from where Jeremy thought Kent was camping, they stopped the Land Rover and walked quietly in file along the road that was dominated on both sides by the towering shapes of eucalyptus blacker than the sky.

"Stop!" Jeremy flashed a torch and pointed to a path that led off the road. "This way."

Cedric wondered for a moment at what might be the outcome of their walk. What would the P.C. say if he came to hear about it? And Garston? In any case, one thing was certain: there was no turning back now.

Jeremy again halted in his tracks, this time at the entrance to a small clearing surrounded by elephant grass and thorn trees.

"The lion's den!" he whispered.

They listened and from a shape that could be guessed at as a white bivouac came the low sound of snoring. An unmistakable smell of smoking wattle reached them from Kent's burnt-out fire.

"Remember! Cedric, you 'owl'; Peter, you 'dog', me, 'torch'," Jeremy said as they split up and went to separate positions in the grass around the tent. None of them was more than twenty yards from the snore.

"Too near," thought Cedric, as he cupped his hands to make the exact owl sound for which he had been famous at school.

Freeman replied with a low, less realistic growl that sounded more like the death rattle of some wandering hog than a man making dog noises. And from Jeremy's corner came a momentary flash of a torch.

The snoring continued unabated. After two more unsuccessful rounds, Cedric took it upon himself to utter an unearthly shriek that attempted to simulate the cry of a hyena. The snoring stopped.

Peter waited a few moments before giving his growl. Jeremy's torch flashed immediately onto the canvas. As Cedric prepared another owl cry, he could hear Kent unknotting the strings on his door flaps. He waited.

Soon it was clear that Kent must be sticking his head out into the night. A low muted owl noise shivered from Cedric's sector. Freeman, according to the plan, uttered the Mamba for 'let us kill him' in a deep African voice. The flash of torchlight caught Kent's agonised face as he retreated quickly inside the tent. They waited.

Suddenly, the night was punctured with the terrifying crack of a shotgun. Jeremy flattened himself into the dank earth as he realised that a cluster of shot had just passed noisily through the tall grass to his right. They were unarmed and had forgotten that Kent shot his own meat.

Cedric looked for the torch beam that never came and wondered whether Jeremy had been hit. Kent had pulled on his trousers and a shirt and was standing by his tent with his shotgun at the ready. Freeman could see him silhouetted against the canvas. He took a handful of earth from the ground and, aiming carefully, lobbed it from the ground at where he supposed Kent's head rested on its long neck. He was accurate and Kent involuntarily shot a second cartridge into the air as the tiny clods hit his face. Then he began talking in Mamba to his unseen foes. Cedric could not understand a word and found time to wonder how Kent had managed to learn so much within a few weeks. But he caught the gist of it. Kent was repeating the word for 'friend' again and again. From the tone in his voice, it was clear that he was stiff with fear.

Jeremy started to crawl forward snake-like having personally abandoned the original plan for a quiet retreat. He reached the tent without being seen, wriggled into the overhang of the flysheet and, stretching out his arm, jerked one of Kent's ankles so abruptly that the body above it fell heavily to the ground where, breating loudly, it lay waiting for a frightful death.

Jeremy ran double-up back to his place in the grass and gave the retreat signal, two flashes. The three met on the path. As they reached the main road, they were horrified by the sound of a familiar voice: that of the local chief.

"I heard shooting, sirs, and saw your car in the road. Is there trouble?"

"No trouble at all," said Cedric, wondering once again what the Provincial Commissioner would say.

JUNE 1962

CHAPTER TWENTY-FOUR

Welcoming Visitors

Bulikiki Safari Lodge Ltd. was registered soon after Garston's visit to Uncle Burns, with Patel, Muljibhai, Jeremy and Burns as its directors. Within three months, The Romba Builders had produced a building by the shore of Lake Menehiya approximating to a detailed plan thought through by Garston. There were five bedrooms, a dining room, lounge and wide verandah. Fastened to the apex of the roof above the main entrance was a rhinoceros skull minus its horn. Burns was a realist over rhino horn and accepted a market price.

"You know, Angela," said Garston, looking at the Lodge from some way along the lake shore, "at last I feel that I've left something solid in the way of a memorial to my passage through this District." In his pocket was a letter received that morning informing him that his post was due to be "Africanised" within two months and that he should hold himself ready to retire immediately after the elections.

Moored to a landing stage near the Lodge were two fishing launches and a few dugouts with outboard motors just as he had planned them. The afternoon sun looked at itself in the lake and appeared to set ablaze a great belt of the water. Some workmen were putting finishing touches to a special wire mesh enclosure for crocodile-free swimming.

That same evening, Burns was throwing an Opening Party for the first guests and most of the Romba notables. Meanwhile, Muljibhai's contacts in the Capital had been active over publicity and the Lodge had already recorded several advance bookings for tourists apart from a large number of applications from government officers who wanted to spend their leave there.

Garston had been genuinely hurt to read that Onyango, always ready to impute a wicked motive, had failed to see what an asset the Lodge could become to the District.

"I have heard it said," Onyango had argued in the Legislative Council, "that the Bulikiki Safari Lodge in my District will enrich the District because it will attract tourists there. And tourists, I am told by the District Commissioner, will spend their money in the District. Yes, but on what? On imported gin, imported whiskey, imported wine! So the Government and the Indians will get the rake-off, not the people of Bulikiki. My people make good spirits that the imperialists ban! And will the Lodge employ much labour? No! The directors have decided on a skeleton staff. I say to the directors of this lodge, instead of building a safari lodge for bloated aristocrats, give the people a dispensary!"

But the Sultan was enthusiastic and, in his old age, warmed to the prospect of fishing in the European manner. He saw the Lodge as a pearl in the midst of his country and told Garston that Onyango was merely jealous that it had not been sited in "his horrible homeland near the river".

The zoo was proving troublesome. Several expeditions had been organised by Willie Ives and Burns and none had returned with anything more than dead meat and the skin of a moulted snake. On that same day, a party was out looking for an elephant. Geoffrey had devised an anaesthetic to be smeared on a very fine dart that could be shot from an ordinary rifle doctored by Ives.

They found a huge bull elephant munching quietly under a tree near the main road.

"A beauty!" said Burns from beneath an old ten-gallon hat. He took the rifle from his bearer and bending low in the long grass, slowly approached the elephant followed by Geoffrey Manley, Willie Ives and Jan Peebles.

The elephant's vast ears were waving gently like galleon's sails in a near calm. As the dart penetrated its skin the sails stiffened, the trunk soared up in sinuous protest and a potent bellow of rage shuddered across to the lake, where Garston heard it appreciatively. Leslie then revealed himself too soon and the monster's beady eye caught an awkward ducking figure. In no time, the whole massive bulk had been turned in his direction and was bearing down upon him almost out of control.

"Run like the hammers of hell!" shouted Burns to the others, while he himself remained slightly to one side of the line of charge gripping his second rifle, a tense grin on his wrinkled face. The elephant bumbled ferociously past him, sending violent tremors through the earth onto which his four trotters crashed.

The fugitives looked back and saw that the beast was gaining on them. They reached the road and someone shouted "Car!" Hotly pursued, they raced down the murram road to where a lorry and Land Rover stood waiting for them. The lorry driver saw what was happening and in a fit of what he conceived as devotion to duty, quickly revved up and moved the vehicle one hundred yards down the road. The Land Rover was their only hope. Only forty yards ahead of the elephant whose breath they could almost feel on their necks, they dived into the open vehicle.

Leslie then saw with terror that the key was not in the dashboard – "Thirty yards away, he's getting closer!" Twenty yards... "The key must have dropped out..." Ten yards... "For God's sake, let's run!"

The men fell untidily over the side of the vehicle and rushed in different directions through the grass in time as they turned round to watch the elephant wind its trunk firmly round the steering wheel, pull the car on its side, kick it upside down and begin to execute a rhythmic tattoo upon the iron underbelly with its monstrous waste-paper-basket feet. Then, beginning to feel the effects of the anaesthetic, it lay down in the road and slept soundly for three hours.

Having, as the expression goes, rallied, the party returned to the Lodge by lorry and convinced Garston that the idea of a zoo was a totally unnecessary embellishment in a country where elephants used one's car as a pillow.

Although the Lodge was over fifty miles from Romba, the cars of guests kept arriving in an undeterred stream. Mavis, Christine and Diana had already been at work supervising the catering arrangements all afternoon.

"I must say I do think Angela might have helped a bit more instead of going on poetic walks with Garston," Diana had commented as she saw the couple approaching the Lodge, secretly disappointed that her grand plan for a conclusive demonstration of

Angela's perfidy towards a trusting husband was fast becoming impossible of realisation.

Already installed in their chalet were Mr and Mrs Simon H. Enderbilt of Maine who were in search of Africa at all costs even if it meant, as Mrs Enderbilt had somewhat enigmatically said, "doing a Hemingway". The Protectorate Tourist Office had taken the opportunity of suggesting the shaky venture in the north of Mamba about which it knew next to nothing. In the next chalet were booked a young lady inscribed in the register as Lise, Comtesse de Roquefort, and her friend, Karl. They, however, were not in search of Africa; on the contrary, they were on the run from the south of it, where a dispossessed husband, not the Comte de Roquefort but a rich delicatessen grocer in Johannesburg, was preparing to follow them to the end of the earth with a wad of travellers' cheques and a revolver. Jeremy, who was handling the booking until a suitable European secretary could be induced to part with a government job and defect to the wilderness, had been intrigued by a note in Lise's writing at the foot of Karl's letter:

"I am passionately fond of nude bathing. It is alright, yes?"

Jeremy had replied that the management would be pleased to deal with any special requirement on request.

Cedric and Peter Freeman arrived with Dorothy. The two men were still under a cloud. Kent had not done the sensible thing and let the baiting incident drop, in which case the officers would have held fire about his behaviour at the baraza. Instead, he questioned all the local witnesses, and wrote a full account of the affair to Garston, defending himself in advance against charges of seditious behaviour and asserting his intention to stand in Mamba at the coming elections.

"The man's an out-and-out troublemaker, sir," Cedric had protested, but all Garston would say was: "I'm surprised by both of you and very deeply disappointed. I shall have to think very carefully what I should do about you. At the very least, this means a posting away from here."

But he did nothing except leave the culprits in suspense and limit his courtesies to cold nods and terse comments. Jeremy, however, whose existence was now charmed by his association with the Lodge, enjoyed a slight measure of familiarity with Garston to the point of being able to plead for his partners in crime. But Garston had not given way. To Kent, whom he had summoned to his office, he addressed a monumental tirade of very British abuse until the anthropologist winced visibly and suddenly to himself appeared as a brash young man playing with ideas he barely understood.

"And what's more, you silly little squirt," the D.C. had concluded, "if you were to stand where I was registered, my vote would automatically go to the best man even if it was Lenin!" Kent had retreated and now lay low, much alarmed.

That afternoon too, as the two Circles in Romba depleted themselves for the migration to Menehiya, Björnsson prepared himself for a second overture to Eleanor Mbuya. Militating against all the arguments that should have deterred him from what he knew was an insensate course, his compelling desire nonetheless allowed him strange prudence in the execution of his plan. Through the complex network of houseboy knowledge, he had been able to discover that Morris would be travelling to Lake Menehiya that afternoon leaving Eleanor alone in the house with her children. He had even arranged for his own servant to bribe Eleanor's boy out of the way.

Eleanor was the first woman to have offered him resistance – all the others had been rented – and he wanted her all the more because of it. But he shuddered at the contemplation of some of the ideas that had passed through his head, scarcely believing that he could have formulated them, trying to pretend that they were merely projections of dreams. His forehead grew beady with perspiration as, from where he sat in the back room of the "Happy Events", he saw

Morris's car leave its garage. He looked at his watch. He would have to wait until dark.

The new faces combined with the delectably novel surroundings all contributed to the success of the Lodge party. Dancing to the same old long-playing records took on a new flavour by the lakeside. Leslie flirted openly with Angela and Diana could not strike back because she was similarly involved with Garston. Thelma looked out to the great lake, a profound black expanse under the brilliant crescent moon, and thought deep thoughts. Jeremy involved himself as soon as possible with the Comtesse de Roquefort, while Burns kept Karl out of the way in a hunting story, huddled round the bar.

"This is such a wonderful place," said Lise, with a long sigh. They were walking between two chalets. "Somehow I feel that if time were to stop now, I could be happy forever."

"So do I," Jeremy risked, as he took her hand gently.

Morris chatted politics with Father Grimaldi, a new look of content in his face. If Garston had just learnt that he was going, to Morris had been offered an intimation that he would be made a District Commissioner after the elections. The Sultan meanwhile cornered Father Cincillati and tried to extract further conclusive proof of the greatness of the Bulikiki Empire.

"I cannot understand you, Musa. You spend all your energy in condemning the imperialistic attack of the British on your country and you want nothing better than to be known as an imperialist yourself!"

Musa laughed and considered the joke worth another Pepsi-and-whiskey.

Brother Pitt fidgeted in his attempts to abandon Muljibhai who was deep in an abstruse proposition over the nature of time that he said was not money at all. He was aching to hear Burns' poaching story and tell one himself.

"Call me Hamer," Mr Enderbilt was saying.

"You know something, Charlotte and I have travelled over 10,000 miles in this Continent since last fall and this is the first time we really feel that here, right here, is the true spirit of Africa."

"Yes," said Peebles, "– have some more whiskey."

"Oh, and another thing," chirruped Charlotte, "coming here this afternoon we saw such a cute thing, a real elephant with what looked like a car seat or something stuck on its trunk! Wasn't that something!"

"Yes," said Peebles.

Dorothy and Peter were nowhere to be found, although nobody was indiscreet enough to look too hard. Cedric was discovering that if Mavis Harriman never talked much, it did not much matter as long as she danced as close as they were now dancing.

"Alright everybody!" shouted Reg Blagdon. "Do you know the 'Muffin Man'?"

At this quasi-interrogation, Harold Harriman was induced into the ring as the station champion.

With a deadly serious expression on his face in the sudden silence, he took a full glass of beer and balanced it gently on his forehead. Sagging at the knees with his arms outstretched as though he were playing at being a glider in an air pocket, he incanted the sacred words. His eyes looked dumbly into space each side of the glass as he descended in an excruciatingly gradual movement to the support of his rump. Then, straining his stomach muscles to the upmost, he increased slowly backwards until he was supine and the beer in the glass had ceased to slop gently over the rim. The whole company asked Harold whether he knew the "Muffin Man" and the reverse process began until, with free beer assured for the rest of the evening, he stood to his full height and, amid loud applause, almost casually removed the accursed glass from his forehead where it had left a distinct red blob. Blagdon tried and soaked his shirt at the first wobble. Lise, having drawn a reluctant Jeremy in to watch the act and having concluded "que c'est rigolo, ces Anglais!" and insisted on trying to do it with a liqueur glass full of Benedictine. She too was sinuously victorious and, during her subsequent hurried passage from man to man, shouted in confusion:

"But Jerry, what does it mean? French 'pecks' all round?"

Björnsson waited until ten o'clock before approaching the Mbuya house. No light was showing. He tapped sharply on the metal front door. There was no reply. He took a stone and banged harder. From somewhere within came the low wailing of a crying baby. Then, as he peered inside, he could see the flickering of a candle reacting on the walls of the front room as the flame approached along a corridor hidden to him. Then the flame went out.

Instead, somewhere along the wall to his left, a window was slowly pushed open and a head looked out at his waiting shape for an instant. The window was quietly closed. Further along, he saw another open window. He darted along the path by the wall and caught hold of it just as a hand seemed to be pulling it closed. As he grasped the frame, there was a tiny suppressed shriek from somewhere near, and all resistance at the window ceased. There were no burglar bars on the window. He hesitated for a moment and then, breathing heavily, hauled himself inside the room. It seemed to be empty except for a few suitcases. He tripped over one of them and swore to himself. With half a bottle of whiskey inside him, he would die rather than give up now. But he still had the wisdom to keep the lights off. Whoever it had been had shut the door on him.

It was not locked and he found himself in a corridor. The baby started crying again from a room that he guessed was almost opposite him. It was joined by the quiet whimpering of the terrified Joseph.

He put his hand on the doorknob and pushed. This one was locked.

"Come out! I don't touch the children. Me and you have a bit of fun, that's all!" Even the boy was quiet now. There was no reply. He felt a great fury rising within him.

"You don't come, I push the bloody door down!" As he struck a match to see where he should start kicking, a line of light appeared under the door. They had lit a lamp. Then came a long fumbling with the doorknob from the other side. He stood back as the door opened, wilting in the light. It was Eleanor's schoolgirl sister. He brushed past her into the room.

"Where's the woman?! Where's the woman?!" Björnsson looked at the girl who was sobbing convulsively and clinging to the open door. Joseph had hidden himself beneath the blankets.

He heard a car outside, and running to the window by which he had entered the house, he was almost caught in a sweep of headlights that gyrated like twin lighthouse beams into the drive. Eleanor got out and talked to her friends for a full five minutes. The headlights stayed on. He would wait for her and get her then.

But behind him in the hall there was a rush of hurrying slipping feet, a shriek of pain as the schoolgirl caught her foot on a door. He ran after her but she was raising the native alarm, and he held back. Outside, they could not discover from her exactly what was happening and Björnsson had enough time to escape through his original window.

He drove through the night to his new borehole site where Fawcett arrested him late the next afternoon.

CHAPTER TWENTY-FIVE

A Temporary Occupation Licence

"Why, just take a look at that great big bird up there!" exclaimed Charlotte Enderbilt, pointing at a fish eagle perched high on a borassus palm that overlooked the narrow papyrus-bound channel which they were negotiating in one of the launches coxswained by an expressionless African with scars all over his touristic face.

"Hamer Enderbilt didn't," said Hamer, who sat trawling his line with a kind of expert facility acquired off Key West although he had never actually caught anything during two big sea fishing trips. About thirty yards away darted his lure and the tip of the rod juddered rhythmically with its swift underwater progress. It was a giant lure decorated with five sets of barbed hooks. From its devilish orange eye painted on an articulated brown wooden body issued a grim sympathy up the nylon line to Hamer's murderous, expectant expression. Then it would foul a weed and have to be stripped for action once more.

Next to him stood Charlotte wearing a great straw coolie-hat, she too held a rod that she would hand to Karl whenever she wanted to snap a scene.

"Wouldn't that bird look good on a picture! My, I can just see it now," she said as though she wasn't actually able to look at the bird before it had been through the processing laboratories. And she made sure of her fish eagle.

Stretched out on the roof of the little launch, Lise sweltered in a black bikini, her back shiny with sun-tan lotion which Karl had lovingly applied. She had undone the straps of the bikini's brassiere and manipulated the pants into a formality. She was trying to forget how cross she was that Karl had tricked her into coming on the launch with the Americans instead of going with the nice Jeremy on the other boat.

Similarly frustrated, Jeremy toyed with plans for drowning Karl. Lise had already said that she would simply love to stay at his little place in the country.

"I come to Africa for relaxation when the London Stock Exchange bores me, Lise."

"Stock market? Ah, Bourse! Mais c'est formidable!"

The second launch carried Garston, Angela, Jeremy and Leslie who had escaped from Thelma and jumped on at the last moment. And while Garston

smoked imprecations through his pipe at all dilatory Nile perch ever conceived, unable to understand
the absence of the death-wish in fish, Angela slipped
down to the cabin with Leslie.

"Look, Angela, we must decide. In two months
or less, you'll be gone for good. It's now or never."
Leslie spoke the words he had rehearsed to himself
so often.

"I don't know, Leslie. I'm so confused about all
this. One minute we're in Africa for good and the
next we're out for good with enough money to buy
some ghastly suburban house while Garston com-
mutes. Imagine it!" She felt the absurd drama they
were acting to its close and resented the time it took.
"I never thought Africa meant that much to you,"
he said, following the wrong tack.

"It's eaten into me, Leslie. For better or for worse,
it's eaten into me. I lie awake at night and listen to
those drums. Some African has died. And out there in
the night that bunch of people bobbing up and down
chanting to the drums while the corpse lies in the
hut… can't you see that it's far more exciting than
anything Surbiton has to offer?" She looked abstract-
edly out of the boat; the sun was catching one side
of the tiny ripples on the lake and turning them into
sequins.

"Look," she continued, "you say that we can
run away to some place in the country, maybe

your aunt's place in Dorset. Don't you see that we should never really be happy? We would be doubly escaping... escaping from ourselves and escaping from Africa by making believe we were somewhere like it."

"I don't believe you know what you do want," said Leslie.

"No, I don't. You're right," she replied quietly.

"So you don't," replied Leslie.

He thought for a moment.

"Angela, I suppose I've never been quite fair to you. When it looked as though there was no more real point in running the Administration rat race... I mean, I knew I'd never have my own District... so I turned to you for compensation. I've never been much of a hand at sweating it out with loyal devotion to duty. That's Garston's line. I need people, not ideals, to love."

She looked at him pityingly. When he was serious and abandoned his rakish pose, he talked like an adolescent. If he'd done this sort of thing to her in the past, there would never have been assignations on the Pimple, she would never have gone through those tortures in the confessional. And now he was proposing the most unromantic thing in the world – an escape to England! He was going to ditch poor Thelma, forget Jill, expect her to leave Garston, a mountain of a man beside him, abandon her own child to the mercies of a public school and a bachelor household. The thought of Garston housekeeping in England would have been comic were it not bitter.

"No, Leslie, I won't do it. Let's leave it at that, shall we?"

He experienced an odd sense of awe in front of her, and suddenly understood that they had each been loving different people from their real selves over the months.

"OK," said Leslie, giving her, despite resistance and admonition to caution, one last lingering kiss, which, as fate would have it, was observed through field glasses by Diana, who had been watching the launch from the Lodge ever since she had learnt that Leslie and Angela were aboard it together.

"That's good enough! That's good enough!" whispered the second lady of the station to herself.

"Hamer! Quick!" Charlotte's line was zipping off the spool at a terrifying rate. "Adjust the strain! Adjust the strain!" said Hamer, taking the rod from her. The launch stopped trawling and Hamer took over the whole operation.

"This requires... great care... Charlotte! My God, it's a strain on my wrists... must be a beaut! Fighting like hell Charlotte... like hell!"

The boatswain came up from his post and pointed at a large piece of sudd that had detached itself from the channel banks. Slowly but surely, Hamer was drawing the diminutive island to himself.

"Take great care, Hamer," said Charlotte, as she photographed an egret floating on the water like a plastic duck.

But Garston on his launch was more successful. "Stop launch!" he shouted, as his line span out from the reel at frightening speed. "Leslie! A whopper!" He put a strain of 100lbs on the line and it still escaped, though sluggishly now and he was able to begin winding in after a few minutes. Then the fish revolted once more and ran away with the stiff line while the rod bent double in an agonised struggle. After twenty minutes of this, the fish tired, and Garston, perspiring heavily, his arms worn out, began to make some progress against the unseen monster. The boatswain and his assistant looked on like hounds waiting for the kill. Leslie took a gaff from one of them as they prepared the rowing boat. The line now entered the water taut as a needle, switched from side to side with the pained remonstrances of the shape caught on the hooks. But it was still twenty yards off and they could only guess at its size. For a moment, it heaved above the surface and dived deep taking more line with it, as though looking for solace in the muddy bottom even though the hooks should wrench harder and harder.

But it was no good. Ineluctably, the lure drew it further in until it swam desperately beneath the rowing boat where a gaff stood ready for its gills. Again, it dived. The sight of the boat sent it down and down. But it came up in the end, and the men in the boat caught their first glimpse of their fish, silver and huge, now a shadowy presence three feet below the brownish water, now a wild and desperate serpent breaking the surface with a furious splashing. Leslie took a wild grab at it with the gaff. The rowing boat wobbled and Garston felt a stinging pain in his bare foot.

"For God's sake, Leslie!" But Leslie had only scratched him.

The fish surfaced again, this time quietly, with a new resignation. Leslie slipped the hook into the gills and only then did the perch convulse its body in some weird shimmy of death. The cavernous mouth gaped open and showed its thousand tiny teeth, and its horny lips tried to pout. Leslie needed help to bring it into the rowing boat. The tail fins drummed the side, then came another great convulsion before it fell heavily into the bottom of the boat and quivered like a panting dog; its golden eye looked up without meaningful expression like that of a Byzantine martyr. They cut the hooks out. Later that day, they found that it tipped the scales at one hundred and eighteen pounds.

The other survivors of the party of the night before who had camped for what was left of the night in the Lodge's cheap armchairs, were now consuming their Bank Holiday Monday afternoon on the drive back to Romba. Cedric had been told by Garston to get back early as a telegram about Björnsson had been received at the Lodge through the Ogi Police Post wireless. He was to be available magisterially to Fawcett. Morris accompanied him and did not say a word the whole way.

H.M. Prison, Romba, was, like the market, surrounded by a great white wall, except that the women's annexe abutted onto it from outside. Cedric approached the great wooden doors, knocked, and a surprised black face – a small shutter slid open – framed the aperture.

"District Officer!" said Cedric curtly.

It was a baking hot afternoon. The duty sergeant, pained out of his reverie over a great ration register by Cedric's untoward visit, slid back the bolts and let the white man in. No, he knew nothing about Björnsson. Cedric decided to while away the time by listening to prisoners' complaints.

As it was a public holiday, the prisoners were not out on the Prison Farm. Some lazed motionless on their blankets on the floor of the long white cells that housed twenty or more prisoners. Others squatted in the compound under the full heat of the sun, talking and joking. A young warder strode up and down officiously, trying hard not to smile at the jokes. Near the ablutions, two prisoners were playing the game known locally as osi, popular over the whole of that part of Africa. It was a kind of draughts played with beans that were dropped into successive small compartments carved in a long board. They were watched by several other prisoners who grunted approvingly as soon as one of the players made a good run. In the centre of the compound stood the kitchen building and the prisoner cooks were preparing the evening meal of groundnuts, beans and vegetable soup in one huge black cauldron and maize meal dough in another. An ineffable lassitude pervaded the whole place.

Decidedly, Cedric was not playing the game by asking to see prisoners on such an afternoon. The duty warder straightened his jacket, took his hat from a hook in the reception office and fumbled through the pages of the visiting magistrates' book. The doubtful amusement of a surprise complaints parade attracted a handful from the cells and compound. The first complainant was a well-built old man with greying hair stubbled sparsely over his head.

"He says that the magistrate did not take his old age into account when sentencing him," translated the duty warder.

Cedric looked at the warrant. The man had speared his brother during a dispute about a cow and had been sent to prison in the capital.

Cedric, like Garston, found it difficult to think about some of these men as one would have done criminals who had committed corresponding crimes in Britain. He was not the first District Officer to look upon their offences as some sort of amoral quirk for which the system he represented was partly responsible. Had not Okot's father, Paulo, told him that in the old days an adulterer for an example would have been castrated and expelled from the tribal fold "pour encourager les autres", as a Frenchman might say! As it was, offenders against the new laws now sojourned comfortably in an official gaol certain of a balanced diet with meat on their tin plates.

"They love it!" Garston would say. Cedric wondered. He told the first man that the Magistrate had amply considered his grey hairs and that he would soon be moved to a bigger and better prison where he could perhaps learn a craft. The prisoner seemed unaccountably content with this assurance and, clapping his hands into an attitude of prayer, moved them up and down in a gesture of gratitude fused with abject humility which Cedric found embarrassing and degrading.

The second postulant asked Cedric to ensure the repayment to him of a remote debt of money contracted three years before by a wife's brother's uncle.

With no confidence whatsoever in the outcome, Cedric fell back on the usual expedient of writing a letter to the debtor's chief asking him to investigate. He was alarmed by the ease with which the simple act of writing a letter signed by a white man appeared to satisfy. In nothing more than in dealing with complaints across a table in the office or in the prison, he had felt the immense, almost romantic, burden of trust that was placed in him and in European officials generally. "In this job, you learn people," Garston had said when he first came.

The parade ceased abruptly as the main gates opened once more to admit Björnsson, closely followed by Fawcett. The driller seemed to be oblivious of his surroundings and submitted pathetically to everything asked of him. Fawcett searched him and conferred with Cedric.

"It's the first time we've had a European in here. A bloody bad thing, if you ask me."

And, as though confirming this view, large numbers of prisoners peered in at the new arrival in the reception room until Fawcett swore them off.

Cedric recalled Morris' almost embittered silence on the drive back from the Lodge.

"I don't see why he should be treated any differently. What did Garston tell you?"

"He left it to me," said Fawcett, who suddenly lighted upon an idea.

"How many women prisoners have you got?" he asked the duty warder.

"Two, sir."

"Good. Put them in the store and keep this prisoner in the female cell."

"Yes, sir."

"Look," said Cedric, "he's committed a serious offence and I think he should be treated appropriately."

Fawcett looked round at the cadet and reduced him to a sense of impotent, if angry, insignificance.

"He's not only not been convicted but he's not even been remanded. You'd better do it now." Cedric did as he was told, crushed.

Fawcett sniffed at the food and decided that it was good enough for Björnsson.

"The man must be a beast anyway, trying to sleep with other people's wives."

That same evening, Garston unlocked the D.C.'s post office box and withdrew a solitary letter. It was from the Ministry of Lands:

I refer to the application for a twelve acre plot at Ogi, Bulikiki, made by Messrs. Bulikiki Safari Lodge Ltd. forwarded by you on January 31st last. In my reply to the Company, LS/352/4/2 of 5th, February, copied to you, I said that the Governor had authorized the issue of a temporary occupation licence in view of the professed urgent nature of the undertaking.

I now regret that consequent on a report of the Lake Menehiya shores, submitted by the Trypanosomiasis Institute, the Governor has reluctantly decided to cancel that licence. I am advised that the area in which the plot is situated will be affected by the Lunduland tsetse clearance campaign due to commence in the coming financial year, and while the area is, of course free of tsetse at present, the Government Entomologist would not be able to guarantee indefinite immunity if clearance is not effected on the scale envisaged for the affected Lundu shores. An area of roughly five miles radius from the Ogi Trading Centre will accordingly be declared a closed area in the near future.

I am informing the Company under separate cover.

Garston drove quickly to the club where he became very drunk and had to be taken home by Leslie.

JULY 1962

CHAPTER TWENTY-SIX

Nomination Day

Mamba District had been allocated three members by the Electoral Commission. Onyango prepared to fight GodiGodi in the first fully representative elections.

The Freedom Party Executive had sent him instructions to produce information for their Schedule A. As he sat in his Romba house that was still unfinished, he found himself faced with all sorts of difficulties. There was no pressing crowd in front of him; he had no need to resort to hyperbole. And his early days in the Mission School and later as a teacher came back to haunt him.

Onyango looked at the form and then at notes in his own little black book. The mantle of his smoky pressure lamp had broken and he was forced to use a hurricane lamp. It was easy enough to write down the names of all Europeans and prominent Asians in the District but to decide who should in fact be invited to leave the country on Independence was less easy, and to fix an order of priority even worse.

So, for the moment, he turned to Section C and gave details of the Government housing facilities on the station, adding a footnote that he would like Garston's house when the time came.

The Government, it was true, was drawing up its own scheme for the premature retirement of people like Garston, the people he, Onyango, had so frequently referred to as 'unskilled labour' in the Legislative Council. Ironically, he would have liked to have seen Garston stay on in some capacity or another. If only he could become Inspector of Works instead of Blagdon, who would be kicked out in any case at the first opportunity. Then he made a list of all the people whom he considered had treated him as dirt because he was an African. He began slowly but remembered grievances flowed back and the list grew in a way that would have astonished those indicted upon it. Almost unaccountably, the one man whom he had constantly condemned as an arch-disciple of every conceivable iniquity, did not figure on the list. On the contrary, he thought, the District would feel empty with him. And in one way or another his whole political development had been linked with generations of the paternalistic whites who sat in the District Office, with or without pipes.

But then, his equivocation was damaging and he chided himself for his weakness. These same whites were, after all, standing in the way of Freedom. He had pledges to his supporters that must be fulfilled. His own motto, 'Democracy on Earth', was no idle threat and combined with the Party's 'Freedom for All', would compound a powerful potion for his coming election speeches. And, after all, what reason did he have for holding a brief for any white?

If they had educated him, it was as a subservient teacher; if they had brought cash crops to the country, it was to reap the benefits in Britain; if they had built roads, it was to police the place more efficiently. The very dispensaries they had built merely underlined the fact that the child mortality figures for the Protectorate were still some of the highest in the whole world.

What reason to accept such a brief, when he was barred from their club, talked down to by uneducated halfwits, sworn at by white men half his age. That day in front of Patel's when he had parked his car so that the bumper was touching Blagdon's in front, Blagdon had called him a "black bastard". If Garston had made Blagdon apologise, it didn't make it much better to hear the oaf say he was sorry and had not realised that the car belonged to him. Black and bastard went together in Blagdon's mouth like "old" and "boy" in Garston's. There had been no apology when the drunks in their club had, according to Chalisi, sung:

"There was Onyango, Onyango

Spewing out a mango

In the Quartermaster's Stores."

Then there was that fool, Kent, who talked to him as though he was a black political heathen in need of salvation by Moscow. As though that sort was any better. The Executive had sponsored him ironically because of his colour and because no Freedom Party African would have a hope in secessionist Bulikiki where he was standing. Kent needn't run away with ideas. Onyango was in overall charge.

Next day was Nomination Day and the ceremony took place in the Elections' Office. Diana was organising. One by one, the prospective candidates filed in with their forms and sponsors. Leslie was acting as Returning Officer.

Onyango came first, with an air of insolent assurance. He had never liked Leslie, never harboured embarrassing reservations about his distaste. Leslie reciprocated. There was none of the banter that passed between Garston and the politician.

"Here are my forms, Mr Farrar. I think that you will find them in order."

"Mm."

Leslie thumbed through the various statutory pieces of paper, irritated by his firm conviction that the whole process was a dignified waste of time. Why bother with all this? In any case, they would have a dictatorship and that would be the end of it! Then he noticed that one of Onyango's forms was missing two supporters' signatures.

He pointed at the gaps.

The politician was furious that he had laid himself open in this way. '*No, Leslie didn't say it but he was doubtless thinking it: Africans never get anything right!*'

"I'll get the signatures within half an hour," Onyango said and disappeared.

Several further candidates passed muster without comment. Some were standing as "Independents", others for the Independent People's Group, and one for a body calling itself the People's Independent Group.

Two were schoolteachers, one a trader, another a lay preacher. None were educated beyond secondary level except for Onyango.

Kent slouched in as though these formalities did not properly affect him. Leslie took his opportunity.

"Please stand in the queue behind Mr Agara, Mr Kent."

Each was required to select a personal symbol that would appear on the ballot boxes. Onyango and Kent automatically had a bicycle, their party symbol; others chose the hoe, the fish, the book, the candle. In the villages, great controversies were to take place about the relative merits of these symbols. Old men argued that since the bicycle went faster than a fish while the other symbols couldn't travel at all, the bicycle should have their votes. Others said that the candle would light up the darkness but young men added that there was no object in lighting it up unless one had a book to read. The hoe stood strong in favour as it went to the core of rural existence, whether they merely grew their own food or cultivated cash crops as well. But Onyango countered the argument for the hoe by saying that it represented traditional old-fashioned policies while he was standing for a new order of things, symbolised by a shiny Japanese bicycle.

Garston and his assistants all went out on safari to explain the functioning of the election to the people. The candidates toured round in borrowed cars, on bicycles, often on foot, depending on the degree of party and local support they could muster.

In Bulikiki, Garston met opposition to the idea of the elections.

Garston would explain how, after the elections, there would be a conference in London to decide on the exact day for the Protectorate's Independence. It was therefore very necessary for each man to be vigilant and to know what was going on in the modern world around him. Otherwise, the people would find that in the unpreparedness they would be robbed of their birthright.

At a mass meeting convened at Ogi, there were murmurings in the five-hundred strong crowd as Garston explained that, whereas in the past they had relied on the constant assistance of the colonial power, they would have to face up to crucial phases after Independence, all alone.

"You have always been our father," remonstrated one old man twice Garston's age, "and now you tell us that you want to abandon your children. Wait a little and when we grow up, then we shall be able to deal with the dangers ahead."

"Of course Britain will always be available to help in whatever ways she can," replied Garston, "but you must run your own affairs. That is what you have asked for, and that is what the Queen has given you."

"I have asked the Government many things but I have never asked it to go away," the old man replied. "We do not want you to go away."

It was odd for Garston to find himself justifying a position that ensured his own redundancy. Somehow, it seemed the final irony in his inconsequential career. He had come too late to be effective in the way he had dreamed he should, too early to realise that he could not carry the dream through. And yet there was that in the voices of old men like this that could be taken hold of as a genuine tribute. Maybe some of them really did think of him as Okot's father, Paulo, thought of Gamage. Maybe his unromantic association with and his implementation of centrally-ordained development plans did count for something after all. Perhaps it mattered that what the District Council, and even that old man, had said 'stay!' He could only hope so. His adventures with the road and the Safari Lodge had not given him grounds for thinking that he had left his mark in any individual fashion although the Chief Secretary thought, unkindly, otherwise. Even at this stage, the hankering to be remembered as a definite landmark in the place had not left him. As he stood there, he felt very much like some beleaguered "Mr Chips"… beleaguered because he could not look forward to a natural retirement after a life of successful self-completion; a life in which the candle had exhausted itself in a candle-long effort to give light. His candle had been blown out half way down, never so bright as in its last guttering endeavours. Then there was that other bittersweet story, 'The Browning Version', odd that he should always think of himself as some sort of schoolmaster – where the boy had given the schoolmaster a translation of Homer. He himself could not look forward to even that. Two lines at the end of a rather vicious chapter in a future school history book locally produced was all he could hope for, and then he would be referred to generically along with a hundred others.

Garston returned to a more cogent reality sharply by remembering that, while he was talking to the crowd at Ogi, Kent was addressing an election meeting some miles further south. Kent, the suspected communist, who was to be deported the minute he started preaching the old, old doctrine: he would let the man discredit himself. And Garston looked at his own audience and, for no very accountable reason, felt an immense wave of trust and confidence in them that they would not follow where Kent would try and lead them. It was an intuitive idea; he had not been in the country for all these years without acquiring the feel of the people and, from there, some notion of their likely reaction to people and ideas. He knew too that that reaction was dependent in large part on all the Onyangos. And, borne along with a self-induced elation behind his words, he prayed by all the gods available to an English gentleman, that if Onyango's party gained the victory, it would use it well.

The Sultan of Bulikiki was making his last desperate effort to secede from the country before it was too late. Surrounded by the best English speakers in the region after the nationalist politicians had been pruned off, he was drawing up a formidable document in impassioned terms, stating the irrefutable in the gloomy certainty that he would be refuted. What would the rest of the country care for the great past of the Bulikiki Empire? They would rape Babuliki traditions, desecrate their hereditary rule, despise their slow, easy-going ways, and quite possibly drive them into slavery. As the Sultan saw matters, these threats meant far more than foreign notions about 'the viability of tiny principalities', a phrase used by Onyango in the Legislature recently when he complained of the Government's failure to curb the "special pleading of the Bulikiki Sultanate with its particularist flavours".

At this time, the Provincial Commissioner called an informal meeting of all the expatriate officials on the station. Brice, who was younger than Garston and who would have been a Governor had he been born earlier, told them all to keep on to the end of the road.

"I know how you must be feeling. The interest has probably seeped away from your job. The Forestry Officer is even less likely than Forestry Officers usually are to see the fruit of his recent labours; most of you must face the fact that standards may drop, often where present facilities and standards are already quite inadequate. It may be that Agricultural Officers will have no more than the right to hope that their work will not be totally effaced over the next few years. Veterinary Officers, who have spent years in a constant vigil against rinderpest and other diseases, may live to read that an avoidable epidemic in Mamba has wiped out half the cattle in the District. The police," he continued, nodding at Fawcett, "may quite possibly find themselves sinking below the level of integrity which as been maintained here over the years. The District Commissioner and his staff may be amongst the first to want to go, and some of the most unthanked. It's maybe the case today that it's easier for people to see the merits of some departmental scheme well put over than the general cohesion and watch a security imparted to a District by a D.C.".

There was some embarrassed coughing as Brice touched on the subject of compensation.

"As you all know, we shall be compensated out the minute Independence comes, some of us, well before. Some again may be invited to stay on with contract terms. Into whichever category you may happen to fall, I want to appeal to you not to do your day-to-day work in a spirit of mere hanging on for 'Lumpers', as I believe the expression goes. It's a short road to Independence. Let us go on to the end of it just as before."

Brice was not given to making this type of appeal. But because he was so obviously involved in the same predicament with the rest, he elicited some response, though, inevitably perhaps, Leslie was to comment bitterly that: "at his salary, he can afford to talk like that."

AUGUST 1962

CHAPTER TWENTY-SEVEN

At Court

"You know, Morris, the more I see of that rag tag and bobtail which pretends to have the right to govern us after Independence, the more I fear for this Country."

Henry Usubura, the Resident Magistrate, from the Provincial Capital, was on a routine visit to Romba – only this time, he had Björnsson on the menu. He was sitting back-to-front on a chair near Morris' desk, with his chin resting on the rim of its back.

"I mean, take that fellow Onyango you've got here. Has he been to Oxford or Cambridge or some respectable place like that? No! All he's done is wet his great black toes in the sea at Torquay! Has he at least got any special qualifications? Has he hell! A weak-minded, power-minded slobberer, that's all he is! By God, if he came up before me, I'd give him freedom in a way that he'd really understand."

Henry overawed Morris. "A second in law at Cambridge and a place in Chambers at Lincoln's Inn – it all read much more grandly than a diploma at the local University College and a year on a special course in Oxford."

"And what will *you* do?" Morris asked.

"Me?" said Henry, as though he had had his attention drawn to a subject so remote from his daily thoughts that it had rusted from disuse, "I will watch, my dear Morris. From my magisterial eminence, I will watch! And, when the moment comes, I will pounce!"

"Pounce?" asked Morris.

"Yes, I will go to the current Prime Minister and say: 'Old boy, you are not doing your job very well, are you? Move over for me unless you want me to spear you and thus remind the whole watching West that we are not after all so very far removed from the savages! The P.M. is dead! Long live Usubura!"

"You are never serious," said Morris, shifting uneasily in his chair, wondering whether Henry was trying to make a fool out of him, as he did out of most people.

"No, Morris, I'm in deadly earnest," said Henry, smiling although not with conviction. "Can't you see that all these wooden idiots going round with the big idea of re-ennobling the savage by getting him to hang up smelly skin cloaks alongside his European suits don't have a clue where they're leading. Not only dress. They have the mental agility to tell you to throw off the old ways of the West and find the African Way to civilisation."

A suppressed snigger played about his nose and Morris felt that, at any moment, it might burst into an explosion of derisive laughter that would not be wholly pleasant.

"Then, when you ask them whether the 'African Way' means a denial of western things, a total boycott of the bloody wheel even, they say no, but we must be selective in an African way! I tell you these jokers don't know where they're going."

The sniggers finally brought on the laughter: "Yes, they do! They're after those new expensive Morocco benches in the Legislative Council and the right to swagger back with your feet on the table, or, if you're not a Minister by some slight oversight, with your feet on a Minister's shoulders!"

Morris never knew anyone more damaging to his rarely expressed, civil-servant ideals than Henry, who seemed already to have mentally savoured the whole experience of "Independence", from the Freedom Night celebrations to the opening of the newly independent Parliament to the first constitutional crisis to the final catastrophe before the assumption of power by Dictator "Zorro". Henry always referred to the satanic being who would crush all Morris' hopes and ideals as "Zorro".

"No, Morris, the day of Zorro is not far off," Henry would say. "In that day, there will be much anguish and gnashing of teeth and the women in travail will wish they weren't. Zorro will have come and the New Age will be at an end. And the enemies of Zorro will be cast into outer darkness, while, to his friends, he will extend a sagacious hand and say, with all the authority of his secret police: 'Get thee, Onyango, behind me and I'll see what I can do for you!'

Henry chuckled quietly, rubbing his chin gently on the rim of the chair.

"And I'll tell you another thing, Morris. Every Tom, Dick or Harry of a candidate in the silence of his respectable, because half-finished European-type house, is saying tonight before he says his prayers 'Zorro, c'est moi!'"

Morris nodded uncomprehendingly.

"You're a cynic and you know it! If it is true that there are many self-seekers, there are just as many educated people trying to find the right way. I believe that we will succeed," said Morris.

Henry looked at his watch and then out of the window.

"God! That bloodhound Fawcett is over there with his manacles and his white rapist! I must rush!"

Henry took up his briefcase and turned for a moment at the door.

"Oh, I'm bloody sorry about what happened to Eleanor the other night." He was as serious as he could be.

"Thanks," said Morris who was now obliterated behind a pile of files which Rodrigues had just brought in for him. He would go to the Court when Eleanor was called.

The Magistrate took his seat quickly in the old Courthouse. Fawcett wore an acid expression but did not take the same sort of liberties with Usubura as he did usually with the District Officers. There had grown up between the two men a gruff, unspoken respect which would perhaps never have matured had Fawcett not been savaged at his first attempt to get the better of the African. On that occasion, he had brought a bicycle thief before him and said that he wanted him remanded for a further twenty-eight days.

"You can have fourteen, Superintendent. Then, if that proves insufficient, I will grant another fourteen when I come next time." Fawcett wondered whether to credit the evidence of his own ears. He had never been refused remands before and now here was this young African magistrate questioning the period for which he asked!

"Your Honour, you must understand that I do not ask for twenty-eight days if I can manage with fourteen."

"Remanded for a further... fourteen... days," said Usubura, writing.

"Your Honour, I demand an explanation!"

Usubura had looked up and stared Fawcett squarely in the face.

"Superintendent, please understand that you will *demand* nothing in my Court. Meanwhile, if I choose to remand a man for fourteen days, surely an experienced policeman like yourself can take a hint and at least endeavour to speed up your enquiries within that time."

From that time, the two had worked admirably together and each man having measured the size of the other, did everything he could to ease their mutual labours.

With Garston's connivance, Fawcett had done his utmost to avoid publicising the day on which the European would be brought up for trial. They both felt that the fewer Africans about to see who had let the side down the better.

As it was, the male prisoners were grossly overcrowded as a result of Fawcett's co-educational reorganisation of the cells. But, despite precautions, the prison staff had kept the public informed and there was a greater crowd for Björnsson than there had been for the Commission. As the driller stood in the box, a shaft of light caught his blonde features as though he were an actor being spotlighted for public entertainment. The people were all looking at him, many with confused feelings. In the early days, the missionaries had come to Mamba and taught the holy life. The older people had not been slow to seize on the significance of the Biblical image of sin as black and holiness as white. They imagined the faraway homeland of the missionaries as a land of shining saints. Then, as some of their sons became drawn into white wars, they had to widen their view of holiness though fighting against brown and yellow enemies did not present the difficulties raised by Italian enemies and the internment of the Mamba Fathers. In the end, they had come to suspect that the heart of the white man was at times blacker than that of the African. But, until the nationalists fanned it into a purposeful direction, it was only an academic acceptance.

Fawcett was charging the driller with "breaking and entering" (lawyers' language for "housebreaking"). Henry smiled to himself as he realised that the policeman would try and steer the case through without a single reference to Björnsson's real intentions. But he felt divided in himself as no Magistrate ideally should feel. For someone like himself to try a white man ought to be inadmissible on the grounds of "bias". In one direction or the other, he would err and the error would remain concealed to himself until it was made.

Fawcett called Eleanor's sister, Joseph and Eleanor herself and Henry noticed the anxious, distant figure of Morris standing by a pillar at the far end of the open-walled hall. They called the Mbuyas' houseboy who began to tell of the previous occasion on which Björnsson had visited the house.

"Your Honour, I protest." Mr da Pinto had jumped up from his bench and objected. Björnsson felt more cut off from those of his own colour than the Asians and Africans around him and had not demurred when Fawcett had suggested putting his case in the hands of the Asian lawyer.

"Your Honour, this incident which is being related by the houseboy has no relevance to the present case. I submit in all humility that you should consider hard before admitting what he says as evidence."

"Mr da Pinto," said Henry, looking down at the squat, white-tied man below him, "why do you always put your points in such an irritating fashion?" Henry, who hated the lawyer's subservience infinitely more than he disliked Fawcett's clumsy arrogance, never missed an opportunity for Pinto-baiting.

"Your Honour…" Pinto tried hard.

"I shall admit the statement," said Henry, and the Asian sat down, reflecting morosely that the laws of evidence had vanished for this Magistrate after Bar Finals.

Da Pinto's cross-examination consisted of a tedious rehearsal of evidence already given by the prosecution witnesses in turn. And, having on each occasion failed to discover inconsistencies in their stories, he concluded the cross-examination of each one with his accustomed words in such predicaments:

"I hope that the Court has had every chance of seeing that the witness was unreliable and that his testimony should be disregarded."

Björnsson took the oath. There was no fight left in him. The undrunken loneliness of his cell had led him to a point midway between an ancient Sunday School desire for cleanliness before God through repentance and a desire to obliterate the record of himself in death.

"What have you to say then?" asked Henry, unmoved.

"I did what the police say…"

"Look, let's have no nonsense!" snapped Henry. "You made a statement to the police denying everything; you pleaded 'not guilty' before me half an hour ago, and now you say you did everything?"

But Björnsson had clenched his fists; his face was contorted into a pattern of crying wrinkles; a convulsive shudder shook his body as the sobs escaped. He started pounding his fists on the bar in front of him, first gently and then more violently as he cried out… "Guilty… guilty… guilty… guilty."

The people in the crowd craned their necks for this unsurpassed spectacle. A great many of them were laughing as loudly as the sight of the nearby constables allowed them. From then on, Björnsson would not say a word.

"This man will have to be deported. I shall look into it," said Henry to Fawcett. "Meanwhile, he will be remanded in custody for fourteen days, pending sentence."

"Yes, your Honour," said Fawcett.

Henry spoke to Morris for a little after the case.

"And now, Morris, I must go off to claim my rights!" He patted the other on the back and drove off with Leslie for a drink before lunch. He was an Honorary Member, the only African so honoured.

Diana nudged Christine as he entered.

"He's really rather handsome, don't you think?"

"Yes, he is. It'd be alright if they were all as Westernised as he is," said Christine. "Do you know, the other day he even discussed that book… oh, what was it… in the library…?"

"*The Guns of Navarone?*"

"Yes, that's it. He discussed it with Jan, you know, quite… intelligently."

Henry leaned against the bar with his back to Chalisi.

"You know, Leslie, the tables really seem to be turning. That driller man. Here am I recommending a deportation order on him while the Governor spends his whole day rescinding restriction orders on our more recalcitrant politicians. Stupid, isn't it?"

"Why stupid? It's the usual pattern," said Leslie, wearily.

"Stupid, because everything I bloody well do, I do by permission of the imperialists. Everything Onyango does, he does by their permission! It's part of a great, elaborate system to bring us into our own without us noticing that it's all very much by permission."

Henry ordered two more beers, still without looking round at the barman.

"Can you wonder that only fools are fooled? And those fools, my dear Leslie, are the very men who believe that they are taking part in some eternal struggle to the victory. Victory by permission! My God, how glorious!"

Leslie felt that they had a common understanding; they were both, after all, frustrated.

Henry went on: "Since you whites started the business of talking to us about souls, I tell you that what you are doing now is bad for our souls."

"And what do you suggest?"

"Usubura for King!"

Chalisi was meanwhile looking through his private profits book. The mechanic at the Romba Express Motors had a car lined up for him at only two hundred pounds. Another two dances and three Saturdays should see him there.

While Reg Blagdon did the accounts, Chalisi was safe. A quick disappearance down-country would be indicated by the time of the half-yearly meeting.

"You are a bloody oaf," said Reg, as he emerged from the store. "How do you think we're going to get through all that gin you ordered when I was on leave?"

"It is good for people to have much expensive drink," explained Chalisi.

CHAPTER TWENTY-EIGHT

Voting

Fawcett's dog was obliged to forego the customary walk over the golf course. His policeman master had left on duty early on Elections' Morning to check the mobile patrols before they left Romba.

As the sun broke over the District, so the Election Presiding Officers emerged from their houses, carefully strapped their polling boxes on their bicycle trailers and made off through the waking villages to their appointed places of duty.

Soon the whole District was alive with this early official activity: Polling Assistants pedalling furiously to their rendezvous with democracy, District Officers sweeping down the roads in fast cars, police crowded with joking constables, their rifles well out of sight, chiefs walking and cycling officially everywhere.

Cedric stood over a Presiding Officer in East GodiGodi. Like most of the temporary helpers, he was a schoolmaster, glad of the chance to earn a few extra shillings. The polling station was in his own school, a classroom with a grass barrier mounted at one end like the veil of the Temple and, behind the barrier on a desk, four wooden boxes, one for each candidate, each with a label bearing its candidate's symbol pinned firmly on the front. The Presiding Officer began to dither under Cedric's gaze. And already the first voters were arriving outside, forty minutes before opening time. Cedric checked the boxes and found that one of them had not been locked. Covered in confusion, the Presiding Officer fumbled for the correct key in the gloom of the inner chamber.

Up in Bulikiki, the Sultan brooded bitterly from his deck chair inside his pallisaded plot. Somewhere in this very territory, the white anthropologist was trying to win himself a seat in the Assembly at the expense of the whole concept of an "Independent Bulikiki". Two years before, the man would have had his car burnt to cinders for such an outrage. But now there was no telling what holds Onyango had secured over the country for the Freedom Party. And, from where he sat, he could see his people streaming to the polls, each one underlining the futility of his efforts to organise a boycott of the elections. The Country Chief himself, his own special agent, had begun to express open doubts about the wisdom of a boycott, judging that the threat of removal that he had received from the D.C. was likely to be more certainly followed up than the fulminations of his senile traditional ruler.

Nowhere was the response to the elections more spectacular than in the Southern Mamba counties. The popularity of the exercise seemed to be fixed in inverse proportion to the degree of literacy generally prevalent. And so in Mamba, where education had made the smallest inroads on traditional life, the elections were greeted with something like awe.

Mothers toiled up the hill to the little school near Burns' quarry with babies strapped in snug bundles on their backs, joining the long queue that snaked twice round the football pitch before the first voter was admitted. On duty as Presiding Officer was Simeon, the interpreter from the D.C.'s office. He went through the movements of preparation with an air of immense importance and clearly impressed the twenty pairs of eyes that were able to glimpse his mysterious ritual behind the uncompromising bulk of the District Council askari who was standing in the entrance with his back to the queue.

Simeon finished his preparations, glanced at his watch, and nodded to his two polling assistants to take their places. After the solemn passage of five minutes, the first five voters were admitted. And more or less at the same time, throughout the whole of Mamba District, and the Protectorate itself, the heavily adapted imported machinery of election groaned slowly into action, while Imperialism watched to see whether a million years of hot sun and ignorance would prove Master in the end.

Simeon's first voter was an old man bent in two with age and wisdom. He leant on a stick one arm and proffered his tattered registration receipt with another. Simeon's assistants laboured for five minutes to find the man's name on the register before looking at his receipt again. He had come to the wrong polling station. They told him to go to a cotton store about five miles away and, with only a moment of regret betrayed on his face, he limped off cheerfully to the immense entertainment of the waiting crowd.

Cedric, Leslie and Morris supervised as best they could. Morris found a station where one of the boxes – Onyango's – had been turned to face the wall so that the symbol was obscured; in another place, the boxes were piled one on top of each other, so that with great difficulty a voter could just insert his ballot paper into the slit on the supreme box. And Cedric was forced to cancel more than twenty papers that had been crammed by confused voters into the inkwell of a desk on which the boxes were placed – unhelpful genius had started that particular error. Leslie, for his part, had been appealed to by the Presiding Officer at Koi to extract a young mother who refused to emerge from the screened compartment. They called her and she said that she would come once she had made up her mind. A further call elicited the same answer. In the end, Leslie went in to the sanctum and found the girl clutching a blank election ticket, almost paralyzed by her indecision and trembling alarmingly.

In West GodiGodi, Onyango was winning a spectacular victory but at a price. Okot had made it known to him by a devious folktale related by a messenger who had brought the politician a gift of eggs that he could arrange that a vote for Onyango could mean peace to the people from the minor Chiefs and the temporary non-enforcement of the whole range of irritating byelaws. Since the riots, their confidence having been restored, these chiefs set to their daily tasks with a conscientiousness approaching fanaticism and zeal bordering on ferocity. So Okot's offers were worth listening to. Onyango had toyed with the idea of denouncing the man once for all but his own stock since the riots had fallen dangerously low and he could not count on popular support.

Yet Okot had not reckoned with his father. Paulo, in common with many white men, had no patience with the latest developments. He could not see the signs that others seemed to recognise as proof that the kiboko whip was no longer the most effective ruler of men. True, one had always in a sense to make people consent to be whipped – that was the great gift of Gamage. There was, after all, no point in whipping people if they were against you; that had been the basic mistake leading up to the riots. It took a rare man to whip and be liked for it.

But as Paulo watched his son submitting to the new corruption, his military scruples surged up within him. The British had implanted very few enduring ethical principles in him but those that remained were rooted as deeply as the sense of the tribal obligations at the funeral of a relative. He had tried to reason with his son.

"You are doing wrong," Paulo had said.

"You day is past," was all Paulo received in reply.

But it was not any searing desire for vengeance on ingratitude that led Paulo to Garston's office and he went there with a heavy heart, reproaching himself with failure. His son had to learn before it was too late.

All the reports reaching Garston confirmed that the elections were going smoothly. The last radio message from Leslie had read: "Thousands are getting drenched outside Mamba polls – what price freedom!" He was not prepared for Paulo's revelations.

"You know you're making some very serious allegations against your son," Garston said through the only interpreter left in the office.

"Yes. But he must learn."

Fawcett drove quickly out on receiving Garston's urgent radio request. Cedric had been touring GodiGodi and had reported nothing amiss. But it was not the first time that the cadet had been misled in that area.

The policemen's contacts seemed to know very little. They had heard rumours that the Chief would relax his regime but they all seemed to adduce different reasons. One said that the Chief had toured the county to let his people know that a vote for Onyango would indeed exempt the voter from three months' work on paths; another believed that Okot had let it be known that he was not in the least interested in the outcome of these elections but, conscious that perhaps he would himself be seeking votes at the next elections, he was trying to introduce a policy of leniency into the Native Courts. A third said that he thought he had seen money pass between Onyango and Okot but just as Fawcett pressed for details he said that he thought it was interest on the car debt which had unaccountably dragged on.

In the end, Fawcett gave up. He returned at the end of the day exhausted and depressed. He had long cherished the prospect of making this particular capture and, although the idea of doing it on a father's betrayal took some of the savour from the exercise, he would nonetheless have enjoyed the sensation of pulling the young chief in.

"There's a forest of impenetrable facts, Garston, and there's very little a white man can do about it," Fawcett explained in the club that night.

The count took place in the three main tribal areas the next morning. At GodiGodi, Onyango turned up early and took his place in the counting hall, a smile of quiet confidence on his face. Kent in Bulikiki was stranded on the way to his counting, wondering who it was had punctured all four of his tyres. The District Officers organised the novel ceremony with a meticulous attention to detail. There would, they knew, be no shortage of failed candidates anxious to highlight any conceivable irregularity in the conduct of the elections in support of a petition to the High Court.

In GodiGodi, they first opened the boxes in which, theoretically, lay the votes cast for an independent, a local fish trader, who was widely denounced by his opponents' canvassers as a selfish opportunist, an allegation which found much favour with the people in his car. And as a damning proof of the effectiveness of the stigma, box after box was opened and upturned only to disgorge a few pathetic ballot papers and occasional twigs. The enumerators, whispering quietly to each other and joking now and again in the esoteric manner employed by people with a unique task to fulfil together, busily piled up their little packets of a hundred ballot papers and passed them to Cedric's large tabletop where the cadet arranged them in rows that were watched anxiously by the candidates. The trader, who had quite obviously lost his deposit ten times over, seemed to be straining in a pitiful manner to take a continued interest in the proceedings. There was little point in his looking for deficiencies in the organisation of the elections. It was clear that he, at any rate, would have to stick to fish. Onyango looked at his watch. It was already half-past ten and the unopened boxes stood in mute piles waiting for the minutes to destroy their secrets. He yawned.

Garston, meanwhile, sat in his Office waiting for the official results to come in so that he could cable them at once down-country. It was a long vigil and, as usual in such vacuums of time, he dreamed. Recently, instead of rehearsing the tragedy of a wasted life at the behest of some ruthless inquisitor inside his confused head, he suffered at the hands of an officious schoolmasterly little man to whom he really had no reply beyond a slightly superior chuckle. The little man asked him just exactly what on earth he thought he was doing, sitting about waiting for the result of elections he had organised with the express intention of ensuring his own professional liquidation. "So what?" Garston replied, sneering the man away. The sun was catching Diana's hair in a very attractive way. He hadn't really noticed before but she was quite pretty in her way. Nothing on Angela, of course, but – er – "quite pretty".

Diana was manicuring her fingers. There was nothing much else to do that afternoon except wait. Garston told her to go home but he would need her when the messages came in, so she waited. She too communed inwardly with herself. Outside in the hot, still Romba afternoon, nobody stirred beyond an occasional cycling messenger condemned to an errand. Angela drove by the office on her way to the shops. She was laying in supplies for the Freeman wedding. The sight of her jolted Diana.

"Angela!" The thought of the sleepless nights that that harmless, irritating, affected woman Angela had caused her! And suddenly it seemed so simple. Basically out of character perhaps, but decidedly simple. It wasn't a question of going to Angela and saying: "Angela, I've behaved like a bitch, dragged your name in the mud through the Station at every opportunity – and of course I know all about you and Leslie." Angela would have found something altogether too noble to say and Diana would have gone away seething, which was no longer really the object. Still less was it a question of flirting with Garston. Garston was not really the type, except at parties later forgotten in the cruel light of the hot mornings. And Angela would probably not have minded. In any case, Garston was the sort of man one could admire at a distance. Whenever she came closer, she had to mother him.

Diana had merely gone straight to Geoffrey.

"I'm not happy here, Geoffrey. Take me away."

The words had to be repeated three times before they penetrated. But her numbskull of a husband had finally reacted. Drained of ambition, with property in Sussex, Geoffrey was left with a shrug-of-the-shoulder philosophy that met most situations that savoured of crisis with an immediate flood of casual good nature. And, in the end, he would cut the situation down to manageable proportions. He had never seen Diana look so miserable since a month after they were married when she had made a complete mess of her first dinner party.

"Alright, my dear. If you're not happy, I shall give notice. I've always wanted to go back to keeping pigs," Geoffrey had said. He had looked wistfully in the direction of his hospital. He had long since succumbed to its inefficiencies, to the welter of poor compromises with insufficient equipment, unconscientious staff, his own lack of contact with developments. Things had never really gone right for him since that famous night when he had, classically, left the wad inside Mrs O'Corcoran. On call, he had staggered out from a club session to the room in a down-country hospital in which the wretched wife of a previous Agricultural Officer lay in the discomfort of appendicitis. It had been an easy mistake to make but it portended little good. Romba had, for years, been his place of exile.

The messages started coming in from the mobile patrols. Kent had polled three hundred votes out of an electorate of twenty thousand; Onyango had scarcely conceded a vote. In Mamba, an obscure and barely literate schoolmaster had captivated the electorate, with his symbol of a bicycle and his promise of "one vote, one bike".

SEPTEMBER 1962

CHAPTER TWENTY-NINE

A Wedding

The big changes came rapidly. The London Conference fixed its deadline for Independence. Onyango drove to and from the Legislative Assembly with a new air of importance. As Minister of Rural Administration, he was in a dream position to bend all District Commissioners to his will. But, unaccountably, he no longer troubled himself with baiting the officials but told himself that he was waiting for Independence Night before becoming harsh. In the meanwhile, he regularly submitted heavy claims for travelling and subsistence allowances and pressed for the upgrading of his salary. The rumour filtered up to Romba that he had fallen drunk into the swimming pool at Government House and the station was delighted when the information was confirmed by a denial in the Party's organ, "*Forward!*"

Romba tried to go about its daily duties with the appearance of being unchanged but everybody from the great Yusuf, still guarding the market like a bald slave master out of a Hollywood epic, to the frail schoolmaster, Hansraj, knew and felt that a new order was coming. And everybody wondered. The Indians feared for their trade, some for their lives. Patel had to face the double nightmare of possible racial restrictions on trade and the imminent dissipation of expatriate custom. He no longer dared to hope that he could cover his losses on "Arpège de Lanvin" by a generous profit on the Supreme Bombay Chutney. And yet home lay here and not at all in India. The few expatriates who were toying with the idea of 'soldiering on' as the expression now went, wondered bleakly about the uncertain future ahead for them. The politicians themselves only played at being confident and, whether they were eager agitators, men of the villages stirring up men of the villages, or Legislative Assembly men sinking contentedly in the back of quietly purring cars, they too suffered their moments of truth and were themselves drawn to wondering.

Only the missionaries appeared relatively unconcerned, involved as they were with issues that transcended the immediate history of nations. Catholic and Protestant alike, they still might have been taken for early pioneers blazing the colonial trail. Just as they were among the first to come, they had every intention of being the last to go.

Leslie sat in his office automatically initialling letters on files that merely required reading and minuting those that required replies to Morris and Cedric. And as soon as he had cleared his desk, he began to write a letter of resignation. His compensation would total about seven thousand pounds and a pretty little cottage within commuting distance of London would, he thought, go a long way to making life with Thelma actually attractive. He was even beginning to think that if he could get her away from the Granthams, Rices and Billmans of this world, she would actually grow pretty. And he already foresaw the time when his years in the Protectorate would have become a mere episode, a short time spent away from the little cottage, and Angela a passing incident in that episode. But, for the moment, he was thwarted and had to serve his period of purgatory. Garston entered his office laughing very nearly uncontrollably and in a somewhat un-English fashion. He left a trail of blue smoke hovering uncertainly in the wake of his pipe.

"Until they are hatched, my dear Leslie! Until they are hatched!" He banged down a telegram in front of his unamused junior.

It read: "FARRAR POSTED IMMEDIATELY. MINISTRY HQ TO UNDERTAKE TRAINING COURSE FOR LOCAL CADETS. ENDS." RURAL ADMIN.

Although Garston and Leslie always suspected
Onyango of foul play, in point of fact the politician
had been ignorant of the move and would have sec-
onded any suggestion that Farrar should leave at
once. Leslie, who had mentally packed his belongings
for shipping, had done copious doodles on his blotter
round the elusive subject of Standing Orders' passage
entitlements, had even seen himself eating ice cream
in Port Said in the same little café where a befezzed
merchant had on his way out, ten years before, tried
to sell him "Spanish fly". He now sunk his head
between his arms and prayed for fortitude.

Thelma, too, prayed. She had long been waiting for
the day when, her back turned on Romba forever, she
would be able to cherish the memory of Gordon as
someone more than a man. The longer she stayed in
Romba, the less tenable this vision was becoming, in
spite of Rice's prolonged and well-meaning wander-
ings in what he called 'the wilderness of the Muslim
country-unbelief' of Bulikiki.

The posting was so sudden and unexpected that
Muljibhai scarcely had time to arrange a farewell
sundowner. And Thelma was, in the middle of their
rushed packing, involved in being a Matron of
Honour in Peter and Dorothy's wedding, already
postponed till then through an attack of cere-
bral malaria which Peter had suffered. Dorothy
had nursed him back to his obligation with loving

care both in Romba and when he was transported down-country in the Protectorate capital.

The wedding had, in the planning stage, long been planned and the various government departments co-operated as never before in contriving a domestic public holiday for the Station. Licensing could wait, rabid dogs would have to froth a day longer, the cotton and tobacco returns could go to the devil, a duty sergeant would keep crime at bay – every office rationalised the holiday in its own way. And if the army of office boys arrived at the usual time, it was only to supervise a massive loading of government tables and chairs onto waiting lorries provided by Blagdon. As a lorry reached capacity, it moved solemnly off to Garston's garden where an immense buffet table was being pieced together. Station females darted about and arranged things in increasing numbers until, by half-past ten, one of them suggested coffee and they downed tools for half an hour speculating on the honeymoon destination which Peter and Dorothy had refused to divulge. Someone suggested that the couple was destined for Mount Buni again.

Peter Freeman stood at the altar with his bride while old Grantham flicked over the pages of his Prayer Book and searched for the wedding service place, out of which a matchstick marker had been removed by the odd-job man on the mission who lit the boilers daily.

Peter thought of the future that he would share with Dorothy in Britain. He had already been offered a good job in a tropical research place in Bristol. There, he would be able to contribute to the development of places like Mamba: but it would be others who would actually put his institute's findings into practice. Somehow that did not feel natural after his solid years of safari in this place. Maybe he would come back himself but he somehow doubted it.

Grantham found his place and began intoning fast as though seeking to alleviate the feeling of slight guilt that attended his ministrations direct from the Prayer Book. Over the years, the Mission had become very low Church and with the intoning, Freeman's nervousness, which had temporarily abandoned him, returned with full force. He developed an uncontrollable twitch in his right knee that he knew must be causing a rhythmic shudder through the trouser leg of his morning dress, borrowed from Jeremy, who sat resplendent in tweeds at the back of the Church.

To Dorothy, the moment was not new. She had rehearsed it to herself for years, first using some shadowy conjuration of a man figure, latterly replacing it with the slight, impetuous and over-earnest Peter whom she had taken in hand and cut down to size. Now she was a little worried that she had cut into his idealism, the very idealism that, beyond the natural propensity of unmarried nursing sisters to lie in wait for single men like undignified bloodhounds, had first endeared him to her.

Diana occupied herself through the service with writing up the details of Dorothy's dress for the *Morning News*, which paid her half a crown an inch for such titbits. Her description of Dorothy's corsage ran to three inches by itself.

The reception in Garston's garden was unique in two ways. This was Romba's first European wedding reception with the unsung exception of a bean feast held in honour of two missionaries married long back by a District Commissioner who subsequently discovered that, at the material time, he had had no powers to effect a legal union but who had never had the heart to tell the missionaries the awful truth. Secondly, it was the last social gathering of its kind that Romba was to know. It was emphatically not all-white – Peter had ensured that much – but it was one of the last functions at which certain up-and-coming individuals could be comfortably excluded. Again, there was an easiness, almost a sense of fraternity, between the cassocked Fathers, always concealing a profound earnestness in their Mission combined with a nearly cynical appraisal of the realities of their surroundings, and the Protestant missionaries, who forgot for a moment their highly demanding concern with the true state of every soul with which they came into contact. That easiness was to disappear with Independence as the political parties aligned themselves along religious divisions and took the mass of the African population with them. The simmering mutual recriminations of the colonial days were to give way to a deeply damaging cold war, pock-marked with house-burnings by night, acts of sacrilege and a swamping of the ancient tents of tribal patriarchs and venerable missionaries alike by the welter of political manifestos that attempted to replace them with false Gods. But that was still in the future and, for the wedding day, the two groups seemed to recognise some sort of validity in each other.

Garston, who had given Dorothy away, was, apart from Peter, the only male in morning dress. He moved from guest to guest with a charm and grace that Angela secretly admired from her own group on the lawn. And, when the time for speeches came, he seemed to be putting more than just the usual banalities into what he said and investing his words with an emotion that she found touching. Cedric fumbled for a few phrases as Peter's best man and sat down, relieved, amid charitable applause. Then Peter spoke, and, without the slightest warning from himself, borne along by two glasses of champagne cider, found himself saying that he and Dorothy were about to leave the country with the greatest possible regret but that he hoped they would return to take part in the immense task that lay ahead for the Country.

"That was terrific," said Dorothy, squeezing his arm, as the guests disintegrated and reformed into groups, slightly muted by another example of the surprisingly naïve pronouncements of which everyone thought Freeman had outgrown.

"When are you off, Mr Moorside?" asked Grantham without malice.

"Booked my passage for November, Archdeacon. We were very lucky to get the cancellations."

"Not very long then," said the old missionary with a look that seemed to recognise that even Garston's long stay in the District would be nothing to his own. He himself thought that, on the whole, he would like to die in Romba, although there was possibly something grander about dying on a safari. He nurtured a secret desire to be buried in a banana grove.

"No perhaps not, but there's plenty left to do," said Garston, halfway between involving himself in a rapid personal stocktaking and just passing off the Archdeacon's remark in the ordinary course of polite conversation.

"I've still got one or two projects to work out," he said half-heartedly. "Have you, Archdeacon, ever calculated just how much bride price changes hands in the course of a year?"

The Archdeacon, who tried to forget that bride price existed as a significant institution and who, in any case, held that it could have no recognised part in Christianity, raised an eyebrow in surprise.

"No… no… Mr Moorside… As a matter of fact…"

"Well, I'll tell you. I've been working out a few figures lately and I calculate that, on average, in Mamba District alone, something like a million pounds per annum changes hands in this way, and that is based on the very conservative estimate of "one man – one wife.""

Grantham shifted his feet disconcertedly. When Garston got like this, he even preferred to talk to a Catholic.

"Now, it's quite clear that in Bulikiki for a start, you chaps have made next to no impression on the monogamy issue, and I don't suppose you will for the foreseeable future. Anyhow… at any rate, not so as to upset these figures of mine too radically…" Grantham coughed.

"The latest census figures for Bulikiki, in any case, show that the number of children they are having is well on the up and, given solid Muslim indoctrination, we can expect that a lot more bride wealth will be raised over the next few years. Added to this is the admittedly smaller uncommitted element…"

"Uncommitted?" asked Grantham drily.

"You know – pagans," said Garston, who had at last realised in some dismay that he was turning the Archdeacon on a spit.

Fortunately, Angela intervened with a second glass of bitter lemon for the Archdeacon, who smiled and looked for comfort into the effervescence. Garston went on: "Anyway, my proposals are for a firm tax on the bride wealth. It's never been tried before but it should bring the District Council in about a tenth of a million a year which would be pretty considerable at a time when they can't even build a bridge without thinking of raising conventional taxes or appealing to the World Bank."

Grantham, who believed himself to be out of the doctrinal wood, began to nod sagely and comprehendingly at the proposal that he hoped secretly would have the effect of discouraging people to pay bride price at all.

"I know what you're going to say… you're going to ask me how collection of this tax could possibly be made effective."

Grantham had not been about to say this at all but he continued to nod in concurrence.

"Well, that's really quite easy, you know. District Council byelaws are ineffectual on this sort of thing, so that's out. The chiefs are reluctant to carry out orders that run so completely counter to accepted custom, not until general approval anyway. No, we make the people their own tax collectors."

By now, a large group had assembled round Garston and individuals within it were winking to each other. He now enjoyed no glory as a prophet in his own or anybody else's country.

"You see, my idea is that while they can go for months without running up against the sub-county chief if they're skilful, they can't avoid going to the local market for very long. Well, as it's obvious to the market keeper which one of the women is married and which one isn't, he will have the job of making sure they have a bride tax receipt obtainable on payment from the local chief. In that way…"

The clouds were gathering above the District and the wedding feast was threatened. Garston's words began to sound hollow and insignificant as the first rolls of thunder were heard from the direction of Mount Buni and distant banks of of cumuli nimbus clouds whipped out spears of lightning. Already out there, the homesteads were being engulfed by furious eddies of orange water chasing and gauging through the balk compounds; and apathetic faces were looking upwards at a hundred grass roofs that had not been mended in time and were letting in great cold drops of water, yellowed in their filtration through the thatch and forming evil black pools on the mud floors. The cotton bowed and swayed as little rivers ran between its rows. And the rain burst into tiny darts and sent up splashes of filthied water to ruin the cotton balls that should have been picked three weeks before.

OCTOBER 1962

CHAPTER THIRTY

Muljibhai's Feast

On a village path in the extreme south of the District, a three-year-old half-caste boy squatted, watching the progress of two beetles attempting to roll a steadily fattening stink ball from one side of their dusty plain to the other. While one climbed up and pushed with a 'to you' motion, his partner, 'to me', walked backwards on the other side of the ball, pulling and guiding as best it was able.

It was a deathly hot, quiet Sunday afternoon and the boy was excited to hear the rumble of an approaching car on the road from Romba off which his path lay. He ran and waited for it to pass.

Peebles drove past scarcely noticing the boy but wondering vaguely whether this was the child attributed by the station variously to Björnsson, Burns and Jeremy. Certainly, nobody had ever discussed the boy with any of these three and, with the Swede's departure, a general assumption had arisen that the child had been his. It had seemed a tidy ending to the rumour.

Soon, Peebles turned off and drove bumpily down a rain-rutted track that twisted now through little centres of habitation, now through swampy patches drained by culverts made out of logs, sometimes through rocky land bounded by great monolithic outcrops that stood bare and grey against the hard blue sky. He found his camp and went down to see what progress his African assistant had made.

Meanwhile, back in Romba, Muljibhai prepared to mount his farewell party for Manley and Diana. For days, he had sent minions about in cars dropping invitations on all the notables. His cards had been specially printed and then steeped in the perfume, "Bint el Aden".

Onyango was in town and had promised to come. He had bought himself a new Mercedes on a government loan and took every opportunity of showing it off to his constituents if not actually emerging from it more often than he could help to defend government policy for which he now had a clear responsibility, however nominal a part he took in framing it.

Muljibhai held his feast on the flat roof of his house on the main street. As his guests climbed twisting stone steps to the top, they were invited to glimpses of his household through open doors on the way up.

Shy smiling Indian women momentarily interrupted from their great cooking labours, girded their many veils about them, the most articulate managing a good evening before retreating to some hidden corner. It afforded a fleeting view of three double-decker iron bunks in one room, part of the answer to the mystery of how Muljibhai accommodated the immense tribe of his family and friends in one room in this excessively modest house. An attractive Asian girl stood pinned to the wall to allow Mavis and Harold Harriman, followed closely by John and Christine Fawcett, to pass on up the steps. And the whole well of the stairs was suffused with the smell sent out by the many joss sticks that seemed to be burning in every room of the house.

A long table had been mounted on trestles the whole length of the balcony and all the Asian young men of Romba seemed to be acting as guardians to the borrowed tubular chairs set alongside it. A dozen pressure lamps wheezed heavily over the scene.

It was a still, warm night. From somewhere in the distance, a muted sound of drumming floated over to Romba, but as the guests arrived and the animation mounted, their tiny illuminated junketing in the middle of Africa assumed its own self-importance, like a lonely airstrip in the desert picked out by planes in the night.

Muljibhai's young men were everywhere, shouting orders, giving shrill advice to the unseen women, ushering and welcoming the Europeans and Africans alike in quiet, respectful tones.

Henry Usubura, the Magistrate, had been on the Romba stage of his circuit at the right time and had received an invitation. Paying very little attention to his Asian hosts, he pretended to engage in furious argument with Onyango.

"… And what do you go and do, eh? You get up and say that under your regime every peasant will run a car! What sort of responsible government is that?"

Onyango listened with a smile crossing his tribally-scarred features. He was well used to abuse and was by now unable to distinguish between well-merited criticism and general mudslinging.

"You will see, my dear fellow, you will see. We cannot expect you bureaucrats to understand these great matters overnight…"

But Usubura had gone elsewhere to present himself from striking the politician. In the end, he found respite with Christine Fawcett and a conversation about "*On the Beach*".

"Not really an African at all," thought Christine, glancing quickly at his fine, well-kept hands.

Gordhandas Jivandas, black in an Australian bonnet, came round asking what everyone wished to drink and trying, with long-acquired skill, to dissuade all the whites from soft drinks. Few of them stood in need of his blandishments.

"Bloody fine hosts, these Asians!" opined Blagdon, stuffing himself with chicken curry, his forehead becoming beady in his pleasurable discomfort.

Harold Harriman nodded and said nothing. He had just bitten into a red chilli.

Muljibhai circulated about his guests, nodding and with a flick of the fingers, a gesture he had picked up by watching headwaiters in Britain, brought a scurry of young men over to any guest whom he judged to be in imminent need of a further helping of anything.

Morris Mbuya was in great form. Constitutional changes and good reports from Garston had given him a new confidence in himself, and the Asians were now left in no doubt that he was worth cultivating. If Onyango were to turn funny, Morris might supply a useful buffer. He might, that is.

Eleanor, quiet and pretty, was expecting another child. She wore a light blue European dress that bared her delicately-shaped brown shoulders. Her hair was done in a new combination of tight, criss-crossed strands. She said nothing all evening.

Muljibhai was, as usual, dressed in a spotless dhoti and it was difficult to imagine him in the suit he was reputed to wear when he did business in Britain, a clerical, grey affair with red velvet lapels.

After the curry had been cleared away, a bowl of a blancmange arrangement tasting of eucalyptus and decorated with rose petals, was placed in front of each guest while the flow of beers, gins and whiskies went on unabated.

Usubura looked at his rose petals and then at Christine.

"These would suit you well, you know," he said.

"Shush," she said, blushing.

"But what does the bloody man expect me to do with all this foliage?" he said, ploughing the petals into the green pog.

Christine developed uncontrollable giggles succeeded by hiccups.

"This is what I call carrying multiracialism too far," Henry went on. "He knows you Europeans are keen gardeners and serves up roses for you to eat."

Next to Henry, the elder Patel was devouring his roses and blancmange unconcernedly. Cedric was deep in conversation with the headmaster, Hansraj.

"You see, Mr Hamilton-Gordon, with Indians problem is very different. You have home and country to go to. But for most Indians, country is here. We are not knowing people in India. India very trouble for us…"

Cedric nodded, trying to imagine the sort of India that Hansraj was depicting, unwelcoming, poverty-stricken and, above all, strange.

"… When I am getting leave, Mr Hamilton-Gordon, I go to India but only for holiday. No interest there."

The uninhibited, self-assured laughter of Onyango broke in on Cedric's concentration. He wondered what Onyango really thought about all these Indians. Would he urge action against the whole race because some of them seemed unable to treat their African houseboys and shop assistants with the common decency that Garston afforded to his office messengers?

"Why do these Indian traders go out into the middle of nowhere, miles away in the bush, far away from people of their own kind?" said Cedric. He had never been able to understand how the Indian bush traders like those at the Koi Trading Centre were able to stand the loneliness and the apparent pointlessness of their life. Why were the evening card games on the pavement with two barefoot friends so alluring?

Hansraj, oblivious of the spiritual maxims on his classroom wall, leaned over to Cedric and afforded the cadet the benefit of his evil-smelling breath as he imparted the secret:

"It is because they want to make profit."

Muljibhai made a short speech about Geoffrey Manley and Diana, and Patel, as he listened, realised that he would no longer benefit from Diana's extravagant toying on his little luxuries counter. In recent years, she had bought many expensive knick-knacks from him in an attempt to assuage her growing but unadmitted desire to leave Africa.

Geoffrey rose, stood swaying slightly to each side of the perpendicular, and delivered a series of slow, deliberate phrases in praise of his hosts. Garston watched him and was not at all sure whether he was looking at a man trying to control inebriation or melancholy. In either case, it was a sad and embarrassing sight, he thought.

As the party quietened to the speeches so the silence of the rest of sleeping Romba became apparent. The only other sound now came from the club's generator pounding away in the distance. From the balcony overlooking the street, one could just see the lights in the club visible between two buildings opposite and half obscured by intervening trees on the golf course. A moon was trying to manifest itself about the night but ragged clouds kept on putting it out.

Chalisi, in the empty clubhouse, looked at his watch and decided that his moment had come. He took a torch from a shelf and signalled into the night from the verandah: it was an idea that had occurred to him as he listened to the trick played on Kent.

One hundred yards down the club drive, two side-lights on a car were switched on and the car slowly made its way to the building. Without speaking to Chalisi, Hamisi, the mechanic at Romba Express Motors, followed the barman into the club. Then, with the lights out and using only the torch, both men began the systematic raping of the club's stock.

When the car was full, Hamisi drove it away and returned fifteen minutes later for a second load. When the last bottle of spirits had been safely stowed in the boot of the car and a case of champagne brandy strapped to the roof rack for good measure, Chalisi locked the club door dutifully, for the last time as far as he was concerned. He put the key in its usual hiding place two yards along the roof gutter under a stone and climbed into the car with Hamisi. Neither man was seen again that side of Independence Day.

"… and all these years in Romba I have, and I say it without the slightest exaggeration, only confirmed the hospitality and gentle ways of Indian people in my estimation: an opinion which I first formulated as a young doctor in the Indian Army…" Manley was interminable.

There was some slight commotion as Peebles was ushered in by one of the young men. Muljibhai leaned over the back of his chair as he passed and said that he was so glad that the geologist had been able to come after all and that, as soon as Manley had finished, he would arrange for his food to come in.

But Peebles seemed excited and preoccupied. He signalled to Garston to join him outside the balcony for a moment and, as soon as Geoffrey was in his seat and was being further lauded by one of the Patels, Garston and he met on the stairs:

"What's up?" asked Garston, disturbed by the geologist's flushed expression.

"Bauxite," said Peebles. He seemed to be trembling a little. There was a silence as Garston took it in.

"You mean… you've found bauxite?"

"What else do you suppose that I'd go down there on a Sunday afternoon for! I didn't want to tell you before because we weren't quite sure. Even now, we don't know the full extent of the deposit but it looks pretty vast."

After the sundowner had broken up, Garston and Peebles discussed the discovery until three in the morning.

As Peebles rose to leave, Garston put into words what he had been thinking ever since Peebles had told him of the discovery.

"I'd give a great deal for the assurance that you will be able to enjoy, that you have made a positive and measurable contribution to the life of the people here."

"Oh, there's a great deal of research to be done before we could start mining," said Peebles as he stepped out to his waiting Land Rover.

NOVEMBER 1962

CHAPTER THIRTY-ONE

Back Home

As he stepped inside the Colonial Office for his appointment with the Resettlement Bureau, Garston remembered, as he had known that he would, the day eighteen years before when he had gone for his interview before the Civil Service Commissioners.

There had been seven of them sitting at one side of the table with himself on the other side and spies watching him from the flanks. They had all bored him through with unsympathetic eyes, except, that is, for the Chairman. The Chairman had seemed to him, on reflection, something of a visionary, and had appeared to nod with approval when Garston had said that he aimed at the Governorship and nothing less. It had been a naive and silly remark and he had kicked himself immediately afterwards for making it. But the Chairman had put him at ease with a remark that the only crime was to aim low.

"Let us trust that the execution goes on to match conception, Mr Moorside," the Chairman had said, terminating the interview.

Now, Garston was back in London and the wheel had turned full circle. He had not become a Governor.

It was some months later that Garston recognised a face from Romba. He was sitting in a bad restaurant above a smart pub, meditating through the yellow-brown translucence of a mug of beer as he waited for his lamb chop and peas. And it was the familiar laugh from behind him that made him look round to see Onyango with another African from the country that had for so long been his own home.

They did not see him and for some reason he could not bring himself to attract their attention. He remembered now that he had read somewhere that Onyango had been posted to London with the new Country's High Commissioner. Maybe that was the High Commissioner with him. If so, it was an odd pub to use.

Garston looked at his watch. "A quarter to two," he said to himself. The waitress brought his meal after a full half-hour's wait. A fat man with creases all over his yellow face sat down at a near table and obscured his view of the Africans with a fully open copy of the "*The Times*".

"Why didn't you go up to them, you ass?" asked Angela from the kitchen of their house in Chingford that evening.

"I don't know…" Garston was looking intensely into the pattern of red-hot coals forming in their sitting room fire. "I had… I really don't know."

THE END